The Most Beautiful Girl in the World

THE MOST
Beautiful Girl
IN THE WORLD

∽ *a novel* ∽

Judy Doenges

Santa Fe Summers 2006

For Kelly, Thanks for being a reader — Judy Doenges

THE UNIVERSITY OF MICHIGAN PRESS
ANN ARBOR

Copyright © 2006 by Judy Doenges
All rights reserved
Published in the United States of America by
The University of Michigan Press
Manufactured in the United States of America
♾ Printed on acid-free paper

2009 2008 2007 2006   4 3 2 1

No part of this publication may be reproduced, stored in a retrieval system, or transmitted in any form or by any means, electronic, mechanical, or otherwise, without the written permission of the publisher.

A CIP catalog record for this book is available from the British Library.

Library of Congress Cataloging-in-Publication Data

Doenges, Judy, 1959–
The most beautiful girl in the world : a novel / Judy Doenges.
  p.   cm. — (Sweetwater fiction. Originals)
ISBN-13: 978-0-472-11561-7 (acid-free paper)
ISBN-10: 0-472-11561-8 (acid-free paper)
1. Kidnapping—Fiction. 2. Fathers and daughters—
      Fiction. I. Title. II. Series.
      PS3554.O346M67   2006
813'.54—dc22   2005035601

for Sarah

What's your name?
Who's your daddy?
Is he rich like me?
Has he taken any time
To show you what you need to live?
Tell it to me slowly
Tell you what I really want to know
It's the time of the season for loving.
   —*Rod Argent,* "TIME OF THE SEASON"

∼

Out of the tree of life I just picked me a plum
You came along and everything's startin' to hum
Still, it's a real good bet, the best is yet to come
   —*Carolyn Leigh and Cy Coleman,*
      "THE BEST IS YET TO COME"

∼

Desire can never be satisfied,
because it is a desire to desire.
   —*Jacques Lacan*

BOOK ONE

chapter one

It was a gentle kidnapping, silent, victimless. Robin Simonsen, barely awake, felt someone roll her into a cocoon of sheets and blankets and carry her from her bedroom. When she and her abductor hit the cold outside air, Robin opened her eyes, saw her father's leonine head, halo of wild hair, and relief of rough whiskers above her, and, beyond him, the inky sky and dull suburban stars.

Without a word, Heath Simonsen installed his daughter behind the seat of his pickup truck, slid a wool blanket under her head, and tucked a sleeping bag around her body.

Robin lay awake while her father drove, watching headlights swarm over the ceiling of the truck and then disappear. The cab smelled of gasoline and Heath's little cigars. After some time, her father stopped to let a stranger inside, a man who talked in a low voice and then lit a match. Thick, sweet smoke filled the truck.

Robin finally turned on her side and pulled the sleeping bag around her, ready to sleep. She knew that a real kidnapping required someone to be taken from. She and her father were all that was left.

Robin awoke, shivering, to a crow cawing in the distance. Outside the windshield lay a vast, flat field covered with dead yellow stalks. A pale light rose from the ground like fog. Snowflakes swirled.

"Dad," Robin said, as she climbed into the front seat. "Dad." Two open beer bottles sat on the floor. A thick stack of rubber bands circled the gearshift.

Spring snowflakes ticked against the sides of the truck. They were wet, half rain, spitting. Robin got out of the truck still wrapped in her bedclothes and the sleeping bag. Heath had parked on a short dirt driveway, the nose of the truck pushed up against a metal gate as if he had tried to crash through to the field on the other side but had given up. Behind the truck was a dirt road, and across that, another yellow, scraggly field. The road had no end points, its brown line sinking into the horizon in both directions. Above the road was a mammoth block of white sky held aloft, it seemed, by the fields, an enormous, pale door hanging in space. Robin was nowhere.

She stood on the sleeping bag and dug her bare toes into its down hummocks. The crow kept cawing, but there were no trees, just barbed wire, which ran in monotonous lines to the horizon. Robin shuffled toward the road, her feet pulling along one edge of the sleeping bag.

No farm buildings, only fallow fields and frosty mud, and the ridged brown road like a long set of ribs. For a few minutes, Robin watched snow accumulate in the folds of her sleeping bag. She sat down to wait. Her father must have fallen off the edge of the world; lately, she'd been waiting for him to tip over, crumple, collapse.

One night just a week before, loud music from the living room hi-fi had pulled Robin out of bed. She had found her father sitting on the couch drinking a beer, accompanied by two men in flannel shirts and a red-haired woman in a nurse's uniform.

"It's loud," Robin had said. Heath and his guests looked surprised. Smoke from something her father held below the coffee table curled around his face.

"Who's that?" the nurse finally asked.

The crow stopped cawing. Snow collected in Robin's lap. Your parents had you, they kept you, and that's who you were—someone held by them. They drew your outline, so when they were gone, you lost all shape. The land around Robin looked as flat as Columbus' nightmare, flat enough for a grieving father to fall off and keep falling.

Out of the whiter sky in the east came a huge box, trembling down the dirt ribs of the road. It might have been a refrigerator, a garage door, a small house, a boat on rough seas, but then Robin heard its gears: a truck.

The box shook and shimmered and then became a shiny red pickup that finally stopped in front of Robin. Heath leaped from the passenger's seat and grabbed up his daughter, her blankets trailing.

"Holy shit!" he cried, surprised, as if he had just remembered Robin and had rushed back to get her. "I'm here, kiddo. Jesus H. Christ." His face smelled of smoke and beer and something else—decay, that sour, yellow odor that had clung to Robin's mother while she waited to die.

Heath kissed Robin and brushed snow from the sleeping bag. He hugged her tightly. A boy's head with long sideburns and ragged skin popped out of the red truck's window.

"Hey, man?" the boy called. His voice had a little twang, a Southern sound.

Heath put Robin down and ran to the red truck. He lifted something from its bed, then raced back to his daughter, slack-jawed and panicky, as if someone were chasing him. Robin smiled: she could wait. After all, when you kidnapped somebody, you were supposed to take them somewhere and then stay with them. But here was her father, gripping his two battered suitcases, running back to her, as if he were the one who'd been stolen.

∼

Patricia Simonsen died in the summer of 1968, right on the cusp of fall, forever ensuring that Robin would mark the boundary between those two seasons by her mother's wasted form in the wide, deep bed, her mother's silence, her mother's sparse black hair sliding from her scalp and lying adrift on the pillow, as if she were drowning.

That left Heath for Robin to follow into the growing cold and dark of the season of her mother's death, a father unlike any other, a dad in disguise. Heath was a tall, stocky man who looked shorter than his six feet, with a head of luxurious and undeserved curly golden hair, permanent stubble, a voice like tumbling gravel, and several large, dark freckles on his right cheek. He rushed around as if he were chronically late for an appointment, though he lived without schedules of any kind. He rose when he wished, worked when he fancied it, and, while his wife was sick, spent countless hours seated next to her bed on a folding chair whose seat was layered with duct tape. Heath Simonsen was a salvager. He ran the business out of the house and yard on Highland Street in Lilac, Illinois, littering his family's lives with others' castoffs. A salvager: someone in the business of salvation, but, to Robin's dismay, someone who couldn't keep her mother from slipping away.

The Simonsens lived at the bottom of one of the few gentle hills in the relentlessly flat land that swept twenty miles east to Chicago and another thirty miles west into the fertile soybean and corn fields of Kane and Will Counties. The Simonsens' neighborhood of a half-dozen ragged and unincorporated streets sat wedged between Illinois Route 53 and busy Finster Road. Bordered on the east, west, and south sides by strip malls and crowned at the north side by Robin's school, Stephen Douglas Elementary, the area was almost superfluous to Lilac, merely a holding pen for people who couldn't afford to live in the suburbs' better houses. At best, most Lilacians thought Robin's neighborhood was a liability, worthy of municipal neglect. There were no sidewalks, street lamps, or snow removal, but the Simonsens and their neighbors had full acre lots, the freedom to burn their garbage in barrels in their backyards, and Heath could keep broken cars and a rotating stock of useless machinery on his property without breaking any zoning laws. The house, like its neighbors, had its own septic system and a private well, like a tiny, isolated village.

That fall, Robin felt as if someone were slowly pulling a hat over her eyes and ears, and before everything went dark and silent, she wanted to see her father one last time. Only now he seemed so decrepit and malfunctioning—as hapless and helpless as the junk he tried to sell. He had trouble speaking to her, noticing her, solving the simplest problems. One night Heath drove the two of them to a fast-food restaurant in one of the strip malls. Back in the darkest part of the parking lot, they ate hamburgers, the truck heater warming their feet in weak, intermittent blasts. After Heath finished, he rested his forehead on the steering wheel and spoke to the floor of the truck, his words dripping onto the mat. He talked about how much money was left in the Simonsen bank—a cash box hidden behind the dryer. He talked about Patricia's medical bills, about how many dollars he had in his pocket— he began to reach for it, then gave up—and he talked about how one less person didn't necessarily mean more money.

There was a lot of business potential in Lilac, Heath said to the gas pedal. Then Robin heard sniffling and the sound of drops hitting the mat beneath her father's face.

"I'm crying," Heath said flatly, as if reading the words off of the truck floor.

"Okay," Robin said. She was impatient, bored. Daily, without reason or thought, and often without real emotion, she'd done her own crying, and daily, the rhythmic heaving of her chest and the seeming endlessness of her grief had lulled her. Her sadness, the hollow sounding of her loneliness, was more comfort than habit. Robin had discovered something she'd never known before, the prim satisfaction of predictability. She'd been brought up on the beauty of chaos, the lesson that there was no point to life except to collect junk and then get rid of it again, no regularity to the cycle of getting and selling; in fact, there was no cycle at all. Things were simply there or not there.

That night in the parking lot, when Robin saw the droop of her father's torso, the curve of his thick shoulders over the steering wheel, she knew he was splashing around inside his grief, hopelessly lost, and she resented him. It wasn't that hard to pen up what you wanted, what you felt, and then visit it, when necessary.

Heath sat up as if he'd been poked awake, his face damp. Robin chewed another French fry while they stared at each other.

"Aren't you going to say something, kiddo?" he asked.

"Like what?"

"Ideas, maybe?"

"What kind of ideas?" Robin asked. So many times, her mother had said to Heath, "*You* figure it out." Heath kept his large blue eyes steady on Robin's face, but behind his stare she could see him banging around, tripping, falling into the darkness of his loss.

"No ideas?" Heath asked.

"You figure it out, Dad," Robin said.

Heath put the truck into gear and pulled out of the parking lot. As they bounced along, Robin felt parts of herself break off and fall into the road. This was a kind of efficiency, a scouring. She felt it clearly. All the emotions and ideas that were too useless for even their junkyard house left her, piecemeal. Robin jettisoned the irrelevant, like hope, so that by the time she and her father arrived home, she could simply pass through the splintered wood of the front door and become a shimmery ghost like her mother, her few remaining desires undetectable.

∼

Heath drove Robin out of the country that snowy spring day, heading north through the southern Illinois farmland, from Benton, Blue Mound, Paw Paw, up into DuPage County, and then to Lilac. While they traveled, Robin rolled up in the blankets and stashed in the foot well under the stream of the heater, her father talked.

"I freaked, baby," he said. "I thought, shit, the kid, the work, all by myself, you know? So I freaked. I had some idea you'd be better off found, like an orphan or something. I just freaked, and then I thought, I'll figure it out. Right?"

Not Columbus, not an explorer, not even a kidnapper, her father.

He just wanted to escape. Robin turned so the heater blasted her face and dried her eyes before her father saw that she'd been crying. She stared at the littered floor of the truck: nothing to bring home, no fortune, no idea, no difference. When she turned to look at her father she saw a man locked between the landscape out his windshield and the empty road in his rearview mirror. A man hanging, suspended, like the cold sky he'd emerged from before.

When they got home, Heath touched Robin's forehead and then placed her in the bed he had shared with Patricia, where for several days she lay sweating and sleeping among the dank pillows and moth-eaten wool blankets. At one point, the redheaded nurse appeared.

"She's sick all right," the nurse said, peering at Robin's face in the weak yellow light from the dresser lamp.

"No shit," Heath said. He lit a Panatela and shook his hair back. "But my question is: what are we going to do about it?"

"Stop smoking in here for one," the nurse said, her rough hand cradling Robin's burning cheek.

"Right," Heath said, fleeing the room. Sometime later—a day? days?—when the house was quiet and the sun was high and bright outside the windows, just a few clouds scudding across a shiny sky, Robin tried to get up. She fell back onto the pillows. "Dad!" she called into the quiet. Her father's dresser listed, the drawers broken open, a tumble of socks and underwear spilling out; the frame for another bed stood upright in the corner, dozens of crossword puzzle books stacked in front of it. A giant stuffed dog wearing a top hat sat under the window. A sign on his chest said, "Happy Birthday, Chester!" Tacked up on the wall was one of Robin's school drawings. Patricia's dresser, the match to her father's, was gone. "Dad!" Robin called.

Later, when Robin woke up again, a tall woman bent over her, a stranger.

"Huh," the woman said. She chewed gum, sending puffs of cool spearmint scent onto Robin's face. "Kind of a tiny tadpole, isn't she?"

The woman had a towering stack of blond hair that looked stiff and soft at the same time and large, light blue eyes. Familiar eyes. The woman reached into the low neckline of her blouse and adjusted her bra strap; plastic bracelets clattered along her wrist. "Huh," she said again. Then she sighed and moved away. "I don't know about this," she said.

A figure sat behind the woman, a hollow-eyed man with hair like a movie star's, slumped in a duct-taped chair. "Kiddo," Heath said. He could have been calling to her from the next room, the next town, or from downstate, some faraway trap; from inside of it, her father's voice carried forward and back. "Robin," Heath said, "say hello to your grandmother."

chapter two

～

She was like a mother with the sound turned up. Stationed in the kitchen, she heated up TV dinners and played solitaire at the Formica table, read movie magazines, and drank tiny bottles of Coke through a straw; she laughed like a beagle on the scent, talked like a jay, and, late at night, sometimes cried, as if she, too, had lost her mother. Her name was Otelia Simonsen, but everyone called her by her stage name, Goldie. She was the only relative Robin had heard of, the subject of past eye rolling and sighs by both Heath and Robin's orphaned mother, who didn't understand parents. Apparently, there was a grandfather, too, a steak house owner far away in Corpus Christi, Texas, whose likeness sat on Goldie's dresser. Rex Simonsen's large, bespectacled, and mustachioed face and pile of white hair made him the generic patriarch, distant and wealthy, a man who had abandoned Goldie when Heath was a toddler but who had the misfortune to be married to a woman who didn't believe in divorce. Rex called every few weeks so he and Grandma, who was a former Minnesota farm kid like him, could argue with each other in a dead Norwegian dialect. Rex gave Grandma a Cadillac, and he sent monthly checks, and sometimes, special delivery envelopes filled with cash.

"Some songs are like boyfriends," Grandma said one night that spring, Sinatra on the stereo. Her eyes filled with tears. "They get right up in there," she added, jiggling her breast with her fist, massaging her heart, as the music did.

Heath's heart splintered that spring; Robin saw it shatter, like her own had, though slivers of her father's heart flew out of the house and beyond Highland Street. One piece Heath saved for Robin. But for Patricia? Robin believed that her father had simply stored that piece away, hiding it in the same place he had hidden Patricia's possessions. The rest of himself he began to pay out in increments to an endless series of women. Robin wondered what was left.

The women came at night, sometimes as many as four times a week when Heath felt like staying home to receive them. Blonds, brunettes, redheads, women with light brown hair, cut short or curly or sweeping to their waists, some with freckles, long eyelashes, clothes right out of a magazine, or just jeans and work boots. The women waited in cars on the street, in lawn chairs in the backyard, in desultory poses by the front door where Goldie and Robin could see them. When the women learned who Robin was, they threw her pointless questions, part of some maddening game designed to make her never want to grow up. "Doing your homework?" the women would ask. "Watching TV?" "Glad the school year is over?" "Know where your dad was last night?"

As the summer ripened, Robin tried to remember some of her father's dates, but in a week or two she forgot them, their faces blending into the ever-changing scrim of junk before her. Sometimes a single characteristic floated out of the female mess like a vibrato note sung by one of Grandma's crooners. A birthmark, the smell of a certain shampoo, a catch in a laugh—anything could sear a woman to Robin's mind. Eventually, though, her memories flickered as quickly as her father's attention, she missed the transition from one woman to the next, and then there she was, blinking up into the face of a long-haired blond who might or might not be Mary, the long-haired blond of several months before, but who, after Robin's question to her father and the embarrassed silence that followed, would instead turn out to be Susan, or maybe even Penny, or Melanie, but never Mary, never again.

~

Anger crawled all over Grandma that morning: it swelled the skin under her eyes, it chipped her fingernails, it pulled tight the turban of stretchy hairdo tape that bandaged her head. Even Goldie's nightgown seemed annoyed: this one was hot pink satin with a marabou collar and hem and a matching bed jacket. A piece of down drifted from Goldie's shoulder and landed in her coffee cup as she harangued her son. Heath was captive in the kitchen. Robin swung her legs, thrilled to see her father in his dirty tee shirt, drinking out of the orange juice carton and sawing at her piece of toast with a steak knife. Business was bad, but here was her father, cutting bread just for her.

"What're you running?" Grandma asked. "Where's the customers?"

"I could open a casino," Heath said, handing the plate of toast to Robin. "Would that make you happy, Ma?"

"Dad," Robin said, giggling. She began to devour her breakfast.

"You're going to go broke, son," Goldie said. Heath didn't reply. He chewed and read the *Tribune.*

"Mr. Hazen came over yesterday," Robin said, referring to the Simonsens' neighbor to the south. "He got some wood from the backyard." Robin smacked her lips, happy to bring good news.

"Don't do that, honey," Grandma said. "Your lips'll get all loose and ugly. Heath, Hazen *took* the wood. Took it because he said you took it from him. Are you nuts? He could have the cops on us from that."

"That old cracker," Robin's father said.

"You asked me to come here and you said it'd be hands off," Grandma said loudly. Her cigarette ash drooped over the newspaper.

Heath cleaned a molar with his tongue. "And?" he said. He turned the page.

"Well, I'm not going to sit here while we go down the toilet and take the kid with us."

"Yuck," Robin said.

Heath blinked rapidly over the paper and rubbed his palms to remove crumbs. Goldie smoothed her nightgown over her breasts. Robin hadn't noticed before how perfectly her father's eyes matched Goldie's, thin blue, large, and clear, like distant planets. "Remember in college, Ma?" Heath said. "When I was home from Berkeley?"

Berkeley meant just the one year, which Heath rarely talked about except to mention that that's where he had met Patricia. When Robin had asked her mother about the courtship, Patricia conjured up a campus full of eucalyptus trees and a young version of Heath charming her beneath their branches.

"What I remember about college," Goldie said, "was that you never went back. So what?"

Heath slid his folded arms across the table, his head leading, his face and eyes wide open as he advanced on Goldie. This was his make-a-sale face. For years, Robin had watched him inch toward potential customers exactly like this, his voice growing louder and more insistent, as if to forestall the buyer's inevitable retreat.

"Yeah, so I didn't go back, Ma," Heath said, close now to Goldie's face. She didn't flinch. "But remember?" Heath asked. "When I was home from Berkeley and Patty was still there and you and I were living in North Vegas and you were between boyfriends? Remember? I said then, Ma, get a hobby, make some friends, learn a business—but get the hell out of mine. However, you'd rather spend your hours reading about who's kissing Charlton Heston's ass. Or maybe you'd like to do it yourself."

"Aw, nuts." Grandma stabbed out her cigarette and crossed her arms. "You don't know a thing about what I do. Where are you all the time?"

"What are you doing, Ma, that takes up your day?"

"I've got to take care of the kid here," Goldie said, pointing at Robin, who quickly picked up her empty plate and licked it.

"Robin's in school all day," Heath said.

"Was," Grandma said. "And when she is, she comes home! Cripes, she comes home for lunch even. I thought kids ate lunch at school."

"Not until junior high," Robin said from behind her plate.

"Don't slobber on the dishes, honey," Grandma said.

"There's your child rearing for the day, Ma," Heath said. "We've cleared your calendar." He leaned closer to Goldie. This is when he loved to say to customers, "You're not going to find it anywhere else," as if the junkyard were some magical repository, choosy rather than promiscuous about what it contained. Now Heath looked steadily at Grandma and said, "*I* know, Ma. I know exactly what you need."

"Don't start," Goldie said. "Don't even."

"Start what?" Robin asked.

"Remember, Ma," Heath said, "when I was home from Berkeley and we lived in North Vegas and you got so antsy? Remember?"

"You try raising a young man all by yourself and work full-time, too," Goldie said.

"I was raised already," Robin's father said quickly. "And you weren't working then. Not dancing. Not seamstress work. Remember, Ma?"

"I suppose you've never heard of a professional injury," Grandma said.

"What's that?" Robin asked.

"Jesus, Ma," her father said, laughing. "Professional injury."

"I was still paying the bills," Goldie said. "Money was still coming in."

Heath nodded. "Money coming in, yeah," he said. "From several sources, too, if I remember correctly." He stuck out his thumb: "Bennie Nigro." Index finger: "Stew Patton."

Goldie gasped. "You're not," she said.

"What's Stew Patton?" Robin asked.

Her father started to raise his middle finger, right in Grandma's face. "Harry Tomczak," he said.

"Don't forget, son," Goldie said, "you're never too old for me to hit."

Robin's father shook his ring finger and said, "Pete Sulli."

"And I'll do it, too," Grandma added.

Heath held up his pinkie: "Did I forget anyone?"

"Uff-da," Grandma said, turning away. "You just want someone to stay home all day and watch you mess around." She had a small, tight smile. "Did Patricia do that for you?" she asked.

"Grandma!" Robin cried. She didn't know what her grandmother's question meant, but her mother's name uttered in the middle of a fight frightened her.

Heath was calm. Robin had seen him like this after the sale, after the customer pulled away. This was counting the money. "Forget the business, Ma," Robin's father said. "This isn't about the business. This is about you wanting my blessing. So, okay: once and for all, Ma, I don't give a damn who you fuck."

∼

Inside the city of Lilac was a smaller city, the unincorporated area where the Simonsens lived, and, within that neighborhood, which was the only place that had ever mattered to Robin, were Highland Street and its ten houses. On Highland Street, Robin's interests grew narrower, focusing on her immediate neighbors: Mr. and Mrs. Corner to the north, both as ancient and broken-down as their house; the Bogat family across the street to the east, who were always having a boat, a car, or a snowmobile dragged off their property in a late-night repossession; and Mr. and Mrs. Hazen across a weedy, vacant lot to the south, the only people on Highland who acted like they lived in a richer neighborhood. Before her mother died and Goldie arrived, Robin thought she and the rest of Highland were the same. She hadn't thought much about her father's work or the state of their house and property. But after Patricia died, the front of the house seemed to crumble, and now everyone in Lilac could see Heath playing loud music all night in his boxer shorts; Robin crying in the bathtub, water up to her nose; and Goldie, shell-shocked, slapping down solitaire cards at the kitchen table. Maybe they were right, then, the parents of all her former friends who had forbidden their kids to play at Robin's house. There *were* too many pieces of rusted machinery, too many sharp objects, too much fire danger in a living room piled high with old newspapers and rags and boxes of Japanese fans or old books. When strangers drove by the Simonsens' place as if they were sightseeing, and paused to gaze at the spread of semi-crushed autos and broken lawn mowers, and the yawning garage full of tools, refuse, busted pinball machines, an old Thunderbird up on blocks, and a dressmaker's dummy, Robin had assumed they were customers shopping on the fly. So the fact that the arthritic Corners refused to wave hello, despite their own poverty and isolation; and the fact that Mr. Bogat was only civil to Robin's father when they commiserated over another visitation from the repo man; and the fact that Mr. and Mrs. Hazen often watched with binoculars as Heath unloaded his truck, the better to report him to the police—none of those facts had told Robin that her family was vastly different from others until Goldie woke up one morning, dressed, primped, "took the bull by the horns," as she put it, and started driving Robin around Lilac in an effort to get legitimate businesses to play dirty with the Simonsens. "We'd starve otherwise, sweetie," Goldie said to Robin.

That was the summer of Grandma's singers on the hi-fi, Grandma's pastel capri pants and tight nylon sweaters, Grandma's amber-colored sunglasses, Grandma's mouth, open, beagle-braying. That was the summer Robin discovered that she didn't have to be out in the boonies with her dad, searching junkyards for car parts, or cruising some service road in far-off McHenry County to really see the sights. Instead, she could slump down in the passenger's seat of her grandmother's yellow Cadillac, her feet pressed against the dashboard, air conditioning on high, because on summer days like this Goldie indulged her, the motherless child, so she sat in an excited crumple eating candy bars, her eyes just level with the side window, while her grandmother drove around Lilac and DuPage County to the lumberyard, the hardware store, and to taverns—every one of them filled with bulky, looming men.

"We'd starve otherwise," Grandma said, putting the Cadillac into gear.

First stop was the Lilac Smoke Shop. Robin loved the heat of the men's bodies, the clouds of cigar and cigarette smoke, all the colorful packs and cartons behind the wood and glass counter, the periodicals, the dusty Mars Bars, Baby Ruths, and Butterfingers in tiered racks next to the cash register. She wandered the aisles, fingering the rows of print-heavy racing forms, then the slicker publications with cover shots of the velvety heads of horses, then baseball, football, and golf magazines, and then newspapers that weren't the *Chicago Tribune,* that weren't in English but in Polish, Italian, and Spanish. Robin even liked Larry Pike, the shop's owner, a man with sparse black and gray hair tangled on top of his head, eyes droopy in deep pouches of skin, and shiny, brightly colored shirts that strained at his belly. He smelled of cigars.

After the Smoke Shop came the lumberyard and sweaty teenagers in suede gloves who could only look away with shy smiles when Grandma unfolded from her Cadillac. Then a few bars, where Robin had to wait outside while Grandma went in to buy a bottle of Old Granddad or Gordon's and to laugh at the proprietors' jokes. Finally, Grandma would stop the Cadillac in the parking lot of Bogdanas Hardware, step out and adjust her clothes, and take Robin's hand. Inside the store, which was redolent with the smells of iron, rubber, and rope, Goldie paused and let the Bogdanas men drink her in: first Old Man Bogdanas, broad and tall, with a wide nose and head, clad every day in black pants and a white shirt; then George Junior, taller and narrower than his father, with sharper features and a brushy mustache that looked dirty. The Bogdanas men always waited for Goldie by the cash register, as if ready to ring her up as a purchase.

There were other men, there were more, all of them huffing and puffing and circling Goldie, trying anything to make her laugh, not even knowing when they first started bringing over extra goods from the stores—seconds, rejects, anything that was mismarked, untaxed, untraceable, unwanted, or unusable by anyone but the Simonsens—that their deliveries meant more to Robin's grandmother than a love song or a diamond bracelet.

By the end of that first summer, Goldie was spending her mornings scratching price tags off of dented wrench sets and setting out shopping bags full of untaxed cigarette packs and dusty pints of liquor. By August, day and night, the house on Highland Street was full of men.

Heath counted stacks of cash into the metal box behind the dryer, shook his head, and said to Robin, "Your granny's got good mojo."

Infants in blue sleepers cooed at Goldie from supermarket carts; little boys on Highland Street watched her back out of the driveway and then ran screaming after her as she drove off; husbands waiting at the post office with their wives winked at her and let her cut in line; even the geriatrics at the drugstore with their sticky-handled canes called her "Miss" and followed her bottom with their eyes. Mojo: another word for Goldie's magic. There was the paperboy, gawky, freckle-faced Jeff from Robin's grammar school, who one morning stood up on the banana seat of his spider bike when he saw Grandma in the picture window and promptly fell off and chipped a tooth. And there was the teenage boy at the Sinclair filling station who shot out of his folding chair the minute Goldie pulled the Cadillac up to the pump. He liked to stand at the car window, all smiles, while Grandma pulled at the opening of her blouse and laughed about giving him payment in quarters, or while she kneeled on the front seat, pretending to look in the back for the purse that was right next to her.

Grandma's mojo was this, too: if I've got it, you can see it—and vice versa. Robin couldn't get dressed without Goldie coming into her bedroom to ask a pointless question, nor could she go to the bathroom without her grandmother banging in to look for cold cream or her comb, only to leave the door wide open when she left. Once, when Goldie walked in on Heath while he was reading the Sunday funnies on the toilet, he rolled up his newspaper and swatted at her until she left. Grandma couldn't keep her hands off of Robin's clothes. She pulled at her blouses until they hung straight on her broad little shoulders, yanked her tights up into her crotch and bounced her. She talked about her own body incessantly, right down to her excretions and effusions; Robin heard the whole history of her grandmother's painful periods, in bright red detail. Goldie reported on her digestion, picked her teeth with a matchbook cover and examined the findings, extended delicate farts into the kitchen as she fried hamburgers on the stove. One night, Grandma opened her blouse at the dinner table and lifted a heavy breast out of her reinforced bra in order to show Robin a mole she thought might be malignant.

Grandma's mojo brought a collection of men to Highland Street that shook themselves out into a steady group after the holidays that first year. The men were Goldie's connections, from her rounds. Every day when Robin came home from school, she found the kitchen table littered with vodka, gin, and beer bottles, cut limes, half-empty glasses, puddles of melted ice cubes, full ashtrays, and, sitting in a circle around the wreckage, Goldie's men: Old Man Bogdanas and George Junior, Larry Pike, and "Tommy Boy" Berensen, who liked to pull quarters from Robin's ears while she sat giggling on his lap. "That old black magic," Sammy Davis sang from the living room. "Fly me to the moon," said Sinatra, "come fly with me," "let's dance." "Girl talk," sang Tony Bennett. "Girl, talk to me."

Tommy Berensen was Robin's favorite. She liked to lean back against his chest and try to follow his off-color jokes and sexual innuendoes, all the talk that caused Grandma to laugh her hound laugh and to jump in with staccato responses. All of Tommy's stained and ripped suit coats smelled of old sweat. He kept a pint of whiskey in his pocket. When he wasn't doing sleight-of-hand or showing Robin card tricks with his dirty-picture deck, Tommy Boy gave advice, just like Grandma. "Show you how to make a quick ten," he would say. "All you needs is a five and a little smooth talk." Or, on another day: "Say you're hungry, baby. You want a meal, but no dinero. What do you do? You remember this: people love to give away free if there's a chance someone'll make trouble. Now trouble can come three ways." But before Tommy could count off trouble on his fingers or explain how you got money to grow, Grandma would say, "Shhhhht, for cripe's sake. Pick on somebody your own size."

Robin finished fourth grade the same way she had started it, as a girl supposedly so fragile that her teacher spoke to her only in whispers, and her classmates refused to throw the dodge ball at her during recess. At home, she felt sturdy, even protected. At home, Grandma threw her in among the men as if she were a grown woman, and they often talked to Goldie through her, as if speaking directly to Grandma were as dangerous as staring at the sun.

"Think your grandma would want to have dinner with an old horseplayer like me?" Tommy asked one afternoon. "Here, baby," he said, patting his thighs. Robin sat and started going through Tommy's suit coat pockets.

"You've got those blue eyes just like Goldie," Larry Pike said, leaning over the kitchen table toward Robin.

"Blue, but the dark came in from her mom," Goldie said. She put numbers into a ledger book, her glasses low on her nose. "And her face is wide, see, and her mouth. Good bones, though. Dark hair, like an Italian, though the mom was a Ukrainian gal."

"Chicago?" Larry asked.

"In my old neighborhood," Old Man Bogdanas said, "the Ukraines had it in for us Lithuanians. Latvians, too. They hated our guts for sure."

"Just yours, Pop," George Junior said.

The old man glared at his son. Robin found a penknife in one of Tommy's breast pockets and opened it. They always did this, the Bogdanas men. Old Man said something, the son bit back, and then he let his father's anger ricochet off his skin. George was the only one of Grandma's men who wasn't afraid to lean into her, to brush against her, or to get her alone over by the sink and put his hand on her bottom. George had never spoken to Robin; he sat with his back to her, as if the sight of her offended him. Goldie said George didn't even like his own kids.

"Give that over," Goldie said to Robin, holding out her hand. "What's the matter with you," she said to Tommy, "letting a kid play with a knife like that?"

"It's okay," Robin said, putting the knife back into Tommy's pocket. "I have a bunch of my own." Heath had given her a box full of cheap aluminum penknives, throwaways. "Use 'em and lose 'em," her father had said. "They're for quick work," he said, winking.

The kitchen was full of baking summer air. Robin heard children riding their bikes down Highland, yelping as they got to the bottom of the short hill and coasted to a stop, usually in front of the Simonsens' house. School was out, and other kids played in the streets, or on the jungle gyms at Stephen Douglas, or even in Post Park in the middle of Lilac, but Robin was at home, in the smoke-filled kitchen, while Grandma cut huge slabs from a bologna one of the men had brought, and Old Man Bogdanas stared silently into the kitchen, and Tommy worked on his pint of whiskey. Peggy Lee sang "Fever" in the living room.

Grandma took off her sleeveless blouse, revealing a white, skintight leotard. She flung one arm over the back of her chair and looked around the kitchen, smiling. Robin felt the men shift just slightly.

"What?" Grandma asked, smiling harder.

Tommy had books of matches from a coffee shop on Diversey in Chicago. "Do you eat here?" Robin asked, fanning out the matches on the kitchen table.

"That's where I meet my probation officer," Tommy said.

"Everything's got to come out of that mouth," Goldie said. "Doesn't it?"

"What's 'probation'?" Robin asked.

"See?" Grandma closed the ledger with a sigh. She turned to Robin. "I knew every probation officer in Vegas," she said. "You couldn't help it in my business."

"I never got that," George Junior said. "You should go away, do your time, and then you're done. End of story. Why have to report then, like a bad kid?"

"Exactly," Grandma said.

The father stared at the son. "That's a stupid idea. You've got to have that in between, so you're ready to go back with people."

"There's an idea, too," Grandma said, smiling and pointing her cigarette at the old man.

"It's not a fucking zoo!" George cried. "You're in jail or you're not!"

"What're you yelling for?" Old Man Bogdanas said. "Christ."

"We're guests here, you know," Tommy said.

"I mean, really," Grandma said, pretending to be serious.

"Sorry," George said. The old man briefly hung his head.

"There's a sulky driver," Tommy said, raising his voice. "I know him from Maywood, and this guy, he can't stay out of jail." He put the matchbooks back into his pocket. "Suspicion of fixing races," Tommy continued. "He's so bad about it, it's like he wants to get caught. He's dumb, really. Everyone around the horses is dumb, except the gamblers. And the horses."

"I knew a jockey once," Goldie said, her voice distant. "Came up to about here on me," she added, pressing a hand to her breasts. "You could find him in the sports book at the Sands morning, noon, and night."

"I know loads of jockeys," Tommy said, sitting forward. "Come to the track with me next week. It'll be like Vegas."

Larry snorted. "Have you ever even been to Vegas?" he asked.

"Yeah, I bet you haven't," George said.

"And when were you there?" Old Man asked.

"My dad was born there," Robin said.

"Never mind about your dad," Goldie said.

Tommy leaned over and whispered into Robin's ear: "Your grandma and I are going to Vegas next year."

Every day Goldie told stories of Vegas, wrapped herself tighter into her clothes and complained about the cold, even in June, swore at the sunlight streaming into the kitchen before noon. Her unhappiness was a threat. Was Grandma moving back? Going on a trip? For how long? "Grandma," Robin said, but Goldie was telling a story about the Sands and a pit boss and a ripped dress. If Goldie left, it would be just Heath again. Robin's father was out now, but for three days he'd been in his room, smoking and sleeping and only coming out for the bathroom and for food. Grandma had kicked at his door and yelled at him until he emerged.

Now the Bogdanas men were fighting about what each of them would have done to the pit boss to defend Goldie's honor. Grandma laughed. Robin got off of Tommy's lap and stood next to her grandmother.

"Grandma," Robin said. She pinched Goldie's arm. "When are you leaving? I have to know."

"What, sugar pie?" Goldie asked. "Honey, hair behind your ears. It looks better."

The Bogdanas men rose from the table.

"All the way up the seam," Grandma said to Tommy, in response to a question Robin hadn't heard. "Ruined it for good. The animal."

"Maybe I can go with you," Robin said.

"Where?" Goldie asked.

George and his father had moved to the other side of the island and were now yelling at each other. "No wonder Ma hates you," George said, and then a pot went flying off the stove.

"That's enough!" Larry said, getting up. "Help me," he said to Tommy.

"I'm staying out of this one," he said.

"Smart man," Grandma said. Larry sat down.

"Maybe Dad and I can both go," Robin said. The crash and yelling of the Bogdanas men could be taking place in another house on Highland; Robin barely heard their voices. You could turn anything into junk, even shouting, make it all irrelevant and fleeting, if you just knew how. It was a matter of putting a frame around what you wanted and ignoring the rest.

"I'm waiting for a call, honey," Grandma said. "I can't take you anywheres now."

"She's talking about Vegas," Tommy said. "Remember?"

"What Vegas?" Larry said.

"I'm telling you, those guys are going to kill each other," Goldie said.

Old Man Bogdanas and his son were in each other's face, whispering and spitting.

"I don't know how they can stay in business together," Goldie said, sighing. "Boys," she said quietly. "Stop this now."

"We talked about visiting my place in Wisconsin," Larry said. "Remember? Last month, we talked."

"You don't have a place in Wisconsin," Tommy said. "You have a brother with a piece of land for a tent. And Goldie's not going camping, I can tell you that."

"Grandma!" Robin yelled. She jumped up and down.

"Sweetheart, what is it?" Goldie put her arm around Robin.

"I don't want you to go to Vegas," Robin said. "It's just me and Dad then, and I can't."

"Nobody's going to Vegas," Goldie said.

"Hey," Tommy said.

"See?" Larry asked. "Wisconsin's not even that far," he said. "Two, two and a half hours, tops."

"Are you going to Wisconsin?" Robin asked. A whole state away.

The Bogdanas men strode out of the house, yelling. Robin heard their cars start up and roar away.

"You know what you call that in Norwegian?" Goldie asked. She paused. "Damn, I can't think of it. It's when the son hates the father."

"Cain and Abel," Larry said.

"That's brothers, for god's sake," Goldie said.

"Oedipal," Tommy said, pouring himself another inch of whiskey. Goldie and Larry just looked at him.

"Grandma, where are you going?" Robin shouted.

"Look, pumpkin!" Goldie said. "Here's your dad in the driveway."

Outside, Heath and a couple of other men pulled boards from the truck. Her father looked heavier, bloated; Robin felt the way he looked sometimes, brimming with tears. Heath's hair was dark with sweat. What would happen without her grandmother? She and her father would simply burst open.

"Baby!" Heath said when he saw Robin in the kitchen. "See what I've got for you?" He didn't wait for an answer but headed down the hall with the other men, their arms full of boards.

In Robin's bedroom, Heath and the men folded up her army cot.

"Something new, kiddo," Robin's father said. "Just for you."

It was a double bed, and it took the three men over an hour to put it together. Heath made several trips out to the garage for tools and fasteners, but in the end he had to hammer a cotter pin into the screw sleeve to hold one side of the bed together and use a clamp to hold the other.

"Don't jump on the bed, Rob," he said, "and you'll be fine." He plucked the Panatela from his mouth and pushed his hair back. The other two men stood around Robin's bed, panting and smiling.

"She needs sheets, man," a guy in overalls said.

"Use the ones from the cot," another guy with a beard said.

Then there was another flurry as the men laid the old linens on Robin's new bed. They didn't fit and instead formed an imprint of the cot in the middle of the new mattress. "There," the guy in overalls said. He had a long red braid and wore a flannel shirt with the sleeves ripped off.

"What do you think, Robin?" Heath asked, opening his arms to her new bed.

It took up most of her room, crowding her dresser over to the closet. The cherry headboard was scratched and gouged. And the sheets looked sad in the middle of the bed, like clothes with the body missing.

"I don't like it, Dad," Robin said. The three men turned to her.

"Aw, honey," Heath said. His face fell.

"We'll wait in the kitchen, man," said the bearded guy.

"It doesn't fit," Robin said, after the other men left. "See? It's all over by that wall and almost over by this one."

"Well, kiddo, there's not much else in here," Heath said, looking around at Robin's tiny dresser and the child's rocking chair that was too small for her now. "What do you need the space for?"

"I might get something I want, or you could put more in here or something." In the kitchen, the voices of Heath's friends rose as they talked to Grandma.

"Get on it and try, honey," Robin's father said. "For me." He leaned against the dresser and plunged his hands into his pockets. How could he look so tired in the middle of the day?

Robin perched on the edge of the mattress. Her feelings for her father sloshed together. She was ecstatic at his attention, yet she was afraid he would bolt, leave with the two men, slam his bedroom door and smoke, maybe take the bed back. This was the first time she'd been alone with her father in months; she had to make it count.

"You have to really try it, Rob," her father said.

"I am."

"No, come on, lie down with me a minute. Shove over." Heath lay down and rolled Robin to the wall.

"Dad."

"Just wait. Here, come back, and I'll put my arm around you."

"It's scratchy."

"Try, baby. See? You've got all this room."

"It's okay."

"Better," Heath said. "Better than okay."

Her father's arm was heavy and hairy across her shoulder and chest. Heath's fingers gripped the edge of the floating blanket. He breathed on Robin's neck. In the living room, Sammy Davis paused in the middle of his song, stopping the music.

Recently, Heath had told Robin and Goldie that he wanted his own floor of the house, his own room with more privacy. And he needed his own bathroom. Grandma had looked at him, taken a drag on her cigarette, and shrugged. "Long as you pay for it," she had said.

Robin had quizzed Heath on where he would really sleep, where the old bed he had shared with Patricia would go. If her father made a new place for himself, it would be pristine, free of any memories of Robin's mother. Robin still saw her mother regularly, in a kind of companion movie that picked up pieces of the past and projected them onto any random minute of her day. One moment Patricia was making dinner, her long black hair swinging as she reached for a pan; the next moment Robin saw her mother in bed, her collarbones standing out like huge scars, her thin-lipped, wide mouth, just like Robin's, forced into a smile. If Robin's father had no pictures in his head like these, or if he rejected them, then he was half-blind, incomplete, a man no longer her father because he had no claim to her mother. To Robin, one could not exist without the other.

Heath shifted his arm and settled closer. He'd already started construction on a second story. So far, he'd built just the stairs. They angled up from inside the back door, slanted over the dryer, and stopped at the ceiling of the back room, which also contained the furnace and the hot water heater. Robin had ascended the stairs until her head hit the ceiling. She imagined her father finishing their construction, one step at a time, breaking through the plaster and wood and continuing into the sky. If Robin called his name, would he come back to earth?

"Dad?" Robin whispered. Her father snored quietly.

Robin had brought him back, that morning on the farm road, and then he'd pulled Goldie into their house, and all the men, and more junk and women, and even this new lethargy. From the beginning, before Robin could reason, Heath had been her father, the only reason she needed. Now, even in his sleep, Robin could feel her father's discomfort, his exposure. All of that buildup, all of the people and trash and distractions were meant to hide her father, so that next time she'd never be able to find him.

chapter three

~

"Kitty Paint is going to make you dumb," Ken Taylor said to Robin. "Just wait." He ran his bicycle tire over the toe of Robin's shoe. "She doesn't even know her times tables," he added.

"Shut up," Robin said, turning to go.

They were walking on the wide lawn in front of Stephen Douglas Elementary. Once they got to the road, Robin assumed Ken would turn left and coast down Highland Street, then turn right toward his own neighborhood. But at the edge of the school lawn, Ken raced from behind and then skidded his bike in front of Robin, blocking her path.

"You're gross," he said.

"Cut it out," she said, trying to go around him.

Ken anticipated her move and blocked her again. "Both you and Kitty are gross," he said. He leaned close to Robin's face. "You don't talk to anybody else," he whispered. "It's queer."

Ken tossed his brown forelock out of his face. Robin was furious: people came at her with their feelings hanging out, demanding she pay attention, as if she were responsible for them.

Robin grabbed the handlebars of Ken's bike and yanked hard; the bike tipped and he fell onto the grass. "I think *you're* queer," she said.

Ken sprang at Robin and they wrestled. A group of kids emerged from out of nowhere and circled them. Robin kicked Ken in the shins. He rolled her around on the cold ground. They grappled. He sobbed into her ear, though Robin couldn't see how she could have hurt him. They continued to struggle, and as they did, Robin's grip tightened, and her knee worked harder against Ken's body. Her palms felt blank with rage, as if she were trying to break an inanimate object. Ken's own anger was mysterious; he acted as if he knew something she didn't, a lie she had inadvertently spread, a misdeed she had forgotten she'd committed. Robin felt as if she were beating Ken's knowledge back inside him. Suddenly, as if by some silent agreement, their fight ended, and they both stood up, Ken weeping, Robin looking beyond him to the corner of the school yard and to the cyclone fence with its angled opening, just room enough for one kid at a time to pass through, and then beyond that to the street that led to Highland and to her home. The circled kids breathed heavily, as if they, too, had been fighting.

Ken, who was still crying, pulled his bike off the ground and put his foot on the pedal. The kids stared at Robin; she was a girl, and she'd fought a boy. She looked down: her green wool coat was smeared with dirt; tufts of grass stuck to her sleeves, and her knee socks had puddled into her shoes.

"God, Robin," Ken screeched through his tears, "you're going to be sorry!" He pedaled off, tires churning across the school lawn. Robin turned without a word and walked away, passing through the fence gap and onto the blacktopped street, her skin still twitching from Ken's grasp. She felt oddly exhilarated, though she tingled with dread, too, like the hero in a storybook heading off to another battle. Coming down Highland toward her house, seeing Goldie's new red Cadillac like a piece of candy in the driveway, her father entering the house with the bounce in his stride that meant a sale was near—Robin finally felt as if she were worthy of her odd family. Since Patricia's death, the family had gone on without her, creating a new configuration and a new method of moneymaking. Now she had her own story, her own fight that ended in her own self-righteous victory over a myopic, narrow-minded enemy. Robin had defended her friend, Kitty Paint! And, in the words of her grandmother, she hadn't given a flying damn how she'd done it.

"Holy smokes!" Tommy Boy cried when Robin entered the kitchen. He pulled her to him. "This kid's got a problem," he said.

"Lemme see," Goldie said, squinting through cigarette smoke at Robin's face. "Why are you crying? You hurt?" "Canadian Sunset" was on the stereo—Dean Martin's version.

"I'm okay," Robin said. The tears surprised her; they seemed entirely physical, uncontrolled leaking without any emotional cause. Tommy Boy's arm was a smoky, comforting bolster, his breath in her face liquored and warm.

"Aw, see, she's fine," Grandma said. She wore her glittery reading glasses, and arrayed in front of her were a stack of movie magazines and an envelope bulging with cash. Grandma pulled the money out of the envelope and began to count it, snapping each bill like a bank teller.

Tommy Boy's red eyes followed her movements. "How much?" he asked quietly. His arm tightened around Robin.

If anyone asked her, she could say that she'd walked home during the light rain that was falling, and that it had wet her face. She didn't have to be crying.

When Goldie finished counting the bills, Tommy's hand shot out, closed around the envelope, and slid it into the left side of his brown suit coat.

"How about a nip now?" he asked Goldie.

She looked over her glasses at him, smirking, even as she pushed away from the table. She came back with a cup of coffee for Tommy. He slid a pint bottle out of his right jacket pocket.

"Hey, Goldie," he said, "I'm balanced." He rocked from side to side, moving Robin with him. "Get it?" he asked. "Left side, right side, I've got everything I need in my pockets."

"Okay, hon," Grandma said.

"Robin, you wanna try?" Tommy Boy asked. "It's a little whiskey. Good for a person."

Robin looked to her grandmother for permission, but she was reading the front of a movie magazine. On the cover, a pretty woman cried into her hands. No one had noticed the mud stains on Robin's coat, or the brown smears across her calves. She wiped her face.

"Taste," Tommy said.

Robin stuck her index finger into the bottle. It came up glistening with brownish liquid, like the oil stick in one of her dad's useless cars. She gave a tentative lick. Sour, strong, with a sweetish cushion and a vapor like strange breath that snaked down her throat. She made a face.

Tommy Boy laughed and took her hand. "No good?" he asked, hugging her to him again. "You left most of it, sweetie." Tommy pulled Robin's finger quickly and gently through his teeth the same way Grandma drew at a chicken bone.

"Tommy, quit," Goldie said. She was watching him over her glasses, unsmiling. He laughed, but with less energy, and he took his arm away from Robin.

"Sweetie pie," Grandma said, "go upstairs and get your dad."

"Where's his truck?" Robin asked.

"Larry borrowed it to go back to the store," Grandma said, just as the old Ford rattled into the driveway. Larry Pike got out carrying a large shopping bag.

"It's pay-up day, in' it?" Tommy said, squinting out the window.

"Go upstairs," Goldie said to Robin.

A month before, Heath had completed the second floor. After months of delay, he had finally burst through the ceiling to the outside. It had been night, the dead of winter, so when Robin came to inspect the noise, she climbed the stairs toward Heath's voice and passed right into a dark bowl of stars. She found her father on a ceiling strut, his breath curling out into the night, smiling and reaching out a hand for her. As they sat on the roof in the cold, Robin thought she could see her mother, her dark hair a shade lighter than the black sky, her long smile in a band of stars. Below, Goldie had clacked around the kitchen in her high heels, looking for the two of them. Later, Heath covered the hole with plastic. The next night it snowed, and he removed the plastic so he and Robin could walk up into the falling flakes, their heads blanketed, their torsos warm and dry.

Robin reached the top of the stairs and stopped in the small box of a hallway. She had carved her initials into the soft wood paneling with a butter knife, on a spot between the door to her father's room and the opening to the bathroom, which was really a closet with a shower, sink, and toilet, all of which rested on creaky subflooring.

Heath's bedroom was the size of the downstairs living room, dining area, and kitchen combined, and it all belonged to him—his "space," he called it. A king-size mattress lay on the floor, covered with Indian-print pillows and a red bedspread; his old, broken dresser sat next to the closet, which had no door and just a tangle of clothes and a snarl of empty hangers on its bar. The dresser mirror sat on the floor across from Heath's bed. When Goldie first came up to inspect the room, she looked from the mirror to the bed, took a drag on her cigarette, shook her head, and said, "Criminy, boy." She hadn't ventured upstairs since.

Heath was moving furniture. "Kiddo!" he cried. He pushed a ripped armchair against the far wall, then dropped into it, sending up a cloud of dust. Robin stood thinking: Lorraine, Trudy, Annie—they were last month; they were the first ones up here. Her father had no pictures of anyone—even Robin—nothing to remind him of who lived downstairs, nothing about these new women except furniture for them to rest upon.

"What happened to you?" Robin's father asked. He frowned. "Come here." He turned Robin around.

"I got in a fight, Dad," Robin said, grinning. Her father's hands on her shoulders were as good as an embrace. They made her weak, giddy.

"A fight?" Heath asked. "With who?"

"Ken."

"That boy who used to come over? Why?"

"He said stuff."

"Stuff about me?" Robin's father took her into his lap, his wool shirt scratching the back of her neck. To Robin's surprise, she began to cry again.

"No," Robin said, wiping her nose with her hand. "Stuff about somebody I know." Heath breathed deeply behind her; his skin and clothes met her back, then retreated. For months, she hadn't thought of her father as truly alive, as someone who had to breathe and blink and keep his heart beating. Instead, he had been more like a cartoon, racing through the house, eating, running in and out with dates, pocketing money, revving the coughing engine of the truck, all of it fast, fast. Now that he was stationary, he seemed all flesh, blood coursing, sweet smoke and dirty hair smell.

"It's good to stick up for your friend," Heath said. "But Ken could have really hurt you. Look, you've got a scratch." Heath held up Robin's arm and shook it gently. A tiny zipper of dried blood lay across the top of her wrist.

"I beat him, Dad, I think," Robin said.

Her father chuckled. "That's my girl," he said. Robin closed her eyes again. My, mine. My girl, he had said.

"Dad, Grandma gave Tommy Boy some money."

"Yeah?" her father asked. His voice was quieter.

She turned and tugged gently at a curl of his blond hair. It was almost as long as hers now; it fell past his shoulder blades, a tangled mane, and when he walked out to his truck it rose and fell like waves of yellow smoke.

"Business is big," Heath said. "We're doing good now."

"Is it because of Grandma?" Robin asked.

Her father was silent for a moment. "Tommy Boy, he's good at finding things for me and Grandma to sell. All those guys, all Grandma's friends, they're resourceful."

Next to Heath's bed was a stack of *Playboy* magazines. A week ago, Robin had stolen one of them. In bed that night, she had examined each page. The roundness of the women's bodies, the circles of their breasts, mocked her when she closed her eyes; they were like balloons she wanted to pop. The magazine made her angry, in the same mysterious way some girls at school, even her new friend Kitty Paint, so slow and so dense, made her want to attack, to kick them all in the shins.

Heath and Robin walked hand in hand downstairs. Robin could feel every spot where Ken had touched her. Her skin seemed to light up, then cool down, an imprint of the boy's fingers left behind. Her leg ached, and the dried mud pulled at her skin. She made a sudden wish: to enter the kitchen and find her mother, long black hair like her own, brown eyes to her blue, waiting to uncomplicate in Robin's life what Robin only suspected was beyond her own ability to correct.

But instead, Robin found another stranger, this one a thin, fidgety man in a tweed hat and a corduroy car coat. Heath greeted him. A wide spiral of cigarette and cigar smoke hovered over everyone, as if it, too, waited for the secret of this man's visit.

Outside, cold dusk coated the French doors. The stranger laid two shapes wrapped in cloth on the tabletop, then unwrapped each bundle like a woman opening her blouse. The first shape became a jumble of sparkling jewelry—stones, gold, silver, rings, bracelets, a necklace with tiny strung stars. The second shape, shining just as brightly, was a small silver pistol.

∼

Kitty Paint had joined Robin's fifth-grade class in October. For days, before the bell and during recess, Kitty had stood alone, bouncing her back against the chain-link fence that ran around the schoolyard, chewing on her cotton gloves, and watching the rest of her classmates through darting eyes. The maples and poplars and cottonwoods spread their bare branches and leaves skittered across the playground. For a while, Robin ran back and forth in front of Kitty, pretending to be a part of the games, until one afternoon she stopped and leaned on the fence, gasping for air. Kitty began talking to Robin as if they had been in the middle of a conversation. Kitty was a tall, broad-chested girl with colorless, flyaway hair, and she had a slight lisp, which forced Robin to watch her mouth while she talked.

Kitty had come to Stephen Douglas, she said that October day, from Immaculate Conception ("Contheption"), also called IC, one of two Catholic schools in Lilac, but already Kitty didn't like public school, she told Robin, because there was too much shoving. Everything Kitty said to Robin came out like the printed words in a comic strip bubble, plain, easy to understand. At home, Goldie's and Heath's sentences had an echo of other words underneath them, but Kitty's speech was as uninflected as her wide, bland face and faded brown eyes. When Robin asked why Kitty had left IC for Stephen Douglas, Kitty said, blinking slowly, "My parents couldn't afford parochial anymore."

Robin walked Kitty home that first day. To Robin's amazement, Kitty lived only four streets behind Highland, in a small brick house in a neighborhood with sidewalks. It had only recently dawned on Robin that there were dozens of other kids attending different schools like tribal villages, all over town, inaccessible because of a few measly streets, yet as foreign as a settlement of Pygmies would have seemed to a clan of Laplanders.

When Robin told Goldie about Kitty, Grandma said that nobody ever went from Catholic to public, only the other way around, and then only if your kid was in serious trouble.

But Kitty was as stiff as a ruler, a characteristic that Robin assumed meant goodness. Kitty barely opened her mouth in class, talked to no one on the playground but Robin, and always stood tall, one of her legs wrapped tightly around the other like a muscular snake climbing a pole. Kitty's whole life seemed predicated on staying out of trouble, or staying invisible. As for Kitty's religion, Robin found it deeply mysterious. She knew about Catholics, in part because her mother had been raised as one and had grown up as the only Ukrainian girl in a Polish orphanage in Chicago. And around Lilac, everyone knew the Catholic kids by sight. All of the students at IC and at Visitation, the other parochial school in town, wore uniforms, along with an air of seriousness. You just knew that these kids did their homework and never talked back; if they misbehaved, the nuns would beat them with the heavy beads Robin imagined them swinging like Olympic athletes doing the anvil toss. There were daily services, too: Robin had seen the tidy, marching lines of students swallowed up by the churches attached to both IC and Visitation. According to movies and TV shows, people chanted and priests sprayed incense inside Catholic churches, and sunlight poured through high windows, plus there were whispered secrets and elaborate ceremonies. One morning during Kitty's first spring at Stephen Douglas, she came to school with a gray smudge on her forehead that she said was ashes the priest had blessed her with. The mark irked Robin—it was just dirt!—but Kitty refused to wipe it off, and her stubbornness was so infuriating that Robin snubbed her at recess. Unmoved, Kitty returned to her place at the fence again, stupid, placid, and alone.

Robin had never had a friend like Kitty, or a friendship like the one she now endured. One day she loved Kitty like someone in a movie would, desperately, in bright color; the next day Kitty was just another girl Robin wanted to pummel as she had Ken. Kitty was like a fever one day, then cool and clean in Robin's blood the next. Every day, Robin worked so hard to get Kitty to understand some simple event, some idea, some emotion Robin wanted to name, that she felt her upper lip prickle with sweat. She promised Kitty an audience with Goldie, who could never remember the girl's name, or a look at one of Heath's *Playboy*s, which made Kitty giggle and hide her eyes, or free reign in the spare room, a treasure hunt guaranteed to produce nothing. Several times, Robin had burst into tears just as Kitty was about to go home, and, after Robin mentioned Patricia, Kitty would break into sobs as well. Then the two girls would sprawl on the double bed in ecstasies of sadness. But all of this was tiring, just hard labor that made Robin wish for something simpler, like a solid shoe and Kitty's shinbone. Sometimes, just walking home from school with Kitty exhausted Robin, and once she got to her own house she could only sit vacantly before the TV while the Three Stooges battered one another, her father went missing, and men yucked it up in the kitchen with Goldie, their wallets thick with cash.

~

Corned beef hash in a worn black skillet, potatoes in a huge brown mixing bowl with a yellow stripe around it, salad in an enormous greasy bowl with three wooden balls as feet, four kinds of dressing in bottles that had been wiped clean, all of it served in the stifling heat of July at Kitty Paint's dinner table. Robin sat fidgeting, unable to eat, worried about her sleepover suitcase, which was just a shopping bag with string handles. Mrs. Paint had watched her carry it in.

"I don't know how we're going to send you kids to college," Mr. Paint said, heaping food onto his plate. A radio played in the kitchen: the treacly sounds of Tony Orlando and Dawn and then jaunty jingles with bleats of horn and a chorus of women's voices.

Mr. Paint was as disconcertingly thin as Kitty's older brother, David. Father and son sat side by side, passing dishes of food back and forth with frightening speed. Both were very pale, with tall pads of brick-colored hair, and they both wore thick glasses with heavy, transparent frames.

"What about your dad, Robin?" Mr. Paint asked, his mouth full of potatoes. "What's he going to do about getting you to college?" Before Robin could answer, Mr. Paint said, "How many brothers and sisters." He looked from Kitty to Mrs. Paint to David. "Did I ask that already?"

"She's an only child, Daddy," Kitty said to her dinner plate.

Mr. Paint flashed Robin a look of sympathy. "Well, that doesn't make it any easier, does it? One child, two, or a dozen. Who can afford college?"

"Who would want to go?" Mrs. Paint said, staring over everyone's heads at the cuckoo clock ticking on the dining room wall. "All that sex and drugs." Her hair, colorless like Kitty's, was twisted into a long, flat bun and secured with a narrow barrette in the shape of a frown.

Robin cleared her throat. "My dad says if I want to go to college I should go to Berkeley, in California, where he went. He says there's not so much bullshit there and everyone's not up your ass like they are at other places."

Mr. Paint scowled.

"My," Mrs. Paint said flatly. Her eyes ran over the walls, which were bare except for the clock and a painting of bleeding Jesus.

David coughed and began choking. He blinked his pale eyes and lifted a trembly, freckled hand to his throat as he gagged, his face flushing crimson. Everyone ignored him.

Mr. Paint rattled on for the rest of the meal. He talked the way a sweeping sprinkler worked: right, then left, a steady spray covering a wide territory. Words rained down from his food-flecked mouth. When Mrs. Paint rose from the table and began to stack plates, he still wasn't done. Instead, he looked at Kitty and Robin and asked, "Now what?"

At Robin's house, this was the time of night when, if he didn't have a date, her father went off to the garage with his Panatela and two fingers of scotch in a coffee cup, or, more likely, when he holed up in his new room until smoke choked the back stairs. Robin wouldn't see him again until the next morning. But Mr. Paint herded Kitty and

Robin into the living room and sat them down on the couch. He was serious about seeing what was next. David tiptoed up the stairs carrying a soup bowl filled with ice cream.

Mr. Paint got out the Monopoly game and set it up, all the while extolling its educational value. He then played with desperate enthusiasm, commenting on every one of Kitty's and Robin's moves as if real skill were involved. Mr. Paint's mood turned somber when he helped Kitty count out her tens and twenties and when he praised Robin's ability to acquire hotels on all the cheap properties within the first half hour. Robin didn't tell Mr. Paint that Monopoly was the only game at her house, and, even though it was missing all but twenty bucks of fake money and most of the playing pieces, her father had been teaching her its ruthless strategy for years. At home, Robin and her father played with real cash, the denominations on the bills altered with a red marker, and they moved pieces of Grandma's costume jewelry around the board. Heath always won.

Mr. Paint's extended stay in Jail gave him the opportunity to inform Robin about Paint family history while she carried on with the game, bankrupting Kitty. Mr. Paint got out a dusty photo album. Inside were thick, shiny photographs of worn-down people and scores of raggedy kids standing shyly in muddy barnyards. The adults' hands were twisted and painful-looking; the men wore caps, the women babushkas. Goldie had pictures of her own parents before they emigrated from Norway, but she also liked to pretend she never had a family or a farm childhood in Minnesota, so she hid the photos in an old Modess box in the back of her closet. Every time Robin got out the box, she heard the pictures sliding around like sand shifting, and she felt discouraged, as if the photos had turned to dust and it would be her monumental task to piece them all back together again. Mr. Paint was proud of his family; he talked of their hardships and poverty. Whenever Grandma mentioned her family she looked sour and tired and her mouth filled with spit and she always concluded by saying that it was her family's fault she didn't talk to them, as narrow and isolated as they were, willing to throw off their very own for nothing. You couldn't fix stupidity when it didn't want fixing, she always said.

Mr. Paint pulled an almost transparent piece of paper out of the photo album. It was written in a foreign language, with a shaky X marked at the bottom.

"These were my grandfather's papers for the Polish army," Mr. Paint said. "See? He couldn't read or write, only make an *X*." He pointed to a separate line on which someone had written two words. "That was his name," Mr. Paint said. "Stashu was the first and then this was our original last name."

He moved his finger over to a jumble of *p*'s and *c*'s and *z*'s that ended with a *t*, a word that looked like a mouthful of crooked teeth. When Kitty said the name, it sounded like a sneeze.

"Say it again," Robin said. Her heart swelled. "Paint" was just a code word for Kitty's secret self, another mystery, like her religion. Robin knew about blood and inheritance; you could never be sure how much of a person was a new collection of traits and how much an echo from grandparents or before: Goldie said she found her own smile inside Robin's. Robin looked at the long-dead members of the Paint family. Kitty chewed her cuticles until they were bloody, an exercise in pain; she had a broad, sprung ribcage like a cartoon hero's, strong-looking, a shield upon which to crack villains' heads: were those traits in the photographs? You had to keep looking at these pictures, just to keep the people in them dark and glossy, tics in your memory like a flapping bird you see out of the corner of your eye. A picture of Patricia sat next to Robin's bed, shining hair framing her face. Her name before Heath had been Petrigala.

Bedtime! The girls pounded up the stairs. In her bedroom, Kitty peeled off her shorts, then her ankle socks. Kitty's legs were the color of bread dough, and sturdy, like fence posts. Her white underpants were frayed at the waistband. Robin stood in the middle of the room fully dressed, remembering suddenly that she'd forgotten to bring pajamas; she slept naked at home. From the hallway came the wet whisper of David's transistor radio playing behind his closed door. The tiny cones of Kitty's nipples showed through the cotton fabric of her undershirt.

Kitty stood in the light from a street lamp outside her window. Her chest was impressive, as wide as a tiny man's, and she had thick, fleshy arms. Looking at Kitty should have been like looking into a mirror, but part of Robin felt she was seeing something brand-new, something she had to memorize and decipher. Kitty was a new species, unclassified.

"We should get in bed now," Kitty said.

Robin took off everything but her underpants. The sheets were rough and clean. She could smell Kitty next to her: meat and potato odors from dinner and a sweet afterburn from the same laundry detergent Goldie used. And she could hear her, too, even though Kitty's face was in shadow. Kitty was a mouth breather, especially when she was thinking hard. Every question their fifth-grade teacher asked Kitty was followed by a long pause filled with the chug-chug of Kitty's breathing as she solidified her answer, her mind working away like a kiln firing a simple pot.

Robin lay on her side, letting her eyes adjust to the darkness in Kitty's room. It was a stark place. Unlike other kids' rooms in which you played, read, or even watched TV, Kitty's was only good for sleeping. She had the twin bed with its lozenge-shaped headboard and footboard, a four-drawer dresser, and a simple bedside table with a clown lamp and a small electric clock with luminous hands. No books, toys, or childish items except for the lamp and a Cinderella night light, pink skirt aglow. A cold wind swept through Robin's belly. This was the same feeling she had when she saw animals in trouble or hungry. This was pity. Kitty's room made Robin sick with sadness. There were Kitty's parents, too, who were sorry enough to decimate even Kitty's stark space, the tops of their heads narrow and vulnerable as they bent over the table to say grace that night. Robin had sat upright and silent through their murmuring, her hands in her lap, unsure how to act, and also angry. You didn't bow down in her house.

"Do you like anyone at school?" Kitty asked, her eyes wide open and fixed on Robin's face.

"Like anyone?" Robin asked. "You mean like friends?"

"No, like boys," Kitty said. She paused. "I like Eric Gromico," she said.

Eric Gromico did his own science projects at home, and he had perfect posture and a loud swallow. He waved his hand wildly whenever the teacher asked a question. Eric could have been from another era, like the perfect student from the ancient school-safety films Robin and her classmates had to watch every fall. He was the boy who always kept the fire drill lines straight and calm, a boy who wore brittle brown shoes like insect casings. In second grade, Eric Gromico had worn a patch to cure his lazy eye, and Robin had thought him sickly ever since. But no boy had ever spoken to Kitty. Robin and no one else had rescued Kitty from her exile by the playground fence.

"*I* like you," Robin said, hoping to end all talk of Eric. The boy was already stepping out of his safety film and leaving footprints on Kitty's liver-colored carpet.

"Let's tell each other everything," Kitty said suddenly, grabbing both of Robin's hands. She sighed deeply.

"I tell you everything already," Robin said.

"You do? Really?" Kitty asked.

"Sure," Robin said. "We're best friends, aren't we?" Kitty didn't even know that when you stayed over at somebody's house and everyone knew it, then you were permanent friends, and even when you were separated by meals or bedtime, you had to keep track of each other. It was like a marriage except you didn't live together.

Kitty pulled Robin's hands up to her chin. Kitty's touch was purposeful, not a tap on the arm during gym or recess, not a grabbing hold to tell a secret. Kitty's pulse bumped against Robin's palm. Kitty breathed deeply, her eyes closed. Since her mother's death, every connection Robin had to another person was like a splinter she had to remove; her feelings for Kitty now shifted between love and hate, relief and pain, with each of her friend's even breaths. Kitty's cheap tee shirt was too tight for her, her dinner smell had soured, she didn't seem to understand the rarity of having a best friend—all of this was like a concrete block Robin wanted to hit her head on again and again.

Kitty was examining her. "How come you don't have any brothers or sisters?" she asked.

"My mom died," Robin said. Kitty knew this, of course, but it had also become Robin's response to any question about herself she couldn't answer. It satisfied most people—or scared them off.

"Was your mom going to have a baby or something?" Kitty asked.

"I don't think she could," Robin said. Patricia had been a skeleton with hair, not the plump, fleshy kind of mother Robin saw listing around, big-bellied.

"My mom says that whenever God takes a lady away to heaven that she was such a good mother on the earth that they wanted her up there."

"That's not what happened," Robin said. She'd heard these explanations before, full of benevolent winged creatures and invisible spirits, all coming from the sky possessed by some selfish and baffling desire to snatch up her mother. But what good was Patricia away from home? She was Robin's mother on earth; separated from the Simonsens she lost color, shape, and purpose.

"Maybe it did happen like I said," Kitty said. "Father Bukowski says God is a mystery."

To Robin, God was like Santa Claus—a cute man in a picture or a story—but it was science that ordered the world and her dad who wrapped the Christmas presents every year. The Simonsens' tree was fake, too, four feet tall and crooked, and covered with nothing but bubble lights because whenever Robin's father got any Christmas ornaments he sold them right away as a holiday special.

"I don't believe in God," Robin announced.

Kitty gasped. "That's a sin," she said. "The worst sin! You have to believe. You just have to."

"Cut it out," Robin said. "No, I don't."

"We can't be friends if you don't believe in God!" Kitty whispered.

"Why not?"

"Because it's a black mark on your soul," Kitty said. "It's a sin, and I'm not supposed to be friends with a sinner."

Every Sunday morning, since recovering from what she called "Vegas time," Goldie sat wincing at the breakfast table, hostage to the endless pealing of Lilac's church bells. "What a goddamn racket," she'd say. "We don't believe," Heath had said when Robin asked why the Simonsens never went to church. And Robin remembered her mother's words: "If you're good, you're good. Reading a book and singing once a week won't help you if you're not."

But the thought of trying to explain all this to Kitty made Robin sleepy. Besides, Robin's sin threatened to distract Kitty from their friendship. Or from Robin herself, who suddenly felt a warm urgency in her chest.

"You can't make me believe anything," Robin said, her voice harsh. She sounded like George Junior, in an argument with his father.

"Father Bukowski says we should save people for God, that we have to."

"How do you do it?" Robin asked, excited. She imagined dangling off the half-shingled roof of her house, her forearm gripped by Kitty's chubby hand.

"I go to classes with Father Bukowski," Kitty said. "You could go with me."

"You could save me yourself," Robin said.

"Robin," Kitty whispered. She shifted closer; her breath moved the hair at Robin's temples. "Father Bukowski says God loves everybody and that God is inside everybody, too." Kitty's large hands were hot and damp; they covered Robin's. "I'll pray for you, since you don't know how," Kitty said. She scooted closer to Robin until their thighs and knees met under the sheet. "Ready?" she asked.

Robin nodded, her forehead hitting Kitty's as she did.

Kitty's mouth began to move. Her eyes were so tightly closed that they looked like tiny scars. Kitty sent words spinning through the air, binding them in a web of letters. Robin's mind swirled toward sleep, and in the space where she teetered between awake and the black of dreaming, her mind hung. In this place, Robin pushed Kitty on a swing. Her small palms pressed into the cotton of Kitty's plaid blouse, hot to the touch as if it had just been ironed. Up Kitty sailed into the summer sky. Kitty looked back at Robin and laughed, and Robin felt at once that they were the only inhabitants of a new universe, a place still and uncluttered. They were girl one, girl two, a swing, and the sun. Nothing more.

"I can't hear you," Robin said. "Move closer."

Kitty shoved up against Robin, muttering into her neck. As close as Kitty was, Robin could feel something separating them, a welcome, fizzy sensation that was entirely new. The feeling faded, and she immediately tried to get it back. Emotions, most of them bad, moved through her so quickly that she never wanted to repeat them. Now, with Kitty, she suspected there was some gesture, some shift she could make, and that sparkling in her stomach would return.

"Amen," Kitty now said.

Nothing had changed: Robin still fluttered next to Kitty, her mysterious excitement beating the girl's face or caressing it. "Is it okay?" Robin asked.

Kitty pressed her warm lips against Robin's.

"Hey!" Robin cried.

"That's a kiss from God," Kitty said, her eyes closed.

Robin's spine grew warm, and the heat spread through every muscle, every vein; she could even see it, a red liquid seeping through a transparent statue of her body, her whole anatomy detailed like an encyclopedia diagram. Every organ pulsed. Kitty gave a little jerk on her way toward sleep and Robin brought her friend's hands to her chest like a hermit crab drawing food into its shell.

chapter four

Robin's father told her everything: his loathing of Richard Nixon, his fury at the Vietnam War, his scorn of drug laws, and his fear of something he called "the fascist boot." The latter made Robin think of her father's own battered work boots, which he left every night at the front door for people to trip over. During meals, Heath told Robin about his dates—Tasha with the long, silky hair, Georgia and her caramel-colored eyes, Sara and her two webbed toes—his litany bleeding into Goldie's stories of her amorous past. "He had my arms in a lock, so I couldn't move," Grandma said. Or, "Boy, *I'll* say he was happy to see me." Sometimes, Robin dropped her cereal spoon and covered her ears, just to escape the stereo of randy bed-hopping and brutal embraces. Heath didn't seem to notice: according to him, Robin was "an old twelve," so she was far enough along to understand right, wrong, and everything in between. Heath didn't believe in secrets, he said, not the kind that kept a kid in the dark, allowing her to miss the gray areas. Apparently, Robin still needed her father's help with that.

One night, Heath canceled a date and told Robin the two of them were going upstairs to his room. Grandma was at the kitchen table, playing cards with Larry Pike. "Remember we love you, kitten," she said, watching Robin pass by.

In his bedroom, Heath got out an old leather mailman's bag. He motioned for Robin to sit next to him on the floor, and then he turned up the stereo: it was *Sticky Fingers* by the Rolling Stones; for months, Robin had heard all the songs crashing down the stairs from her father's room.

Heath dug around in the mailbag and removed a stubby smoking pipe made of metal, a packet of what looked like tissues for cleaning eyeglasses, a small kitchen scale, a plastic bag full of shredded green leaves, and a pack of Panatelas. "Have you had the drug lesson yet?" he asked. He meant school.

"We had the sex lesson," Robin said. The girls had to watch an ancient cartoon on the menstrual cycle and then endure a presentation by the school nurse, a woman so short and wide that she couldn't secure a perch on the teacher's desk. She talked for an hour, shakily tapping a pointer against a poster of the reproductive system, male and female versions. Kitty was excused from all of it because of her religion.

"You knew about the sex, right?" Heath asked. He spread some of the green leaves onto a piece of newspaper.

"God, Dad," Robin said. "Grandma."

They both laughed. Just the other day, Goldie had said, "Remember, peanut: clean undies every day in case of an ambulance ride, a doctor's visit, the curse, or, you never know"—here Grandma had winked—"someone tall, dark, and handsome."

"Here we go," Heath said, spreading his arms before the display on the bedroom floor. "*I* want to explain what I've been doing because somebody else might tell you wrong."

Sex was first, in September, then drugs came later; that's what the nurse had said. Robin couldn't identify all of the articles in front of her father. This was like one of those picture tests you took as a kid: what doesn't belong?

Heath cleared his throat. "Robin, I've been selling marijuana for a while now. Pot. It's a lot of money. Grandma knows and everything."

The leaves, the pipe, the smoky stairwell: her father was right, she was older, but she hadn't seen what she should have. This time, she had covered her eyes. "Dad!" Robin cried. "That's illegal!"

"Well, it shouldn't be," Heath said. "We talked about that, remember?"

"You'll go to jail!"

"Only if I get caught, honey." As Heath spoke, he crumbled the pot leaves between his fingers and began stuffing them into the copper bowl of the pipe.

"This is why there's a gun, isn't it?" Robin asked. Outside her father's bedroom window, the fall sky was a patent leather blue, a promising, lying kind of color that lulled you into thinking your life could be something you could count on, like a picture or an ad.

Her father stopped filling the pipe. "What gun?"

"The one the guy brought with the jewelry. A long time ago."

Heath thought for a few seconds. "Oh, no, kiddo. That was something else. I don't have a gun for what I'm doing. I don't need one," he concluded happily, turning his attention to the kitchen scale. "Now I buy it in pound bags and weigh it out on here," he said, placing the instrument in front of his daughter. "Then I put it in smaller bags for people to buy."

"But if the gun wasn't for the pot, then what was it for?" Robin asked.

"Well, jewelry is a different story, I guess. That guy was someone Tommy Boy and Larry and them knew." Heath scooped a handful of leaves off the newspaper and placed it on the scale. "How much does the scale say?" he asked. "Can you read it?"

"Where did the gun go, then?" Robin asked. This is what her father did all day? She liked it better when he brought home broken water heaters and then sold them as brand-new.

"Honey, I really don't know about the gun. Really. Don't worry about it, okay? Now these are rolling papers," he said, picking up the packet of eyeglass cleaners.

"Dad, on *Dragnet*, guys who sell pot go to jail." Just a few weeks ago, Robin and Kitty had watched while two "joy boys," so named by Detective Friday, got busted at their pad with several miraculously unscathed joints hidden in the back pockets of their corduroy jeans.

"*Dragnet* is a bunch of narrow-minded bullshit," Heath said, filling a tissue paper with pot leaves. "We talked about that, too. In fact, I don't want you watching that show. Okay, so what I'm doing right now is called rolling a joint." He ran his tongue along the paper. "See? It's simple. Just like making a drink for Grandma. Remember when she taught you how to make a Tom Collins?"

Goldie had said: "Summer is for white shoes, white handbags, and Tom Collinses; after Labor Day you go to black for shoes and purses, and you only drink Rob Roys." Robin wanted desperately to lie down on her father's bed, or go downstairs and read, but now her father was lighting the joint. Smoke curled up into his hair.

"Dad, I don't *want* to!" Robin cried. She knew her father watched out for her, even when he wasn't looking. Just the other day, he had replaced her cracked school shoes with a fancy, patent leather pair. They were a half size too big and Robin hated them, but she clacked to school in them every day and showed them off to Kitty.

Heath shook his head as he let out a long breath and an even longer stream of smoke. "Honey, honey, honey, listen: I don't want you to do this, okay. I'm not making you do anything. I just want you to know so you'll know. Remember, no secrets."

In movies, a prisoner's only contact with family members was through walls of thick, clear plastic embedded with chicken wire. Yet here her father sat, eating smoke, oblivious to the fact that every intake of breath brought him closer to abandoning his daughter.

"Now, kiddo," Heath said. "You know without me saying that you can't tell anybody what I'm doing. I have no secrets from you, but you, me, and Grandma have to keep secrets from other people. So you can't tell that little friend of yours."

"Kitty."

"Right. Or anyone else at school. Or salvage customers, or anyone when you're out on your rounds with Grandma." Now Heath pulled a large manila envelope from his mailbag and poured money out of it.

The jumble of cash, all creased and dirty and worked over, agitated Robin more than the pile of pot next to it. Seeing the tens, twenties, even fifties, was like witnessing the manifestation of a threat, a monster that had previously existed only in the abstract. How many times had Robin seen Grandma counting money at the table or barking at one of the Bogdanases' poor jokes, just so a bottle of Chanel No. 5 would show up later on her dresser? Robin had seen her father stacking money in the cash box, folding it into his pockets for a date, collecting it from someone who had just bought a reconditioned carburetor. Money was the end point, always. "Dad!" Robin said. "Who'll take care of me?"

"Robin," Heath said, holding the joint away from the two of them and pointing it toward the speaker and the chiming guitars of "Gimme Shelter," "you've got to calm down. You know, most kids would be happy their dad was so honest with them. It's because I trust you that I can tell you these things. And your mom dying automatically makes you older."

That was impossible. If anything, Robin felt younger. A motherless child had no one to measure herself against, no one to monitor her character or maturity, her length of hair, care of teeth. Since her mother's death, Robin was the lone observer of two new lives, both of which progressed inside her own house, but neither of which depended on her for their proximity or their existence. Her father and grandmother performed a life for her benefit.

Heath sipped at the joint. "You know, Robin," he said, "it's not like I haven't thought about what it means to be your dad since Mom died. I've really considered it. That's why Grandma came, mostly, and that's why I think it's really important that there shouldn't be any difference between parent and child. I mean, what is it anyway but some artificial social expectation that you, the little person, needs me, the big person, to tell her what to do, draw the lines, lay down the law, build all those shitty boundaries? Right, kiddo?"

Fall wind rattled the windowpanes. A few leaves blew past. Kitty Paint's parents still spanked her.

Heath was talking, blowing out smoke. "The parent-child relationship is just a smaller version of the relationship between government and the people. It's fucked up. It's all about who's got the power, the big stick, the money! With parents and kids, it's really all about money. The parents dole it out. They buy love. Here, kiddo," Heath said, pulling a twenty-dollar bill out of the pile in front of him. "We don't have to do that. I know you love me, so here. If I trust you with my job, I trust you with my money."

The richest kid at Stephen Douglas, Tamara Sole, got a dollar a week from her parents. She was saving up for a midi coat with fake fur trim from Marshall Field's. "Dad, I don't want it," Robin said.

"You know what your mom used to call extra cash?" Heath asked. "Funny money." He shoved the bill into the pocket of Robin's jeans. "Get anything you want with it," he said.

Robin's father had that look. Robin had seen it burned into the face of every adult Simonsen, including Rex's in the studio photo on Grandma's dresser. The look wasn't a smirk, exactly, just a modest version of a knowing smile, some craft to the set of the lips and the height of the chin. Robin knew it as the after-the-sale look, the new-date look, the I'm-putting-one-over look. And right now, for Heath, mixed in with that look was genuine pleasure: here's what I can give my daughter. Mixed in was pride.

∽

It was any warm night that year. Lying together in Kitty's bed, David Paint in the garage tinkering with radios, the Jackson Five on WCFL drifting through the open window, Kitty's whispered talk felt like a gesture to Robin, calling her closer. But Robin also felt a physical hesitation, like a palm on her chest keeping her out of a room. Someone older saying, don't look.

Before sleep, in a blind, confused sweeping of small hands and arms, they touched each other. Every time, Robin thought it wouldn't happen, Kitty would just stop or forget. Inside, she remained twisted and sour until the girl's hand brushed her chest or her arms circled her. Sometimes Kitty fell asleep or started talking about her family or other kids at school, and then Robin might turn away or sniffle or start an argument about a teacher, until Kitty, what seemed like hours later, would finally lurch into a caress, her face as empty as a clean plate.

There were crises. Like the time a few weeks after sixth grade started when the Paints came to pick up Kitty from a sleepover at the Simonsens. Primed for church, prim in their sedan, they pulled into the driveway and found Heath and one of his dates in lawn chairs in the front yard, laughing and sipping coffee. The date wore only underpants and one of Heath's long tee shirts. Robin saw Mr. and Mrs. Paint's horrified faces, and David, slack-jawed and wounded-looking, staring in fascination from the back seat. For weeks afterward, Kitty's parents forbade her to come over to Robin's or to let Robin visit. During that time, Robin called Kitty daily, sometimes hourly, only to have Mrs. Paint hang up on her. She sent Kitty a card, gave her an old bead necklace of Goldie's, found a working bicycle in the garage and rode it up and down the Paints' street. They met on the playground like secret lovers, but all Robin could do was cry while Kitty bit her nails and shook her head at Robin's suggestions that she lie, sneak out, rebel. Finally, in desperation, Robin pretended to make friends with two other girls. She shunned Kitty, laughing and leaning into the new girls whenever Kitty walked by. One day after school the girls dragged her to uptown Lilac to look at brightly colored knit dresses she would never wear. Robin listened to one of the girls go on about some boy who glanced at her in the hall, and then she feigned illness and ran home, throwing herself onto her bed and bursting into tears. She called Kitty's house and sobbed until Mrs. Paint relinquished the phone to her daughter, and then Robin put into motion a plan she'd saved for weeks. She didn't know why, she told Kitty, but she thought there was a spirit visiting her, someone who in the dead of night looked like her mother. Was it a dream? Robin asked Kitty. Was her dead mother a Holy Ghost? Maybe Kitty needed to save her again, and if she couldn't, then Robin didn't know what might happen. She could hear Kitty's locomotive breathing, but when she finished talking, her friend hung up the phone without a word.

The next day, Kitty showed up at Robin's house after school, without explanation, as if nothing had happened, as if Robin's treachery with the other girls had taken place in another town, as if Kitty had been cooking up her sudden return even before Robin's pleas. That was one thing about Kitty: what looked like slow thinking on her part was sometimes just her assumption that Robin knew exactly what she, Kitty, was doing; she took a lot on faith and she expected the same from her friend.

Robin and Kitty's school friendship continued, but then there was nighttime, which they never talked about, and the touching, the almost wretched closeness that always carried, for Robin, the threat of dissolution. All day, she wore a pocket of feeling sewed into her chest, a special envelope of flesh in which Kitty rested at all times, hidden and thick, like a long message she could take out and read at whim.

Robin thought she should be satisfied with Kitty's love, but she had to work so hard to get it and keep it, and there wasn't much else coming in. Goldie and Heath actually worked to make sure everyone on Highland disliked them. The only thing Robin saw in her favor was her status as a motherless kid. The neighbors clearly felt sorry for her; when they did see her, they waved slowly, their faces droopy with regret and awe, as if she were leading a funeral procession. Only the Hazens next door were reluctant to ignore Robin, so every few weeks she visited Mr. Hazen in his garage, a tidy enclave full of every kind of electrical wire and old radio tube and TV tuner. While Robin chattered at him, Mr. Hazen tinkered silently at his workbench, two pairs of glasses balanced on the end of his nose because, he told Robin, trifocals were too doggone expensive. His eyes bulged behind all the lenses. Mr. and Mrs. Hazen both had gray hair and wrinkles and looked more like the grandparents of their only child, Martha. During the summer, when Martha came home from college, Robin often saw her stretched out in a lounge chair wearing American flag shorts, a red bikini top, and huge sunglasses, a thick book open on her lap and her blond hair in a ponytail. Mr. Hazen mowed the lawn around Martha's chair, and her mother stirred the soil in the flower garden. Strudel, the Hazens' dachshund, yapped and trotted around the yard's perimeter. The Hazens were more like Martha's servants than her parents. Lately, though, Robin had caught Heath in the backyard watching Martha across the vacant lot that separated the Simonsens' house from the Hazens', so she wasn't surprised when Martha appeared one afternoon in the Simonsen kitchen. Heath rushed around her while Grandma watched and Robin worked on a map for school. It was the fall of Robin's sixth-grade year, and the weather had shifted. Martha wore a suede jacket with fringe and carried a suitcase. She smelled like a saddle.

Grandma stared at Martha, cigarette poised. "How's your dad?" she asked.

"I'm driving Martha back to Champaign," Heath said, his head in the refrigerator. "Don't we have any Coke?" he asked.

"Why?" Grandma asked.

Heath closed the refrigerator. "I'm thirsty, Ma," he said. Martha laughed.

"No," Goldie said, "why isn't Frank driving Martha back? It's usually the dad that does that."

"I'm going down there anyway," Heath said. He took a colored pencil from the box Robin had open at the table and handed it to Martha. "Here, write down your phone number," he said to her, "and your address, in case I forget to ask before I come back up."

Goldie scowled. "Take Robin with you," she said.

"I don't want to go," Robin said.

"Sure you do," Grandma said.

"She's doing her homework, for Christ's sake," Heath said. "I'll be back for dinner. I'm just dropping Martha off."

Martha took a pack of cigarettes out of her purse. The purse was suede, too, with a braided strap, and she wore suede desert boots. There was a claustrophobic smell from all the cowhide, like being trapped inside a shoe. "Do you mind?" Martha asked, holding up the cigarette pack. "My parents won't let me smoke in the house."

"Huh," Goldie said. "What are you studying in college?" she asked.

"Sociology," Martha said. "Inner city stuff. I'm doing work in Chicago this summer at a housing project."

"You're nuts," Grandma said. "I've heard about those places."

"Martha's smart, Ma," Heath said. "She can hold her own, too." Martha grinned at him.

Robin had mapped out part of Bolivia's border with her pink pencil, and now she drew a row of brown carets for mountains. Just two weeks ago, another college kid had visited the house, and he and Heath had spent all night in the garage. That one went to Northwestern. Then there was an art major from Elmhurst College who'd bought some stretched canvases and old dresses from the 1950s and returned a few days later just to see Heath. Everything led back to the mailbag. Robin's pencil broke.

"Ready?" Heath asked Martha.

"Of course I am," Martha said.

No date, Robin thought. No date, no date. Martha was the first neighbor to see the mailbag. There was the rest of Lilac, then the other suburbs and Chicago, then the whole state of Illinois for her father to pick on. The neighborhood was what Robin had to walk through to go to school. She turned over her map and drew Highland Street in red pencil, then drew herself, running up the hill and away.

Whatever happened in Champaign, Martha Hazen must have kept it to herself because after her first trip with Heath downstate, she came home almost every weekend and visited the Simonsens, clomping up the stairs to Heath's bedroom in her wedgies and miniskirts, but then descending too quickly for a date. And now, even when Martha was at school, Mr. Hazen looked through his binoculars across the wild and weedy vacant lot that separated the two houses, as if to glimpse the last place he'd seen his daughter before he lost her.

Robin stared back one Saturday morning, trying to see into the wide lenses of Mr. Hazen's binoculars, while Kitty stood in her bedroom and laid out the rules of a new game. Robin thought that she and Kitty were older than the other kids in the sixth grade, more knowing, but about what, Robin wasn't sure. She was infinitely patient with Kitty, indulgent, as if, like Grandma with the Bogdanas men, she was waiting for a big payoff. Robin wasn't even annoyed that afternoon when Kitty announced she wanted to pretend something, and wear special clothes to do it. Robin had recently read an article in the *Tribune* that explained how children on the brink of adolescence often regressed—Robin had to look up the word—and acted immature in order to show their reluctance to leave childhood.

"So it's okay if we play like this now," Robin explained to Kitty that Saturday. "But we can't keep doing it."

Kitty was holding up an old garment the girls had stolen from

Goldie's closet, a red dress composed of a dozen scratchy petticoats and a bodice of lace that didn't look big enough to cover a woman's rib cage.

"It's pretty," Kitty said. "You wear it and be the sinner and then I'm the nun."

All of Kitty's games involved church. One time she tried to get Robin to engage in a race for who could genuflect the fastest. "I'm not wearing that," Robin said.

"Come on. *Please.*"

Kitty looked prettier when she pleaded. Her usually pasty cheeks flushed, her smallish eyes sparkled, her lips parted. When she looked like that she looked older, too, and Robin had to glance away. They should have been too mature for this, no matter what the *Tribune* said. Robin unzipped her bell-bottoms and stepped out of them.

"Someone'll see!" Kitty whispered.

Robin looked out the window. Mr. Hazen had moved away from his vigil and was pulling a weed from the lawn. Grandma and her visitors laughed in the kitchen. Robin pulled her shirt over her head and stood facing Kitty, naked except for her underpants. Kitty handed Robin the dress, and she drew it up over her hips. There were no straps or sleeves, nothing to hold it up except what Grandma had on top.

"I look like a dope," Robin said, watching Kitty.

"It's fancy," Kitty said. "I like it. Pull it up more."

Robin tugged at the lace bodice, surprised to find that she could stretch the material all the way up to her neck.

"Okay," Kitty said, taking the pillow from Robin's bed. She pulled off the pillowcase and draped it over her head. "There."

Kitty stepped out into the hall and closed the door halfway. "Get on the other side," she said.

"What for?" Robin asked.

"This is confession. I'm not supposed to see you. Really, the Father can only do confession, but I can't be a priest, even in pretend."

Robin sat cross-legged on the floor.

"Tell what you've done," Kitty said from behind the door.

"What do you mean?"

"Confess. Tell your sins."

"I haven't done anything." Robin's small feet stuck out from under the acres of red material.

"Come on, Robin, we're pretending." There was a hard bang on the other side of the door. "Ow," Kitty said.

"Okay." Robin paused. "I swore," she said.

"Say, 'Father, forgive me, for I have sinned.' No, say 'Sister.'"

"I'm not saying that!" Robin cried.

"You say no about everything. Just do it."

Robin took a deep breath. "I swore, I kept a secret . . ."

"That's not a sin!" Kitty said.

". . . I didn't finish my homework," Robin continued. "I put my TV dinner in the garbage."

"Sins are bigger. Think of more."

"I can't think of any," Robin said. "I never do anything."

"Make. Them. Up," Kitty said. "I'm getting bored."

The freezer door opened and closed in the kitchen, and then Robin heard the chime of ice in a glass. It was still morning. She couldn't remember if her father was home or not. He'd crashed his truck the week before, so while it got fixed he had to depend on other people or dates for rides, and he often just stayed wherever they took him.

"Okay," Robin said. "I stole. I did drugs. I broke the law. I swore. I neglected my child. I forgot somebody who was dead. I drank too much. I had sex with girls when we weren't married. I lied. I hid things. I threw good stuff away and kept bad stuff, on purpose. I looked at pictures of naked women."

"Wait, wait!" Kitty said. "I'm supposed to forgive you and then tell you your penance."

"I had sex with two men," Robin said. "One was a father and the other man was his son."

"Nobody can do *that*!" Kitty said.

"I had sex with a lot of other men, before," Robin said. "I lied so I could get a man to give me a present. I didn't cook dinner for two weeks. I kept a secret. I swore at my husband on the phone. I have a driver's license with a different name on it. I lied and said I voted when I didn't. I broke stuff when I got mad. I didn't pay any taxes. I swore a lot, all the time. I changed the prices on stuff when people were about to buy it. I neglected my child."

"Stop!" Kitty cried. She shoved the bedroom door, just missing Robin's forehead. "Nobody's got that many sins."

"Maybe I do," Robin said. She felt faint, as if she'd been sick. She wanted to be on the other side of the door, to grab Kitty's wide waist, to look into her placid, utterly fathomable face. Robin pushed her hot, damp forehead into the wood. She had that anxious fever again, the one she got every time Kitty looked distracted, every time Kitty didn't call her back right away, that same kind of fury that gripped her running feet as she crossed backyards and opened gates and climbed fences to get to Kitty's street, to get to Kitty. That same fever that gripped her father and grandmother—she saw it on their faces—when every atom of wanting someone or something squeezes through a pinhole. All you needed was one drop in your blood. Then there was the one and only thing you wanted, the one and only, coupled with not caring about anything else. Then there was desire.

"I kept a secret from my best friend," Robin said. "I looked at somebody nude. I touched myself. I liked it. I stood in front of the mirror with no clothes on a ton of times. I loved somebody, and I hated them at the same time."

"Wait a second," Kitty said.

"Okay," Robin said, breathless. "Forgive me."

~

Robin was at the Smoke Shop with Goldie, angry, feeling too old to go on rounds but dragged anyway by her grandmother, who now laughed in the back room with Larry. Grandma was mad at Robin just because she'd asked, "What's he doing here?" when she found George at the kitchen table and her grandmother in a negligee. But Grandma had forgotten that George's visit came just days after Robin found Old Man cooking bacon and eggs too early in the day for him to have just arrived. Robin stood fuming in the Smoke Shop while everyone ignored her, and until her anger took a different shape. She glanced around. She knew where the magazines were, the ones she wanted that she wasn't supposed to have; you couldn't miss them, even though they were in the far corner of Larry's store. She'd looked at their covers, each one bearing the smooth, powdered face of some young woman, hair streaming down her back or over her shoulder, her breasts high and tight inside something skimpy, her eyes always catching Robin's as if she'd been waiting for her to pass by.

Officially, the Smoke Shop was closed. Larry had pulled down the blue plastic shades and turned out the lights over the front racks. But in the back, the fluorescent tubes buzzed, and the magazine covers, rippling in the blast from the store's heater, waited for rescue. Robin still looked at her father's *Playboy*s, but somehow the fact that the photos were for him made the whole enterprise of sneaking them downstairs and into her room, then back up again, too much like stealing books from the Lilac library, something Robin had also started doing that year.

She took down a magazine that had a woman on the cover sitting cross-legged and dangling a cat by its front legs. The cat's body covered the woman's breasts and crotch. Inside, the pages were filled with more women, honey-eyed, silky-haired, hopeful. They lay on beds, on dirty carpeting, across the hoods of cars; they even lay next to grinning dogs, and all of them were naked, nothing on but high heels and earrings. Outside the Smoke Shop, winter gave way to spring, but inside, the heater clanked and surged, ruffling Robin's hair and undulating the pages of the magazines in a kind of beckoning.

One woman took up two whole pages. She was long and blond, her skin ivory and pink, her hair and body spread out on black satin, her pubic hair a dull spot between her torso and her legs. There was something about the woman's creamy skin, her softness, her hair on the silk, the way you could make your fingers feel exactly what she felt even while you held the magazine. The woman was rounded like Goldie, whom Robin could hear laughing and yelping in Larry's back room.

Robin held the magazine open. She could be a methodical girl—a "neat nut," her grandmother called her—especially since her mother's death. She kept her room clean, dusting and even shoving the vacuum around between the cartons of spice racks, the bicycle tires, and the dead Coke machine her father had stored there. A clean room was like homework or a question from the teacher: it required a plan, some process of sorting and organizing that could push her father's junk, or her own ignorance, out of the way. You could even use a plan to figure out how to properly *see* something.

She started with the woman's hair, which fanned out across the black satin, but something about the white-gold strands, tangled just so, and the reaching quality of the ends was disturbing, as if the woman's hair, too alive to be attractive, could slink off to a life of its own. Face, neck, shoulders, breasts, a swoop to the waist and back out to the hips, which took Robin's eyes to the woman's hands. The fingers stretched across the satin, a fan of pink nails, the index finger of her left hand pulling at the smooth surface of shiny black fabric, bunching it, marring it. The finger, too, seemed to want to escape, to crawl out of the photograph and maybe take the rest of the woman with it. The finger looked wormy, inhuman. Robin's stomach curled, though not unpleasantly. The thick vein that ran down the center of her body, that twisted string that since her mother's death had announced every one of her emotions, began to thrum. Fear surged through her, but she kept her eyes on the woman even when the magazine began to tremble in her hands.

"Let's go!" Goldie said, clacking past Robin and heading for the door.

Robin wobbled out to the car, ill, elated. She had abandoned the woman in the magazine. Kids at school made fun of nude pictures, but they didn't know how to look at them. You *could* plan how you saw things. You could take them in.

"Pumpkin," Grandma said, as she pulled the car away from the curb. "Sweetie. Don't cry, honey. I didn't mean to get mad before." She shook her head. "Those two guys, those Bogdanases. Boy."

Goldie pumped the gas pedal and peered at the traffic. You could see your grandmother as a savior, as a protector, but that would take too much planning. Goldie wore her hair in a burnished, cloud-like mass, her skin was pink and ivory, her pants tight; she wore high heels and a white blouse open to her breasts. The nerve running through Robin gave her grief, fear, anger, all of the ingredients of wanting. She looked at Goldie, her fears descending, coming to rest on her grandmother's body, hair, face, hands. This wasn't the same as Kitty, or even the same as the woman in the magazine, but in its own way, this, too, was falling in love.

Grandma stopped at a red light and pulled a pack of gum from her purse. "Not again, sweet pea," she said, glancing at Robin's wet face. "Not when everything's good news! Did I tell you the new deal I made with Larry? Here's some Juicy Fruit." She fiddled with the buttons on her blouse. "Hon bun," she continued, "did I tell you this yet, because this is the kind of thing a woman has to know: *always* carry a spare ten spot on a date, just in case you've got to get out fast." Grandma reached between her breasts and pulled out a folded bill. "See? Lookit here."

∼

Many times during the summer before junior high school, Robin felt like those college kids on TV, the ones who tried to go to classes while the rest of the campus exploded into riots and shouting and tear gas. You could see the obedient ones on the edge of the screen, smooth-haired, arms clutching books, flinching as their ragged classmates dashed past, pursued by police. One night on the news, Robin watched a young woman step over the body of a man who had tripped while running up the campus green. The woman's eyes fixed on the white columns of the building in front of her, and she lifted first one loafered foot and then the other, until she was clear of the scrambling man. She adjusted the shoulder strap on her purse and walked on.

In June, Heath got an ancient school bus, rounded like a butter dish and completely defunct, and had it towed to the backyard, where it finished out the row of dead cars, the last link in a perverted evolutionary chain.

Young people came. Kids, Goldie called them. Robin figured most of them were college age, friends of Martha Hazen who were home for the summer. They gathered in the school bus, lighting it up with candles, smoking pot, and playing the radio at all hours until even Goldie stomped out in her mules and flowing satin gown to tell them to knock it off.

At night, light from the candles flickered through the slats in the shed wall outside Robin's bedroom window. Watching the light, or watching the trail of pilgrims to the bus, made Robin yearn to join her life with her father's, to feel less like a girl who existed alone in a room crowded with cartons of off-loaded goods and the leavings of other people's lives and more like a daughter who had a place, if not a plan. Her father spent one evening helping the kids put up sheets to cover the bus windows, and then he stayed with them, whooping until dawn.

Robin sprang into action soon after that. First she cleaned her own room of junk, anything for sale—besides furniture—and broken items. One Sunday morning, she stood in her doorway and looked at the vacuumed carpet—she'd found the machine, dusty and lying on its side, in her father's old room downstairs—and at the wide expanse between pieces of furniture, the cleared closet—except for a few dresses and a pair of fancy shoes she'd never worn—and she saw a monk's cell, a place too full of a solitary life. Even Kitty was gone, visiting her grandmother in Chicago for a few weeks. Robin couldn't look anymore, so she pushed the vacuum into the hall and started on the rest of the house.

"Stop already, cupcake," Grandma said two weeks later. "You're making me dizzy. Are you all right?"

Robin had her head in a kitchen cupboard. She ignored her grandmother and pulled out the contents. Two identical aluminum saucepans, a cast iron frying pan without a handle, a porcelain egg cup glazed with cracks, and then, in the back, a stack of board games—the old Monopoly set, Clue, and Twister, the latter two unopened. The shelves were littered with spider and beetle carcasses and a mousetrap, empty but sprung.

"She's practicing to be a wife," Tommy said.

"A wife," Robin said. "Ugh."

"Oh, just wait," Tommy said, laughing. "Just you wait."

In July, Heath announced that Robin had been personally responsible for hundreds of dollars in sales, all without him lifting a finger. Old Man Bogdanas had bought a huge box of quilt batting and fabric scraps for his wife; George got a cache of Maybelline for his; Tommy Boy took an ancient wagon yoke Robin had unearthed from the shed and drove around with it in the back seat of his decrepit Roadmaster. "He's got no yard to put it in," Goldie whispered to Robin, as they watched Tommy pull out onto Highland.

One night, Robin's father, lacing his work boots for a date, said, "I'm proud of you, kiddo."

She kept working. Every day, new boxes of junk littered the driveway until Goldie's men arrived, and then they either stored them in the garage or took them away. After returning from Chicago, Kitty came over a few times to hang in doorways and watch Robin's labors, but Robin barely acknowledged her. After she cleared out everything, then she could really see Kitty, as she never had before. Her friend went off to the Wisconsin Dells with her family. Robin moved car parts, inflatable beds, bowling pins, sewing machines, towers of pallets, and then she dusted, swept, and put back what she had to. At the end of two months, having washed her way up the stairs and faced with the doorway to her father's off-limits room, her bare feet slick with water and suds, she dropped her mop. For two months, she realized, she'd been looking for evidence of her mother, and now, having reached the edge of the frontier, she'd yet to find a thing. Any object would have satisfied her: clothes, books—her mother liked romances—even headbands or a note in Patricia's handwriting. But Robin had found nothing. She'd been afraid to ask her father what he'd done with her mother's possessions. But sometimes when Robin studied the studio photo of her mother that she had rescued soon after the death, she wondered if this Patricia, smiling as Robin remembered her, her two front teeth slightly overlapped just like her daughter's, with her long, smooth neck, her shimmering plaits of almost-black hair, her brown eyes, and her pixieish face and shoelace mouth, was just reconditioned junk, part of her father's trade with some long-forgotten customer, and over time Heath had managed to convince Robin that this woman was her mother. He was already so good at making Robin believe that she'd just conjured memories of Patricia, of her smell, her touch. But they had to come from somewhere, and they had to be in the house.

Robin's last site for evidence was the garage, the final outpost for the most neglected Simonsen possessions. Goldie was afraid of the whole structure. She got hives, she said, and had to sit down and have a cigarette, every time she even looked into the maw. Robin was determined to have her father's help with the garage. That way she could confront him immediately when she found her mother's stuff.

"This one," Grandma said one night at dinner, pointing her cigarette at Robin. "Most kids play in the summer, but not her. You could go shopping, kitten. I'd drop you at Oakbrook for the day, give you some money for a top or something. You're old enough to start buying for yourself."

Heath was making a rare appearance at the dinner table. He pulled hamburgers from a bag. "Where's that girl you like?" he asked.

"Kitty," Robin said. "She's on vacation. Dad?"

"You know, Rob, that screen door you found? I've been looking for it for a year. Years. Somebody was asking for one a while ago. Where'd you find it?"

"In Grandma's closet."

"Jesus H. Christ." Heath shook his head.

Robin didn't add that it was also in Goldie's closet that she'd set aside an empty carton to hold the dozens of unmarked cigarette packs from Larry Pike and the shoebox of jewelry pouches from Tommy Boy. Filled with earrings and rings and bracelets, the bags lay in

Robin's hand like tiny animals with broken bones. Robin also didn't mention the small silver gun, which she had gingerly wrapped in a hand towel and placed at the bottom of the carton. Someone had lied. Or kept a secret.

"Dad?" Robin asked. "Do you have a date?"

"No. She's had enough of me, whoever she is. Do you believe it?" Heath looked at Robin wide-eyed, his mouth ajar, then he laughed.

"She got a whiff of your ways," Goldie said. The headline in her movie magazine read BRANDO'S INDIAN GAL SEZ STAR GYPPED HER. "I swear, son," Grandma said, "I see these girls all over town. There's probably cat fights in every part of DuPage County because of you."

"Dad, I want you to help me with the garage," Robin said.

"Can't," her father said, glancing at the kitchen clock.

"Listen," Grandma said, "you oughta be ashamed, making your kid do all this work."

"Nobody made her, Ma," Heath said. "And don't start with me."

Robin locked her father in a stare. His eyes were red and squinty as he chewed the last morsel of two double hamburgers and two orders of fries. Stay, she thought. Stay.

"Okay," Heath finally said. "We'll tackle the beast."

Outside, Robin's father rolled up the big garage door and switched on the fluorescent lights. Inside were sawing crickets; a paper wasps' nest, silent in the dark; boxes of Robin's baby clothes; her father's old suits with their skinny lapels; the intoxicating odor of oil, wood, and rubber. Strings of dirty cobwebs netted the ceiling. Robin surveyed a spread of tools and small engines, a collection of appliances, compromised antiques, a dressmaker's dummy wearing a fringe vest and panties over its neck, and, quiet and smooth as an egg, the old Thunderbird that Heath had driven during his one year at Berkeley. The car sat on its blocks like a sleeping cat. Robin suddenly felt shy, as if she were facing a classroom full of strange kids and a teacher full of expectations. Her father waited.

"Let's do tools first," Robin said.

Heath began sorting screwdrivers, but when Robin checked on him a few minutes later he was smoking and staring out toward Highland Street. She ignored him and continued to drop wrenches into a deep box. Some of the wrenches were so heavy that Robin could barely lift them; others were tiny and delicate, as if her father used them to tighten birds' wings. Heath turned on the radio; Buffalo Springfield, then Canned Heat, then Bob Dylan echoed off the garage ceiling. Pinned across the back wall of the garage were pictures of musicians Heath had cut out of *Rolling Stone* or *Creem* or right from album covers. Mick Jagger sneered down at the wrenches Robin sorted, along with Hendrix, and the curly-headed singers from The Who and Led Zeppelin—Robin could never remember their names.

Heath abandoned the screwdrivers and picked through a pile of yellowed newspapers on the hood of the Thunderbird.

"These are some Patricia saved," he said. "I have no idea why."

"Let me see," Robin said. She tripped over an oil pan in her hurry to get to her father.

"They're just old stuff," Heath said.

"What do they say?" Robin flipped through the stack: Lyndon Johnson addressing Congress, Mayor Daley cutting a ribbon, an astronaut attached to a spaceship by a cord. This was just the air around her mother, the buzzing, the breeze. It wasn't really her.

"Who knows, we might need these later," Heath said, dropping the pile on the floor with a loud slap and then pushing it under the Thunderbird. He looked at Robin. "Kiddo," he said, "you know I loved your mom, don't you?"

Robin felt a flash of jealousy: her mother—scrubbed face, silky black hair, scent of laundry soap and well water in her sweatshirt and dungarees; Robin had created her, so she no longer belonged to Heath. "How can you even remember her?" Robin asked.

Heath's face dropped. "What do you mean? She was my wife. We were together ten years, you know." He gave another kick to the papers under the Thunderbird, ensuring they'd never be found again. "I think you're the one who's going to forget your mom," Heath said quietly. "You're the young one."

Robin's anger was so overwhelming that she couldn't speak. Instead, she returned to the wrenches, touching their cool surfaces to calm herself. Just that afternoon, filthy from cleaning, she had crouched next to the outside faucet, her dark head sizzling in the heat, and let icy well water fill her cupped palms. She had tried to drink it all before any spilled, but she couldn't keep up, and bright streams of water trailed to the ground. Maybe her father was right: this was how pieces of her mother fell away from her even now; after all her labors, this was how memory betrayed.

"Do you smell something?" Heath asked.

It was the scent of leaves smoldering, or paper. A fire. "It hasn't rained in weeks," Heath said. He ran out of the garage and around to the backyard, Robin following.

Ragged orange flames leapt from the burn barrel behind the cars. The sky was moonless, one light on in the house, Sinatra singing out the living room windows.

When Heath got to the burn barrel, he began throwing dirt onto the flames.

"Hey, hey, hey," a man's voice said from the bus. "That fire's working."

Robin's father responded, unruffled by the man's presence. "It's too dry, Tom," he said. "The house is too close."

"That's all my papers, man," the voice said. "Maybe it's even my draft card," he added, laughing.

"You can burn whatever you want, just not right now," Heath said. He picked up a piece of sheet metal and set it over the mouth of the barrel. Robin stepped forward, trying to get a look at the man. There hadn't been anyone in the bus for weeks. "Careful, kiddo," her father said, holding her back from the fire.

"Who's that foxy little thing?" the voice asked, and then Robin saw a figure descending the bus stairs, someone with a huge head of hair and narrow shoulders.

"This is my daughter, Robin," Heath said, rearing back and punching the sheet metal with his boot so that a few flames leaked out.

"Ah-ha," the man said, coming into the firelight.

He had a crooked smile, slung up on one side and pinched down on the other. The bus was dark inside. The only other lights in the neighborhood came from the fire and from the Hazens' security light across the field. Heath pushed at the sheet metal, moving it further aside so that a deep orange glow washed over their faces.

Robin didn't see any scars on the man's face, only the twisted, drawstring smile. Was he trying to look that way? His face seemed to go with his voice, which slid away from you almost before you were aware you'd heard it.

"Fucking old renter's leases, orders from the army, AWOL papers, hospital records, motherfucking marriage license, Heath!" The man cackled.

"All right," Robin's father said quietly.

"Where's the *big* fox tonight?" the man asked.

Heath snorted. "She's inside working her fingers to the bone, like always. Where else would she be?"

"I got something for you," the man, Tom, said, jerking his head back at the bus. Just a few streets over, where Kitty Paint lived, there were streetlights, so you could see people coming and going.

"Give it to me later," Heath said. He put his arm around Robin.

"Not to give, to share," Tom said. His mouth opened, then closed. Or so it seemed. There could have been a second, thwarted speaker inside of the man, one who made the movements of talking but who possessed no more than the promise of a voice. Heath turned Robin around and they walked away.

"Don't forget me," Tom called. His voice came out of the dark like a frog's snatching tongue, just touching the base of Robin's neck.

Back in the garage, Robin waited for her father to explain, but he returned silently to the tools, his back to her. Either her family told her more than she wanted to know, or they told her nothing.

"Who is that guy?" Robin asked. She stayed in the doorway, as if her father's answer might give her reason to flee.

"His name's Tom McAfee," Heath said. "He came just last night."

"Who is he?"

Heath was silent. His hands were busy, but he did nothing. This was new: her father, embarrassed.

Heath took a deep breath, but he didn't turn around. "Tom's been in the war, honey. You know. So he came home and he's supposed to stay with his parents, but he can't, so I said the bus was empty."

"What about all the kids?"

"They know Tom. They don't care. They'll share the space."

"So he's, like, living in the bus."

"Yes," Heath said.

"What's wrong with him?" Robin asked.

"He had a stroke."

"Like Kitty's grandma, a stroke?"

"Yeah, except he's young. It was a stroke from the war. From how horrible it all was."

Kitty said her grandma's stroke had completely laid her up, and now she yelled Polish out of the little space she could open up between her lips. Tom had enough strength for two voices, one of which he reserved for the silent twitching of his mouth.

"We have to be nice to him, Robin," Heath said.

"Where does he go to the bathroom?" Robin asked. "He's got to take a shower, too."

"He can go outside sometimes. And he can use our shower." Now Heath faced Robin, and she saw he wasn't embarrassed anymore. He looked angry.

"You didn't say anything, Dad. Neither did Grandma."

"What you don't understand," her father said, "is that there's so many guys like him and nobody'll do anything. So I did."

There were only two intact seats in the whole bus, springs sticking through the cracked vinyl, and the rest was garbage you could wade through and a mattress with the buttons popped off and sheets over the windows. Robin didn't see how her father had given Tom McAfee much of anything. The night behind her was a soft, black, oozing wall.

"You don't like him," Robin said. The thought had flashed into her mind as bold print, a fact from a book.

She saw that her father was going to answer, angry again, but before he could, headlight beams hit the garage. A car pulled up and stopped in the driveway, Jim Morrison growling from its radio.

"Heath!" a man yelled.

Her father strode out to the car and spoke into it. Someone inside lit a cigarette and Robin saw three people, two in back, and one in front smoking, a man with long hair in stringy brown sheets on both sides of his face.

"Dad?" Robin called. The radio in the garage played the Beatles, the cheery crash of their instruments laid over The Doors' organ. Heath laughed.

"Kiddo, go inside," Heath said. "This is just business."

Just business, again, always. Robin walked through the headlight beams, back to the dark corridor between the garage and the house. She didn't even look at what she and her father had done. It was a waste anyway: nothing but old newspapers her mother had touched once, long ago. The bus was dark. Was Tom McAfee sitting on the steps watching her? Kitty Paint said that a stroke was a silent thing; it hit her grandmother one day, made her bow her head, and then parts of her seemed to turn off. You almost couldn't tell, Kitty said.

The house was dark, Grandma in her room, though she'd left the hi-fi on. Robin came in through the back vestibule, then the kitchen, her hands out to feel the walls. "It never entered my mind," Sinatra sang from the black hole of the living room. The dark clung to Robin like a shawl, comforting even in the heat. Her hands skimmed the kitchen cupboards. Could a stroke make you blind, too? Or cut off your feelings, those in the fingertips and in the heart? Perhaps her father had had a stroke; perhaps that was why memories of Robin's mother drifted away from him, evaporating in the ever-thinning air he breathed.

chapter five

~

Girls looked different in junior high. Robin thought the transformation had occurred over the summer, but then she realized, noticing one classmate's rounded breasts and another's darkening leg hair, that girls had been turning into women for years.

Girls smelled different, too: like grown-up sweat, brothy and moist, sometimes like iron or blood. Robin opened her locker, took out books, put them back in, and all the while a new army of girls marched by behind her.

Even Kitty had changed over the summer. She was thinner, browner, and there were red strands in her mouse-colored hair. Her waist was slightly pinched. There was a new line of sinew in her arms.

For her part, Robin had moved in the other direction, toward being a boy. After her summer of cleaning and hauling, Robin had packed an athlete's strength into her lean, tight arms and her short, compact legs. When she caught her long, dark hair into a ponytail, it felt like a muscle in her grip. The rest of her was still tiny, except for her mouth, which stretched too wide when she smiled. Every morning Robin ran from home to the bus stop and then raced back in the afternoon, her lungs burning and eyes watering.

At Larry Pike's, there were a half-dozen magazines for girls her age and older full of photographs of beautiful young women in stylish clothes, in bathing suits, even in underwear. Goldie got Robin a subscription to *Seventeen* for her birthday that summer. Robin threw the copies away until she received an issue with an article called "Best Friends—How to Stay Close."

At school, girls were put with girls in gym class, in home ec, even in health class, with its redundant explanations of sex. Classes themselves were out of it, irrelevant. Nothing but Lincoln and more Lincoln, the Mississippi River and St. Lawrence Seaway, division with fractions, and Old Jules and his sod house on the prairie. Nothing on the *Tribune* story Robin had read about a father in Chicago who shot his son dead because he refused to cut his hair; nothing on the scores of people marching, wanting Nixon out, even Nixon dead; nothing on the chain of bombs Robin had seen exploding on TV that sent up ottoman-shaped clouds among the palm trees and lazy rivers of Vietnam. And, most strange: not one teacher in all of Lilac Junior High ever remarked on the existence of black people, the denizens of Chicago, Our Neighbors to the East.

At home, Robin's family operated exclusively on impulse and desire. Goldie and Heath were blind to the simplest facts about people, dwelling on casual statements and throwaway jokes, turning them inside out until they got angry or felt betrayed. Goldie banished Larry Pike from the house for a month because she said he didn't protest when Tommy Boy, at the tail end of a bender, sat at the kitchen table and questioned Goldie's virtue. Tommy Boy got to stay. Heath got into a screaming match that fall with some nervous and sweaty school bus regular, a teenager who went shirtless in all kinds of weather, because Heath thought the kid had ripped off Tom McAfee. But Robin had caught Tom in the laundry room, digging around behind the dryer where they kept the strongbox full of cash. When she told her father about her discovery, he responded by giving Tom a heater for the bus and a stained down comforter. Robin could smell the kerosene fumes every morning when she left for school. When she came home, Tom was sitting on the bus stairs with a cigarette or a joint, oblivious to the falling temperatures. He waited for Heath. That was Tom's job, waiting for Heath. Once Robin's father invited him in to yell at the TV news, but Tom was nervous the whole time, like a yard dog that had never been inside a house. Tom waited until Heath came home to take his showers, and then the scent of his grimy jeans and smoky flannel shirts overpowered Goldie's gardenia bathroom. Robin thought Tom looked like a hibernating animal. One side of his face drooped, his right eye slumped in isolated sadness; his crooked features were framed by a growing cascade of rough brown hair. When he came out of the bathroom after a shower, he looked feral, his hair plastered to his large head like an otter's fur.

Robin loaded boxes with junk and moved them out to the driveway, moved furniture around, even tried to keep a list of what the house contained, but every gesture she made was superseded by more junk. She kept her own room pristine, just a collection of wretched furniture, no pictures or knickknacks or stuffed animals. Only books. She studied and read like one possessed, sometimes until it was so late Goldie swooped down in a cloud of gardenia and gauze and escorted her to bed. But even there, Robin planned and organized: she thought about where to move junk, what should stay and what should go, she reviewed class lessons, but mostly she remembered Kitty, parts and whole, and she thought up new ways for them to spend the night together. She could clear out a space in the backyard and they could pitch a tent; they could sleep in one of the abandoned cars, maybe the old Bel Air, which had sunflowers growing through holes in its roof; they could sneak up and spend the night in Heath's room when he was out on a date or had disappeared for a few days. Underneath the organizing, the planning, and the scheming was simple pining, for Kitty's hot breath and heft in bed, for her determined stupidity that drove Robin crazy, for her bouts of illumination that made up for it. Robin began to live for order and understanding, but then she would run down Highland toward her house and see the unpainted second story and the rusting cars and broken mowers and Goldie's latest shining Cadillac, and she would know that the girl who left for school was different from the one who came home. She was like the contradictory twins on Grandma's soap opera who were played by the same actor.

In November, early snowfall hit Lilac, dusting the school yard, softening the yellowed grass and soaking the stitching of Robin's and Kitty's shoes as they stood against the building, cringing in the raw wind.

Before them, kids talked in loose groups. They straggled off the busses, boys with boys, girls with girls, all of them emitting a low hum of hormones, growth, and seething insecurities. Robin was working on Kitty, trying to get her to stay over both Friday and Saturday night during the coming weekend, but Kitty just shook her head and said, "Church on Sunday," and "Mom won't let me."

"We could go through Grandma's closet," Robin said. "There's Milky Ways in the freezer we could eat. Come on."

"I can't," Kitty said.

"Okay, you have to help me with something."

"What?" Kitty said quickly, turning to Robin.

"It's too hard to tell you now. Come over and you can help me."

"I don't know."

"Your parents can pick you up for church."

Kitty just looked at Robin. She had told Robin that her parents blamed the Simonsens' permissiveness for David's turn toward wild living. Robin had seen him hanging around Highland with one of the Bogat boys, smoking in their backyard and playing chicken with a switchblade.

Kitty's response to Robin's arguments was interrupted by the sudden and almost total silence of all the students in the school yard. Even the idling bus engines seemed to quiet as a new boy walked toward the school doors. His back straight, he stepped carefully, consciously lifting each foot as if there were small, evenly spaced obstacles in his path. He wore shiny shoes, a red plaid coat, and a black watch cap on his short black hair. His skin was the same color as the underside of tree bark. He was a black boy, and he was coming to Robin's school.

"Who's that?" Kitty asked.

The boy made his way toward the school entrance as if the ground were littered with trash. The bell hadn't rung yet, but this kid moved forward anyway, against the rules.

"What's he want?" Kitty asked, her voice rising. The bell rang just as the boy pulled open the heavy door, so all the kids came running and yelling behind him. Robin and Kitty pushed off the side of the building.

"He's just a new kid," Robin said to Kitty, but she was nervous.

"New kids don't come in November," Kitty said. Her brow wrinkled. "He's not a new kid."

"What else would he be?" Robin asked.

"I don't know," Kitty said.

Robin and Kitty separated for their homerooms. When Robin entered Mrs. Corning's classroom, the black kid was standing at attention by the teacher's desk. He smiled out at the students taking their seats.

Mrs. Corning stood next to him, her knuckles resting on her desk, while she directed a strange expression at the bulletin board in the back, which was empty except for copies of test keys. The new boy beamed. His two front teeth crossed at the bottom, just like Robin's, just like Patricia's. He wore a long-sleeved red polo shirt, black dress pants, and stiff church shoes, a boy's version of Kitty's Sunday mary janes. The boy's shoes looked brand-new, like him, and they anchored him to the floor.

"Everyone," Mrs. Corning said, after the students had taken their seats, "this is Freddie."

"Hi, I'm Freddie Eakins!" the boy cried. Mrs. Corning started and gave a little squeak.

"I just moved to Lilac, Illinois, from Chicago, Illinois," Freddie said at the top of his voice. "We used to live on the South Side, about near 113th and Aberdeen." He stopped speaking and smiled, as if his old street address might stir some recognition. To most kids in Lilac, Chicago was less familiar than Vietnam.

"Thank you, Freddie," Mrs. Corning said. "You may sit down."

Freddie started down the middle row of desks, but then he stopped at the empty seat next to Robin. He hesitated, facing the class, his hand trembling slightly at his side. "I'm glad to be here!" Freddie yelled. Grinning, he sat down.

Robin turned around. Until today, Lisa Giassi had sat next to her. But there was Lisa in the back row, her head on her new desk. She hated school, which was why she'd been up front. All the kids near the homeroom teacher's desk were troublesome in some way, querulous, bored, slow, with chronic coughs, bad clothes, or clothes that were too revealing; Robin didn't really know why she was up near Mrs. Corning, but she suspected it had something to do with her family. Now there was Freddie. Robin squinted at him, smearing his features against the panorama of white kids, their dark and light hair, bringing his own brown face, black hair, and red shirt into the foreground. When Robin opened her eyes all the way, Freddie was smiling at her.

"I have to tell you something," he whispered.

Robin listened for Mrs. Corning's homeroom instructions. "Tell me later," she whispered out of the side of her mouth.

Freddie was all the students could talk about that day. They whispered at lockers, before the bells rang for classes, behind books, even behind their hands in the lunchroom. Freddie wandered alone with his tray, a smile taped to his face, his back straight. But the minute school was over and Robin hit the outside with all the other screaming kids, Freddie was at her side.

He said, "You live on my street."

Robin stared at him. "No, I don't," she said. How could a black boy be on Highland without anyone knowing?

Freddie said, "I saw you in your yard when Daddy and Mama and me drove by once last week. You had a lady there with some tall hair."

"That's my grandmother," Robin said.

Freddie stared openly at Robin, trembling, as cold seeped up from the melting snow. "Let's walk home," he said.

"I take the bus with Kitty," Robin said, just as her friend came bursting through to the outside. "She's over there." Kitty saw Robin and stopped, remaining still while students flowed around her. "You should take the bus, too," Robin added. "If you live on my street."

Freddie wouldn't stop smiling. Robin felt embarrassed and looked away. He acted like he knew her.

"What's your parents like?" he asked.

"I don't have a mom," Robin said.

Freddie gasped. "How come?"

"She died."

"You got a daddy?"

"Yeah."

"Okay."

"And my grandma lives with us."

"Does she cook good?"

"No."

"My grandma on Mama's side does," Freddie said. "Her name's Mabel. That's an old-timer's name from South Carolina. She's always talking about, be my strong grandson, before we moved from Chicago."

Two eighth-grade boys ran by, and one stuck his arm out. He hit Freddie on the shoulder, sending him spinning backward so he almost fell. Freddie righted himself and reapplied his smile.

"Mercy," he said.

The school yard quieted again, but only for a few seconds. The screaming and scuffling continued, and Kitty caught up to Robin, eyeing her warily, and then Robin herded all three of them toward the bus home.

~

Robin knew it was a mistake right away. As soon as she told her father about Freddie Eakins and his parents moving in up the street, he acted like it was his idea.

"Finally!" he said at dinner.

"Finally what?" Robin asked.

"He thinks it's good we got a colored family here," Goldie said, sawing at the meat in her TV dinner.

"They say 'black' in the *Tribune*," Robin said.

"'Colored' was good enough when I was coming up," Goldie said. "And in Vegas. There was this colored fellow there used to clean our dressing room at the Horseshoe. We loved him to pieces."

"It's about time this fucking town got integrated," Heath said.

"Listen, son, this is one colored family in a white town," Goldie said. "That's not integration, that's trouble." She touched her fork to her applesauce and then set it down.

Heath had on his scheming face, the one he got when he watched a protest on TV or when he closed a big deal and then stacked cash in the metal box. Heath loved it when people misbehaved, and Robin knew that he thought the Eakinses' presence was a rebellion.

"And you're friends with this Freddie Eakins?" Robin's father asked her.

"I guess," Robin said, her mouth full of bologna sandwich. She had recently announced that she would never eat another TV dinner. There was something so sad about all the little compartments full of food that told you you only got so much, whether you wanted more or not.

"Good going," Heath said.

"He's nice, Dad."

"It's a new world, Ma," Heath said. He finished his beer.

"I've lived in this world longer than you have," Goldie said, "so don't tell me a thing, not one goddamn thing."

"We should have them over," Heath said, tossing his empty beer can into the garbage.

"Oh, come on!" Goldie said.

Heath left the offer hanging. "I've got a date," he said. And then he was out in the driveway, starting up his truck.

"He doesn't mean it, sweet pea," Goldie said. "About having them over."

"I know," Robin said.

Heath forgot about the Eakinses, but he was the only one in Lilac who did. Every morning, Freddie, the one and only black boy in town, got off the school bus and wandered with his pasted smile through the pale blob of junior high kids. Every afternoon, all through the winter and spring, as he walked between Robin and Kitty on their way to

Highland Street, curtains and shades lifted, eyes peered out in Freddie's wake. Sometimes an older boy followed the three of them on his bike. Sometimes a boy spit in their direction. But there was no yelling, no slurs, just finally a band of tension on Highland Street that caught up the three of them. Freddie left Robin at her house and continued up to his, but he often left trembling, walking in a stiff, careful way that filled Robin with pity. Now she lay awake at night and reorganized Freddie's life. She gave him other black kids in Lilac, a whole row of them to accompany him up the hill, down the halls at Lilac Junior High, out on the playing fields during gym class, but in Robin's fantasy all the other kids, girls included, looked just like Freddie. He was still the only black person she knew.

One spring afternoon, Robin came home from school and found her grandmother, Tommy, and Larry in the backyard, sitting on lawn chairs inside a small room made out of flexible screens and a vinyl floor. The room opened in the front with a huge zipper, like a colossal pair of jeans. Grandma and the men looked out on the car graveyard and the bus, and on Tom McAfee, who watched them from the stairs.

"What's this for?" Robin asked. Inside, everyone looked veiled and slightly gloomy, despite the sunlight that warmed the top of Robin's head.

"This keeps the bugs out, sweetie," Goldie said. "Larry brought it over for us. Just pull down that zipper." Clouds of cigarette smoke filled the tent.

"I hear you got a colored kid in your school," Tommy said. He had a voice like a dog scratching.

"Yeah, we do," Robin said.

"They're friends," Goldie whispered.

"Naw," Larry said.

They waited for Robin to explain Freddie. If Heath had been there, he would have been happy to explain the Eakinses to Grandma, Tommy, and Larry because he seemed to think an explanation was necessary. Robin didn't.

"Do we have any food?" she asked instead. She knew the answer: it was only Tuesday, groceries came on Friday, and they were mostly gone by Sunday.

"I brought over a summer sausage," Larry said. "You know how your Grandma loves it."

"Is it opened?" Robin asked.

"Not yet, honey pie," Goldie said.

"Forget it," Robin said, walking back to the house.

She called Kitty instead. "Come over and bring something to eat," Robin said.

Kitty arrived with a bag of grocery-store cookies that she said David had made her mother buy. "She got really mad at him and said he could just skip all his meals at home if he'd rather eat what a store makes," Kitty said. "Then she threw them in the garbage, but I got them when she wasn't looking. The bag's not even broken."

"Did she scream and everything?" Robin asked. Mrs. Paint fascinated her; she seemed like the worst possible mother. Her thousands of injustices and inconsistencies were purposeful, unlike Goldie's or Heath's, which were accidental.

"Mom's mad about David's hair and everything," Kitty said. "She does nice stuff for him and then gets mad and takes it back."

"Open the bag," Robin said. "I'm starved."

Kitty hesitated, looking out the kitchen window toward the bus. "What does that guy eat?" she asked.

"I don't know," Robin said. "He buys food. Sometimes my dad gives him stuff." Robin had seen Tom cooking outside over a tiny propane stove, kneeling near it like somebody at a campfire.

"Can we talk to him?" Kitty asked, chewing a cookie.

"Why?"

"I'm just wondering, is all. Maybe he'd want some cookies."

"He's kind of weird," Robin said.

They had to walk past the screen tent. Goldie, Larry, and Tommy were playing cards on the bottom of an overturned barrel. They never looked up.

Tom was waiting for them on the bus steps, half of his face smiling. "Well!" he cried. There was a jump in his shadow voice. "What an honor. And who's this sweet baby?"

Kitty blushed and nearly tripped over a tire hidden in the long grass. "We're having cookies," she said, giggling. "I'm Kitty."

"I think you're Little Red Riding Hood," Tom said. "Gimme what's in that basket."

Tom was smoking a joint, which he made no attempt to hide. "Girls," he said, sweeping his arm backward to the bus.

"We can stay out here," Robin said, her hand on Kitty's arm.

"I want to see," Kitty said, following Tom into the bus.

It was transformed. Much of the garbage was gone, and Tom had pitched many of the broken bus seats. At the back of the vehicle, where the hazard lights were exposed, wires dangling, Tom had set up Robin's old army cot, with a tin cracker box for an end table. A kerosene lantern sat on it. The oil heater, pushed back beside the cot, looked rusty, incendiary.

The rest of the bus, like Heath's bedroom, was set up for a party. Huge Indian-print pillows, all of them stained, lay scattered across the floor, along with ashtrays and empty baggies. The driver's seat was gone, and in its place sat a huge kettle filled with water, a smaller pot floating in it, and several sealed canning jars of yellow liquid. The bus smelled of pot and cigarettes and dirty feet.

"Wow!" Kitty said, her mouth hanging open and her eyes wide. "This is neat."

"Have a seat, darlin'," Tom said. "Robin," he said, pulling a lawn chair from behind some pillows and snapping it open, "you can sit here."

Tom put his hands in his pockets, then took them out again, as he watched them get settled. A breeze blew into the bus and then out the other side, like a thought shooting through an empty head.

"Here," Kitty said, holding up the bag of cookies.

Tom took one and then turned on a transistor radio that sat on a makeshift shelf behind Kitty's head. Kitty watched Tom's every move, her fascination with him so infuriating Robin that she gripped the seat of the lawn chair until her fingers broke through the rotten webbing. What was so wonderful about some guy who could barely take care of himself? Kitty acted just like Heath's dates. They brought food for Robin's father or sewed buttons onto his shirts, or drove him around when his truck wasn't working. They seemed to like the cripple in Robin's father almost as much as he liked it himself.

The radio played only a pop station: "Tie a Yellow Ribbon."

"I like this song," Kitty said.

"Haven't seen your dad since a few days ago," Tom said.

"Nope," Robin said. A photograph of a naked woman with long, chestnut hair was taped over the water kettle. The woman bent forward as she poured a jug of water over her long, smooth calf.

"What do you do in here?" Kitty asked.

"Nada, baby," Tom said. "Right, Robin?"

He looked at her sideways, as if he were afraid of her. Then he slipped a bag of pot from his back pocket and shook it while he got out his rolling papers. Robin panicked, but it was clear Kitty knew exactly what Tom was preparing to do. Her mouth gaped like an idiot's.

Tom leaned back against the wall of the bus and lit the joint, drawing in a huge lungful of smoke. To Robin's horror, he offered it to Kitty.

She looked down and shook her head, then glanced coyly at Tom. "Were you in the war?" she asked.

Robin resisted an urge to clobber Kitty.

Tom McAfee nodded as he pulled on the joint. He held it between drags, never offering it to Robin. "Yes, I was in the war. *That* war."

"What was it like?" Kitty asked.

"The war was like this," Tom said. He took both hands, pushed up the fallen side of his face, then let it drop—a puppet with one severed string. He laughed.

"We have to go," Robin said, standing up.

"I don't get it," Kitty said.

"Come on," Robin said. The image of Tom's face, dangling in a forced smile, remained on her eyes, like the impression of a lightning flash.

"Let's just say, sweetheart, that I returned a different man from the way I left," Tom said to Kitty.

"Have you been on TV?" Kitty asked. She sat cross-legged. Robin wondered if Tom could see up her dress.

"Like marches, you mean?" Tom asked. "Or protests? Or did I get a medal for my valor?" Tom stuck the joint in his mouth and swung his arms as if he were marching. You had to get through two faces, his dodgy talk, and now clowning to guess what he was really saying.

"Like any of that stuff?" Kitty asked.

"Nada," Tom said.

There was a long silence, and in it, Robin felt Tom McAfee's life crash to the floor of the bus like a dead bird. All anyone knew about him were two things: the war, and the fact that he was living in a bus at the discretion of a junk man. What was it like to have your life stop while you went on living?

"I've had this one thing happen," Tom said. His eyes were red, his face pink. Robin thought joints worked like tiny heating coils; they dispersed warmth inside smokers with each inhalation. "Just the one thing in the war," Tom said. "What else could there be after that?"

Voices and footsteps approached the bus.

"A fresh battalion," Tom said, rising from the floor.

"Uh-oh," said the first kid onto the bus, once he saw Robin and Kitty.

Two girls followed him, walking straight back to Tom's bed. That left three boys to huddle around the host and breathe in the smoke from his joint. One of them looked no older than Kitty and Robin. He had brown hair the color of cooked mushrooms, which fell to his shoulders. He was already tall and broad-shouldered, and his wide suede belt strained at its last hole. He turned to Kitty and Robin, examining them as dispassionately as if they were chairs he was choosing between.

"What are you looking at?" he asked Robin.

"You're the one who's looking," she replied.

"What school do you go to?" the boy asked.

Robin said, "None of your business" at the same moment Kitty said, "Lilac."

"That's the shit school," the boy said. He pulled a pack of cigarettes out of his back pocket. "Dirksen's better."

Everett Dirksen Junior High, the richer school on the other side of Lilac. It had once been Otto Kerner Junior High, until the former governor got accused of taking bribes. All the new kids on Tom's bus looked rich. Their clothes were styled to look dirty and torn, and the way they ignored Tom and Kitty and Robin came out of indifference rather than fear.

"Hey, McAfee," the boy said, "these two dogs your new girlfriends?"

"The little dark-haired one is Heath's kid," he said, nodding at Robin.

"Gotcha," the boy said, turning away. Angry-looking pimples dotted his cheekbones. Any other boy would have been embarrassed by them.

"Stevie," one of the girls in the back called, and the boy turned, all smiles.

Robin had thought both girls were from high school, but the one who had called to the boy only looked older because of her thick makeup and her utter lack of self-consciousness. She didn't seem to care that she looked like a girl on TV or in a magazine, fresh and dazzling. Robin watched her: the more the girl talked and laughed with Stevie, the younger she looked. She had long, shimmering blond hair and blue eyes, and she was tall. She could have belonged to Grandma and to Heath; she could be more a Simonsen than Robin was.

"Ask Tom here, Lynnie," Stevie said to the girl. "He'll tell you straight."

Robin looked away. Gazing at the girl reminded her of something.

"Kitty," Robin whispered, leaning over. Her friend sat on the pink pillow, her mouth still hanging open. "Kitty, we've got to go."

"Nuh-uh," Kitty said.

"Yes," Robin said, grabbing Kitty's hand. Kitty shook her off.

The three boys sat on pillows; one of them rolled a joint from Tom's bag of pot. Lynnie and the other girl whispered on Tom's bed, their long, thin legs extending into the bus. They let their sleek hair fall over the sides of their faces, the better to tell secrets.

Kitty, her face flushed with excitement, said to Robin, "My mom would *kill* me if she knew I was here!"

Robin stood up, wanting to say something over the music from the radio. Out in the screen tent, Goldie, Larry, and Tommy continued playing cards. The windows of the house reflected sunlight. The dead cars steamed in the afternoon heat. All of this silenced her thoughts.

The other girl at the back of the bus lifted the blanket that hung over the side of the cot and revealed several large plastic bags, all of them filled with pot.

"Break one open!" Stevie said. "Come on, Tom."

"Are you crazy, boy?" Tom asked, laughing. "I'm the security guard here. The perimeter officer. The doorman with a gun."

"You have a gun?" Kitty asked.

Tom and the kids laughed. "Sweetie," Tom said, "I didn't want one when I had to have one. Can't stand still enough to point anyway." He held up his hand, which shook violently.

A young man with a crew cut stuck his head into the bus. His hair was so blond and short that his skull looked naked.

"Roger Dodger!" Tom yelled. The man bowed his head.

More joint rolling followed, plus the lighting of a pipe for the gossiping girls in the back on the cot, their crossed legs pumping, flip-flops snapping against the soles of their feet. If the blond man had been older, he could have been an army buddy of Tom's, just out of the service, but he looked too shiny, too happy, too sure of himself.

"Hey, McAfee," Stevie said, standing up from the smoking circle and taking the joint with him, to cries of protest. He peered out the window. "Doesn't it make you nervous out here? I mean, Jesus, we're just in the fucking backyard."

Robin had the distinct feeling that she was watching someone else inside her life. Kitty was no help. Now she was mooning at Stevie.

"Shouldn't be scared of the cops," the crew cut guy said. He kneeled and looked out the window. "I left my cruiser down the street. See?" He pointed up Highland.

"What the hell!" Stevie cried.

Now everyone got up and looked out the bus window. Just past the Bogats' house, as the street began to rise, Robin saw a purple and white Lilac police car parked next to the ditch. In the driveway, Larry, Tommy, and Goldie were saying goodbye.

"Man, there's that sexy Goldie," the cop said.

"Watch it," Tom said.

"Sorry," the cop, Roger, said, turning to Robin.

"How do you know my grandma?" Robin asked.

"Everybody knows your old lady," Stevie said.

"It's her *grandmother,* if you can believe that," Tom said.

"I don't think your grandma's old, Robin," Kitty said.

"She's not, she's like younger than my mom," one of the other boys said.

"I gotta go," Roger said.

"Here. Shit." Tom dug through his pockets. "I'm short."

"Oh, god, who cares," Roger said, taking some bills from Tom.

Roger was healthy, exercised, as if he had something to keep up with, maybe a goal. But what should have made him more attractive seemed like arrogance. Snobbery. Robin wondered if that was why her father didn't like cops. All except this one, maybe.

Roger left the bus, cutting his eyes at Robin as he went by. Robin didn't wait to get Kitty or to say goodbye to Tom. She ran out after the cop, but he had already reached the driveway, laughing with Goldie and the men as he jogged by.

Kitty came up next to Robin. "I'm going to have so much to write in my diary," she said. "I can't believe it. Can you?"

"It wasn't a TV show, you know," Robin said. "This is my house."

Kitty breathed heavily for a moment. "I know," she said quietly. "But I like you, so I think of the other stuff as just pretend."

"Really?" Robin asked.

"It doesn't matter," Kitty said. "Just say that and it's okay."

Roger pulled his cruiser into the road and roared up the hill. After kissing Grandma on the cheek, Tommy got into Larry's van.

Robin bent down. There was a ten-dollar bill on the ground. A few feet in front of her was a five. She followed a blowing trail of paper money that led to the zippered door of the screen tent and then past it. It was Grandma's pinochle money, hopping and tumbling toward her on the driveway, where she waited for Robin.

∽

Robin had seen Freddie's mother wheeling big-bellied through the Eakinses' yard and house, but she still didn't think it possible that a friend could have a baby sibling. Nor was she prepared for Freddie's devotion, a brotherly version of her obsessive love for Kitty.

Antoinette was born in September, soon after Freddie and Robin started eighth grade. Freddie missed a day of school, then came back carrying a Polaroid photo of a wrinkled, somewhat pale shape swaddled in a flannel blanket. A swirl of thick black hair covered the baby's head. Freddie kept the picture of Antoinette in his locker, and he gazed at it like a pining suitor.

In late September, when Indian summer brought baking sun and dry breezes that curled the edges of the fallen leaves, the Eakinses planned a celebration of Antoinette's birth. Robin, Goldie, and Heath could come, but they weren't to bring anything.

"Mama's been cooking all week," Freddie said.

As if her family would ever come with anything but themselves, Robin thought.

By noon on the Saturday of the party, there were so many guests at the Eakinses' that two parallel lines of cars descended from the crest of Highland hill all the way to the front of the Hazens' house. Robin left early for Freddie's in order to get away from Goldie and Heath's argument. None of Grandma's men friends would go with her to the party, and she said it was "cheap" to have to go with her son. "Just don't make any of your stupid comments about black people," was Heath's response, as he piled cans of Old Style into a paper bag.

On Robin's walk up Highland, she passed Mr. Hazen and Mrs. Bogat and several other neighbors who were pretending to work in their yards. They swept their spotless driveways or mowed their shorn lawns, all the while craning their necks at the parade of what Heath called "city cars," most of them rusted and clunking, all of them carrying strangers to a stranger's house.

When Robin topped the hill she thought she'd stumbled into a different neighborhood. Black kids swung from the branches of the apple tree in Freddie's front yard and played catch on the grass; in the backyard, old, white-haired men and women—all of them black—sat in lawn chairs, while more people the Eakinses' age milled around. Mr. Eakins poked at meat on a new grill, and, in the shade of a maple tree, Mrs. Eakins and Freddie showed off Antoinette to some more elderly women.

Robin followed the sound of Freddie's chatter. Other kids at school hated their siblings and even wished them dead, but Freddie was a boy in love. Every day he told Robin something new about the baby's range of motion, the extent of her gurgling and noises, even the frequency of her spit-up.

Freddie stood with his hand on Antoinette's fuzzy little head. Her color was almost as dark as Freddie's now, and she had her solemn eyes open, staring up first at Mrs. Eakins and Freddie and then at all the other women, and finally at the half-naked maple tree branches above their heads.

"Isn't she precious?" Freddie whispered to Robin. All the women laughed.

"This is Freddie's best friend, Robin," Mrs. Eakins said to the ladies. "She lives down the street."

The women looked Robin over, then turned back to the baby.

"Are your father and grandmother coming, Robin?" Mrs. Eakins asked.

"Yeah, maybe later," Robin said.

Antoinette had begun to cry, her eyes squinched shut and her mouth, a little slot in her face, distorted and narrow. Mrs. Eakins started to unbutton her blouse, and the group of women tightened their circle around her, squeezing out Robin and Freddie.

Freddie took Robin to the front of the house where some girls were jumping double-dutch on the driveway. Freddie lifted his hands before the two twirling ropes and leapt between them. He was a dazzling jumper, jigging between the competing ropes even as the girls accelerated their twirling and their rhymes, chanting so fast that Robin couldn't understand the words. But she did understand Freddie's slack expression—that giving over of the body that leaves you stunned.

Freddie leapt free of the jump ropes and joined Robin. "Double-dutch's what I like best," he said, wiping sweat from his forehead. "We did that all day long in the summer in our old neighborhood. Right, Tammy?" he called.

"Right," said the girl jumping rope. She had a fierce expression.

"Tammy's my cousin's cousin," Freddie said.

Just then Heath pulled into the Eakinses' driveway, his chugging truck stalling right at the edge of the jumpers. They stopped their game in a tangle of rope and legs.

"Your dad didn't want to haul me," Goldie said, rolling her eyes as she put one sandaled foot on the blacktop and then the other. Heath slammed his door and took off for the backyard without a word, two new packs of Panatelas and the bag of beers in his hands.

"Hi, Mrs. Simonsen," Freddie said, smiling. Freddie had told Robin he thought Goldie was "sparkly."

"Walk up that hill?" Grandma said, ignoring Freddie. "Forget it. It's hot, too," she said, fluttering the front of her black blouse, which was tied around her middle, just above the waistband of her red capri pants. Around her hips she wore a chain belt with large silver coins dangling from it. When Grandma walked, she sounded like a piggy bank full of change.

"You kids take me on back," Goldie said. She grabbed Robin's hand. "You have a big family, Freddie," she added, scanning the staring kids in the front yard.

"It's friends, too," Freddie said, running to keep up with Goldie's long strides. "And you haven't seen Antoinette."

Grandma's heels punched holes in the Eakinses' well-groomed lawn, her tall, frosted hair threatened to tangle in the tree branches, and all the way over to Mrs. Eakins and the baby she jingled like a waitress's pocket.

"Here! Here!" Freddie cried, running ahead of Robin and Goldie to peel the baby's blanket from her sleeping face.

"This is my grandma," Robin said to Mrs. Eakins.

The women standing around Mrs. Eakins moved back, frowning. At the same time, a phalanx of men moved forward and set up a field of palpable interest behind the arc of females.

"My name's Goldie Simonsen, *not* Grandma," Goldie said, looking over Mrs. Eakins' head at the men.

"Pleased to meet you," Freddie's mother said. She looked surprised.

"What'd she say her name was?" one woman in the group whispered to another.

"I don't want to smoke around the baby," Goldie said, holding up her vinyl cigarette case and matches. Her belt tinkled. She still hadn't looked at Antoinette.

"Anywhere over there is fine," Mrs. Eakins said quietly, waving her hand behind her head, her eyes still on Goldie.

Grandma picked her way across the yard to the grill, where most of the men stood by with beers. Mr. Eakins, spatula poised, watched Goldie puncture the earth between his wife and him. One elderly man in a suit and a straw hat stood and gave Goldie his lawn chair. Heath had disappeared.

At sunset, Freddie and Robin lay sick and happy and full on the cool grass at the edge of the Eakinses' lawn. Robin could smell the dark scent of turned earth and the sharp green odor of spent tomato foliage in Mrs. Eakins' vegetable garden. The warm air wore a cold border, like a wool blanket with satin edges. The lightning bugs were sluggish, barely twinkling. Goldie laughed from her lawn chair.

"My dad was scared about today," Freddie said.

"How come?" Robin asked. She caught a lightning bug and let it go.

"You don't know what's going to happen when you're the only one," Freddie said. "People can act crazy, Daddy said."

"Even like your own family," Robin said, sighing.

"I'm not talking about that. I'm talking about everybody else in Lilac." From a record player somewhere the Isley Brothers sang at high volume. Freddie paused. "Come on," he said, rising and pulling Robin off the ground.

Robin and Freddie danced face to face, arms churning with the gyrating fury they'd seen among the stylish Los Angeles couples on *American Bandstand*. The rest of the Eakinses' guests twirled more languidly, and at a distance, off in the darkest part of the yard. After the Isley Brothers, someone put on Sly and the Family Stone. By dusk, even Freddie's older relatives danced, swaying slowly to music that demanded much quicker steps.

The whole party was working on "Everyday People" when Robin's father strode into the backyard, followed by two policemen. Both cops were heavyset, breathing hard, the back porch light illuminating streams of perspiration on their temples and cheeks.

"What's this?" Mr. Eakins asked, speaking over the music. He stopped dancing. As Freddie's father moved toward the cops, Robin watched a whole group of young male guests turn and drift further into the dark.

"Ron," Robin's father said, stepping between Mr. Eakins and the cops.

The cops dodged Heath. "What's going on here?" said an officer with long sideburns. Both cops rested their hands on their gun belts, and the one who hadn't spoken, the one with the wedge of hair like an actor in one of Goldie's old movies, watched the now silent party.

"We're having a few people over, officer," Mr. Eakins said, smiling. Robin's father stomped around behind him as if he'd stubbed his toe.

"Who are all these folks?" Sideburns demanded.

"Well," Mr. Eakins began, still smiling.

Heath rushed between Mr. Eakins and the cops again. "Can't a man have a party in his own backyard?" he burst out.

"Now, Heath," Mr. Eakins said.

"We're looking at a car, a goddamn car, out on the street," Heath said. "Since when is that illegal?"

At the word "goddamn," the other cop turned his full attention to Robin's father and began walking up behind him, his hand still on his belt.

Goldie's voice came out of the dark. "Oh, brother," she said.

"Do you live here?" Sideburns asked Heath. He looked behind him at the Eakinses' house. "In this house here? Do you?"

"I'm a friend," Heath said.

"Then I don't think there's any need for us two to be talking, do you? There's no need for me to explain to you, since you are not the resident, that there's been complaints about noise here."

"My wife," Mr. Eakins began. Suddenly the record stopped.

At that moment Antoinette began to cry, and everyone waited as her howling came closer, traveling from the back of the house and into the yard, until Mrs. Eakins stood before the cops with the baby, whose little face had seized up; she shook her fists.

"You woke up my daughter," Mrs. Eakins said sternly. She held the baby in one arm and hugged Freddie to her with the other.

Sideburns looked down at Antoinette, who was taking a deep breath preparatory to a scream, as if he'd never seen a baby before.

"Seems to me," he said loudly, as Antoinette carried on, "that music you were playing woke her up."

"She was sleeping just fine until you showed up," Mrs. Eakins said.

Mr. Eakins gave his wife a panicked look. "Jacqueline," he said.

"Now, ma'am," Sideburns said.

"Jesus, leave her alone!" Heath cried, stepping forward and grabbing Sideburns by his shoulder.

At this, the other cop rushed Robin's father and pulled one of his arms behind his back.

"I don't fucking believe this!" Heath yelled. He swung around, his eyes just grazing Robin. He looked instead at the rest of the party guests.

"Heath, man, oh, God," Mr. Eakins said.

"For Christ's sake!" Goldie's voice again emerged from the dark. But she didn't get up or come forward. "Get a grip, son!"

The cop pushed Robin's father out of the backyard.

"Dad!" Robin cried, running after them.

Antoinette continued to scream. "Excuse me," Robin heard Mrs. Eakins say, "I have to feed my baby."

The cop moved quickly for a heavy man. He and Heath gasped for breath, their shoes slipping on the driveway.

"Dad! Daddy!" Robin called behind them.

"Kiddo," Heath said, turning his head and trying to look at her, "listen now. You go with Grandma, okay? This is just bullshit."

"Arrogant hippie son-of-a-bitch," the cop muttered, shoving Robin's father up against the side of the squad car and putting him in handcuffs.

Robin stopped on the driveway and watched. It looked so permanent, the cop's anger so irreversible, the way he shoved her father into the back seat. Heath tossed his head to get his hair out of his eyes. His mustache looked sad, but the rest of him was tense and flexed, angry. The cop sat in the passenger seat and wrote on a clipboard under the dome light.

"Go in the back now, girl," a voice next to Robin said. It was Sideburns, on his way to the squad car. He took off his hat.

Sideburns got behind the wheel, and then the car swiftly pulled away from the Eakinses' driveway, no light, no siren. Robin's father never looked back.

~

They had to leave the truck. It was still in the Eakinses' driveway the next morning, another warm day, as if Robin's father, reluctant to quit the revelry, was the last to leave the party instead of the one whose arrest broke it up.

Robin had returned to the backyard and roused Goldie from her lawn chair, and on their way past the house she had seen Mrs. Eakins through the back window, nursing Antoinette in a chair, her head held at a stiff angle that seemed to support every word she'd spoken to the cop, as well as Antoinette's little body, and even the Eakins house itself.

Sunday morning, Goldie and Robin drove uptown to the Lilac jail to bail out Heath. Grandma wore all white, stretch pants and a bolero over a tank top, and her big white sunglasses. She stopped at the donut shop and made Robin run in and get her coffee, and then she drove the Cadillac one-handed to the jail parking lot, where they sat while she finished her cup and Robin jiggled her legs. Would there be a trial, then her father in jail for a long time? Robin saw Heath in a striped uniform, like a convict from one of Grandma's old late-night movies; she saw him testifying in court in an ill-fitting suit from ten years ago. Then she saw him the same, red-eyed, distracted, his hand on her head at the breakfast table while he ate his toast, his gesture a replacement for talking to her.

Robin looked up to see Roger Dodger in full uniform walk past the Cadillac. He winked at Robin's grandmother. "Morning, Goldie," he said.

Grandma raised her cup to him. Robin leaned her head against the window, suddenly more tired than she'd ever been. Her father and his great head of hair under the interior light of the police car: just hair, no face turned to her, no look back to where he'd been.

The charges were dropped, for reasons the sergeant refused to reveal, so they just had to pay off Heath's load of traffic tickets. Bailing him out didn't take long. There was only the ritual of Goldie pulling a money roll from her purse, snapping off the rubber band, then peeling some bills. No one in Robin's family believed in banks. You kept everything on you.

chapter six

∽

Kitty found Jesus in eighth grade, which meant she lost Robin and Freddie. She thought she knew God before, Kitty told Robin early in the school year, but it was really Jesus who was calling her. She joined a group of Jesus Freaks, Protestant kids who got together and prayed and sang hymns and did wholesome activities. Some of them played guitar, but never loudly. No smoking, no drinking, no sex, no thoughts of the kind that pinged through most adolescents' heads every minute of the day.

Kitty said she had to keep her participation in the Jesus Freaks a secret from her family. They were Catholic, but now she was Jesus' child.

"What's the difference?" Robin asked. She, Freddie, and Kitty stood in a clump at the bottom of the bus stairs, a sea of sour kids rushing around them.

"Catholics don't believe in Jesus," Freddie said.

"That's not true!" Kitty cried. She grabbed Freddie's sleeve. "No, they do! It's just now I call him Jesus instead of Christ. And I don't like the Virgin Mary anymore."

A group of seventh and eighth graders arrived and gathered up Kitty. They looked happy in a kind of manic way, like bad actors modeling joy. Some of them wore crosses made from thick pieces of wood that hung from long leather shoelaces. Kitty still wore her communion crucifix, because she had to, she said, or her parents would find out about Jesus. Like he was her boyfriend or something, Robin thought.

Kitty's Jesus Freak friends swept her away from the bus door. It was five minutes to homeroom.

"Mama said you can be a godly person, but you don't have to wear a sign about it," Freddie said.

"Right," Robin said, watching Kitty walk away.

There was an early morning fog, but already the sun was burning through, warming the damp air. At least Kitty had a group. Robin had

Freddie; he had her. Robin's family blew in and out of the house like balls of dust.

The bell rang, and Robin and Freddie split up to go to opposite sides of the building. They were in different homerooms and different classes, each of them blazing a path of perfect grades and attendance, Freddie facing the hallways like a soldier going to battle. Once, while delivering a note to a teacher, Robin had seen him in class. He looked stricken in his desk, stiff and sweaty, his hand halfway raised in anticipation of a question. Robin had never seen Freddie in his old neighborhood in Chicago, but she caught glimpses sometimes—with his parents, on the phone to his grandmother, playing with Antoinette—when Freddie's body and voice and speech relaxed and he looked like a boy who could really be happy instead of one just getting along.

For a few months that fall, everything seemed tarnished. Robin felt Freddie's fear like a layer of dirt on her own skin, and she finally gave up waiting for Goldie to become the benevolent queen of Simonsen salvage. When Robin slept over at Kitty's, they fought in the bed rather than explored. Kitty pushed her off, Robin advanced, Kitty laughed; in the morning, Mrs. Paint glared at Robin as if she could read her thoughts, while Kitty slurped her cereal and watched cartoons. Robin knew she had to adapt to new situations, but her whole life was new situations; there was nothing standard by which to measure all her efforts to keep up. Everything was off, compromised: Robin lay awake at night, pondering the borderlines within which she lived, the physical life on Highland and at school and her stature as the small, dark-haired girl walking next to Freddie and Kitty, both of whom seemed to be growing at a clip. She could have been shrinking. Robin had Heath, she had Goldie, she had memories of a mother that played as soft and fuzzy as the dream sequences on Grandma's soap operas, yet nothing from her daily life hooked her. Nothing was permanent. Everything was hard work.

~

"Dad, wake up," Robin said. "Come on."

There was something hard and drowned about her father's body on the sofa, as if, deep inside his skin, Heath had sunk, and the anchor of his submerged consciousness had dragged his body along with it.

"Daddy," Robin said quietly, sitting down next to his body.

She'd been at Freddie's, working on a history project, and now she'd come home to a dark house, her father barely visible in the moonlight, his feet tucked between the couch cushions, his head threatening to dangle off the side. Goldie smoked at the kitchen table, the red ember of her cigarette the only light in the house. Now Grandma appeared next to her and shone a flashlight on her face.

"Cripes, do you believe this?" Goldie asked.

"What happened? Did the fuse box go again?" Just a few weeks before, Robin had spent most of Saturday afternoon screwing in new fuses while standing on a piece of plywood in front of the box with Tommy Boy at her elbow offering advice, most of which he immediately contradicted.

"Guess who didn't pay the bill for how long," Goldie said.

Robin sank into the easy chair and placed her books next to her on the floor. "Well, don't we have candles or something?"

"Tommy and Larry are on their way over," Goldie said. She lit another cigarette, the flashlight resting on the coffee table, its beam shining out the picture window and into the dark front yard.

"What are they going to do if it's the company?" Robin asked.

"They're bringing money, sugar bear," Grandma said.

"Give me the flashlight."

Robin turned the beam to the wall behind the couch, so she could watch her father sleep. Heath didn't snore, he didn't twitch, nothing moved except his shoulder as he breathed. Over the past year, Heath had grown thin, then thinner, then Robin had seen his eyes sink further into his skull and his skin grow rough and blotchy. Her father acted like an invalid, wandering around for days in the same clothes, sometimes wrapped in a blanket at night, coughing and spitting into the sink and the toilet, growling into the phone at people. But seeing her father on the couch now, barely illuminated, Robin thought again how most of all Heath looked deeply alone, almost enclosed, as if some invisible net held his features, his breath and his hair, even the fizz that used to be his energy. Something outside her father's control embraced him. Robin could feel it counting his breaths.

She picked up the flashlight and followed Goldie into the kitchen. "You're just going to sit here in the dark?" she asked.

"I wish there was TV," Grandma said.

"Do you want me to get another flashlight?" Robin asked.

"That's the only one."

"I'm going upstairs with it."

"Why?" Goldie asked quickly.

"Dad probably has candles, don't you think. And just to see. Why's he asleep like that?"

"Oh, you know," Grandma said, waving her hand with the cigarette.

"I don't like it," Robin said, starting up the stairs.

Heath's bed was a tangle of sheets and blankets, pillows stacked at the bottom and the Indian bedspread balled up at the head. Robin swung the flashlight around to the stereo. In the midst of Heath's dirty clothes and overflowing cardboard boxes and mattress on the floor, his stereo looked near death, another discarded piece of junk. The whole room smelled of sweat.

Robin rifled through the boxes. Dirty clothes, spent matches, even Panatela butts: her father must have swept up what was on the floor and dumped it there. Why? His dates didn't care anymore. On a card table sat her father's scale, some matches, an empty pack of razor blades, two opened bottles of Pepsi, and a candle.

It took an archaeologist to figure out her family's detritus, and a daughter could only know so much. In the dark, with just the flashlight and the pale moonlight outside, and no view of other houses on the block, Robin could convince herself that she was in someone else's home, that she was a spy, that she wasn't the daughter of a man who had probably moved beyond selling pot. She felt nervous, as if her father were present, ready to jump out at her. The room smelled bad, not like pot, more like sickness, like the yellow odor that had surrounded her mother before she died. Robin moved the flashlight beam around the room. No sign of her father's pipe or papers. No baggies. He had changed jobs. The people she'd seen come and go every day, they looked like the same ragged folks; in some ways they were animated versions of all the junk on the property, just as expendable, just as interchangeable.

Robin shone the flashlight around at the bare walls, a cracked windowpane, an ancient coat rack in the corner from which her father had hung his one tie, a skinny, striped model from the early 1960s, and back down onto the stereo and the crates on their sides full of records. In one of the crates, the bottom row of records sat halfway out on the floor.

Robin got down and pointed the flashlight beam into the back of the crate. She dragged out the records. Behind them were two large plastic bags. The first one held dozens of hypodermic needles, a red cap on each point. She gasped. But there was no need to feel surprised, she told herself a moment later, taking a deep breath. If you added up all the evidence, if you thought of your family as a problem, a collection of smaller dilemmas you could tick off, then you could be ready for anything. *Begin* to be ready. The one piece of logic Robin's father and grandmother had taught her was that desire was nothing more than a cause, and a cause had to have an effect. Robin picked up the other plastic bag. She opened it and poured a pile of money onto the floor, an even bigger pile than the one her father had shown her years before. Twenties, fifties, hundreds, dozens of tens and fives, and a score of crumpled one-dollar bills, the effect of desire, of business well done. Robin scooped up the cash and took the bag down to her grandmother in the kitchen, the flashlight beam bouncing before her.

∼

Robin couldn't see more than five feet in any direction. The trees were taller and thicker on this side of the clearing, and they hung over Robin's and Freddie's heads like huge green parasols. After an hour of searching, the two of them had found this area alongside the Prairie Path that was free of flattened ground cover or busted bikes or cigarette butts or even couples making out. They were finally alone, branches tossing overhead in the wind, and, beyond that, the hot blue sky, washed out and pale.

The leafy enclosure felt right. In the past few weeks, Robin had all but boxed up her family and put them aside. She would no longer look to them for answers or even questions, no longer hope for anything useful from them. Just a few days ago, while Heath languished silently upstairs, Goldie had said, "No boy wants boobies hanging down to the navel. It's time we got you a bra." Now, Robin thought, she would make up her own life.

In the rustling shade, Freddie's skin took on golden highlights. He had grown more wide-eyed in the past year. He looked perpetually surprised, or maybe alarmed. His hair was lush and springy, though he complained that his dad made him keep it just short of an Afro. Robin wanted to press down on the crown of his head and feel the hair come back up under her palms.

"You wanna keep going?" Freddie asked, looking around.

"We've looked enough," Robin said, though she was nervous, too. She and Freddie had planned for today as if it were one of their school projects, discussing timing, protocol, place. Freddie was Robin's match in ability to organize and make priorities and to work toward a goal; the only difference was that Freddie was in love with the *idea* of the goal, not the goal itself. Robin could never get him to say what he wanted.

She felt the ground with her hands: a blanket of dry leaf litter in the shadows touched by sun and the patterns of shifting leaves.

The Prairie Path was not a prairie, or even strictly a path, but a ribbon of cleared ground that had once been train tracks running west from Melrose Park through a half-dozen suburbs, including Lilac, then stopping in the town of Geneva. Bicyclists and joggers used the path itself; on either side of it—the only part that could conceivably be called prairie—were overgrown stands of sumac and maple saplings, the occasional cottonwood or poplar or tangle of bushes and brambles and tall grass. Here eighth-grade kids smoked cigarettes, high school kids smoked pot, got drunk and threw up, or had sex, or sometimes did all three. Despite the lingering creosote smell of railroad ties, the piles of dog waste, and the occasional pair of underpants in the weeds, there was a storybook quality to the Prairie Path. To get to their hiding place, Robin and Freddie had crossed an old train trestle, scrambled up embankments, crashed through several stands of foliage, and encountered hostile gangs of kids. Now all that was missing was a flash of light and someone to cast a spell. Robin looked at Freddie, handsome, friendly and open, petrified: no witches here, unless Robin herself was one.

Freddie sat cross-legged, ripping leaves into tiny pieces. "I don't know how I'm going to do in science next year," he said.

"Just because it's high school—that makes no difference," Robin said. "You got an A in it this year."

"But it's different things: biology, chemistry, physics, I think. It's separate and different."

"Fred," Robin said.

"Okay," he whispered, looking down.

They had agreed to be honest about what they were going to do, call it what it was, avoid slang. Before today, Robin and Freddie had had several reasonable, rational conversations in Robin's room while they drank Cokes and ate Goldie's Snickers bars they'd stolen from the refrigerator. Robin approached her and Freddie's plan with logic. She rejected the Simonsen tendency to overreact, to relate everything only to oneself. She tried to see things clearly: Heath was no longer much use as a father; if she had been an old twelve, she was an even older thirteen; she would make up her own life. Robin wondered if her grandmother had guessed what she and Freddie were up to because for the past month Goldie had fiercely lobbed nuggets of useless advice at Robin. "Slips are only good if the lace shows just a little under the hem of your skirt," she said. "When a man gives you a nice bracelet, wear it on your right wrist; the left is for husbands." "There's nothing wrong with wearing a bra that's one size too small." "If you get a pimple, stay home and make excuses to your date." "A good hairdo is timeless; think of it as a fingerprint, something that says YOU." And finally, "A pretty woman's corpse always gets a better funeral than an ugly one."

Freddie stared at Robin. He laughed. "I'm going to high school, and Antoinette's like, just a baby. Being that little looks kind of good sometimes, you know?"

"Not really," Robin said. "Babies have to do what everyone tells them to."

"Food whenever, and what you like, and just naps and toys. No TV, though."

"Your parents hardly let you watch it anyway."

"Daddy says, you see a black man on TV, and it's just a pimp or a crook or whatever."

"Is he still mad at me?"

"Who?"

"Your dad! About my dad."

"Naw. But I'll tell you, when I come home from your house or from us doing stuff, Daddy asks me right out what we did, where we went. He's keeping an eye out. He knows it's not you, though. He says kids can't help their parents."

"Are you going to tell him about today?" The leaves moved small patches of sun over Freddie's face.

"Are you nuts?" Freddie laughed, ripping up another leaf.

Robin scooted close to Freddie. He drew back, just slightly.

"Okay," Robin said. "If you could have sex with anyone, who would you have sex with?"

"God, can't we just do this? Do we have to talk about everything?" Freddie swept the leaf shreds off his lap.

It was true that her father always went right upstairs with a woman or straight over to her place. And Grandma talked a lot to men, except the Bogdanases. Their visits embraced a blank space in Goldie's days, a time when all the other men were gone.

"But Fred, remember?" Robin asked. "We're doing this just to see. We might as well talk first anyway. What difference does it make?"

They'd made a list, sitting on Robin's bed while Perry Como played in the living room. (1) Get to Prairie Path. (2) Find place. (3) Warm up. (4) Kiss. (5) Take off clothes. (6) Do it. The whole enterprise seemed so manageable, so far beyond the crash and clutter of the Simonsen house.

Robin decided it was time to skip steps. She leaned over and kissed Freddie on the mouth. He kissed her back, and then they spent a few minutes pressing lips, without touching in any other way, and with their eyes open.

Finally, Robin pulled away and looked at Freddie. He didn't look any different. He was a friend, a boy. "What do I look like?" she asked.

Freddie wrinkled his brow. "You've got a leaf in your hair," he said.

Robin pushed her face toward Freddie and kissed him again.

This time, after a few kisses, Robin gently pushed Freddie onto the ground, where they continued kissing. Soon, Freddie pushed Robin off of him and sat up.

"I think I'm ready," he said, staring into the surrounding foliage.

Robin immediately peeled off her tee shirt. She didn't feel excited or frightened; the blood wasn't leaving her legs like it used to in bed with Kitty. She liked Freddie's taste. He was sweet and a little stale, and his lips were warm and soft. But these were observations. She felt just as happy about a bright-eyed wren on a nearby branch. It twitched its tail and then flew off.

"Don't you wear anything underneath?" Freddie asked, his fingers on the buttons of his shirt.

"Why would I?" Robin asked.

Under Freddie's plaid shirt was an undershirt. He paused before taking it off, and Robin wondered for a moment if he'd have something under that, and then another garment and another. Once, after several Rob Roys, Goldie had explained the art of striptease, the slow removal of a dozen tiny scarves and hankies, the gentle revealing of first one part of the body, then the other.

"Now I'm nervous," Freddie said.

"So am I," Robin said, lying, "so hurry."

Freddie took off his undershirt, then his sneakers and socks. Robin took off her shoes. Then she jumped on Freddie again, pressing her mouth to his, waiting for pressure in response, and, when he didn't return her urgency, shoving him onto the ground.

"Ow!"

"Sorry, Fred."

They grappled for a while. Every touch Robin and Kitty had shared now seemed like an accident or instinct.

Robin stood up and stripped off her shorts. She shivered in her blue-flowered underpants. They were worn down to the elastic around the legs and at the waist.

Freddie wasn't even looking. He fiddled with the zipper on his shorts.

Of course, Freddie's briefs were perfect: pure white, no frayed edges or stains; they could have been ironed. Freddie's nipples looked almost blue in the dim light of their enclosure. "What if someone sees us?" he asked.

"Why would anyone come back here?"

"We're here," Freddie said, pulling off his briefs in one quick movement, like ripping off a bandage. Between his skinny thighs, his penis hung short and limp, looking part pale and part dark.

Robin stood with her hands on her hips. They had a plan. Okay. They could learn.

"You lie down," Freddie said. "On the bottom."

"Why do I have to be on the bottom?"

"That's where girls go," Freddie said.

Robin decided not to argue. Now she was getting nervous. Nearby, she could hear the crunch of bike tires on gravel. The ground no longer looked comfortable, so Robin spread out her tee shirt and shorts. They lay there bodiless, like the outfit of a ghost. She placed herself on top of the clothes, a paper doll undressed. Freddie kneeled next to her.

"Get on," Robin said.

"I think we should kiss more first," Freddie said. He put one leg over Robin's thighs and left the other curled next to her, hovering over her in a half straddle. Then he leaned down and kissed her lips. He hung over Robin's body, as if held up by strings.

After a minute of kissing, Robin was bored. She even counted how many times the branches overhead blew back and forth. "Here," she finally said, grabbing Freddie's penis. "I'll do this to you, and you can do it to me. That's a way to start."

"No!" Freddie cried. He pulled away from Robin and fell on his back. "I don't want to touch you *there*."

One night, Robin scooped her hand down into Kitty's crotch and held it there. Her hand had fit right around Kitty's bone and flesh and tissue, her body keeping Kitty's intact.

But Robin and Freddie had a plan, and a plan must go forward. "Come on," Robin said. "We can do it any way we want."

"I don't. I can't." Freddie stood up and began gathering up his clothes, not looking at Robin.

"Are you mad at me or something?" Robin asked. She thought Freddie might cry.

He had his briefs and his shorts on, but he stopped dressing, his undershirt in his hand. "You know, Robin," he said, "people don't have to do everything they want all the time."

Sometimes when Robin was with Freddie, she wanted to scream, to roar. Hot and indecipherable feelings collected behind her sternum and made her want everything, just to want it: food, sugar, money, books, order; or she wanted to run as fast as she could down a hill, her legs churning, her heart pumping against her clogged emotions. Robin wanted. It was the Simonsen way: now, for me, for always.

"Fred!" Robin cried. "Please."

"Richard Roundtree," Freddie said, dropping to the ground. He wiped his eyes.

"What?" Robin asked. "Are you crying?"

"You asked, before," Freddie said. "Who would I like to have sex with if it could be with anyone."

"Who's Richard Roundtree?"

"*Shaft*," Freddie said. "The movie. You know."

"He's a guy, Fred."

"Duh." Freddie faced Robin and looked at her. "Duh," he said again.

Robin sat up straight, still naked, not caring how much of her flesh Freddie saw. "Oh, shit, Freddie! Shit!"

"Okay, all right. Don't have a cow."

New muscles had taken shape in Freddie's arms, hard ones, small and tough. Robin hadn't noticed them before. "I thought you didn't want to be friends with me anymore," Robin said. "I thought you didn't like me or something. I hate crying, Freddie," she added. "So cut it out."

"What am I going to do, Rob? I mean, God."

They were both just babies, Robin thought, looking at Freddie's shivering body and feeling her own tininess underneath the shadows of the great cottonwoods. Robin said, "When I was friends with Kitty, my dad told me that sometimes kids loved each other and it was okay."

"Your dad's so cool," Freddie said.

"Not really," Robin said. "Not all the time anyway. Mostly he's just not around." What would her father say now? He didn't utter a word when he came downstairs and opened the refrigerator and found nothing in it. This wouldn't move him either. And Goldie? Robin had the boy and girl part with Freddie right, but the details were wrong, as usual; Grandma would be displeased in the same way she was about Robin wearing high tops and boys' jeans.

"You can't tell anyone, Robin," Freddie said, gripping Robin's shoulder. "Promise."

"You must think I'm a mental case," Robin said. "I know you can't say that kind of stuff."

Freddie sat silently, just looking at her. She stepped into his thoughts, as she often did. And, as usual, Freddie was asking for some kind of trade, for another step up in their friendship. "Kitty and I used to do stuff," Robin said.

"Yeah, I thought so."

Nothing had ever made Robin happier than the sight of Freddie smiling. It would be all right now.

The foliage in their enclosure smelled of cat pee. A full bush to Robin's right was called a bridal wreath. Some scraggly sumacs stood to her left, no doubt started by wayward birds or the wind performing its planting duties. Another bush had rounded leaves, like dogs' ears. Robin would remember this place. And she'd remember Freddie's beaming face. She started to get dressed. There was always a secret to keep, Robin thought, watching as Freddie buttoned his shirt. She was getting to be an expert at secrets. "Let's go," she said.

Freddie didn't look at her. "Let me leave first," he said.

"Why?" Robin's stomach tightened. Nothing in the plan had worked. It was like homework left undone.

"It's safer," Freddie said. "It just makes sense."

Before Robin could protest, Freddie pushed his way through the foliage and disappeared. She sat in the green cavern of trees and bushes, so quiet and empty, she could have been alone the whole time.

BOOK TWO

chapter seven

Robin and her grandmother followed Heath into the backyard. Beyond the roofs of the dead cars sat Tom McAfee's school bus; the shanty he'd built the year before leaned hard up against it. Overhead, Heath and Tom had strung an illegal utility line, fragile as a thread, from the house to the shanty. Tom had lights. A new day dawned at the Simonsens.

Heath led them into the garage. He'd adopted a peculiar shuffle lately, what Tom called a "junkie walk." He rarely changed his baggy tee shirts or loose jeans. He was like a drop of mercury in a bowl: malleable, yet toxic.

Heath approached the old Thunderbird, its wheels on blocks, its body covered in parachute silk and tarps. He grinned at Robin, his hand on the hood of the car. "Happy seventeenth birthday!" he cried.

"What," Robin said.

"That's worth a pretty penny," Goldie said.

"It's a classic, kiddo!"

Her father's smile. It forced Robin's eyes to the floor. Heath had lost some teeth a year ago, perhaps he fell, or maybe he got into a fight, but it wasn't the gaps that Robin couldn't look at. Heath Simonsen smiled like a man who'd be ever so grateful if you didn't kick the shit out of him.

Robin's eyes began to ache. "Dad," she said, "you're kidding about the car. Aren't you?"

Her father's smile leaked out a warning, too: you don't want to see what happens if you rattle the old man.

"Daddy, it's a wreck," Robin said. The muggy morning air clung to her head.

"It's great under the cover!" Heath said. "And how often have you watched me work on cars? Huh?" He squeezed Robin's shoulders. "We've got the tools right here. And I'll help you." Her father smelled of Panatelas and beer and acrid sweat. All at eight A.M.

Heath hadn't touched an engine in years. He barely left his room now because he'd found someone who was willing to score for him, no questions asked. Even the women had all but disappeared from her father's daily life, unless they were the using kind. The new ones had to steady themselves against the walls when they climbed the stairs. They all had chronic head colds, too.

"God, Dad, when are you going to help me?" Robin asked. "When? Also, I don't have a license. Remember? Driver's ed cost extra last year."

"You've been driving the truck since you were like twelve," Heath said.

"Tommy Boy can get you a license," Goldie said. "Nice chunk of change in that T-Bird," she added.

"Kiddo, really, this is a great car," Heath said. "You know that. I saved it for you, for this."

"Nobody else wanted it," Robin said, rubbing her eyes. Fifteen minutes ago she'd been asleep, in the middle of a dream about a girl at school, a perfect girl she knew, whole and sleek and almost hers.

"I had plenty of offers," Heath said. "But I wanted the car for you. It'll be fun, Rob. How many girls do you know get to work on cars? Most dads would never let them, but your old man's a feminist."

Goldie looked from Heath to Robin. "I told you this was a bad idea," she said, walking out.

On the garage wall, Jimi Hendrix nibbled the strings of his guitar. Robin could barely remember her father's old restlessness, his flowing golden hair like a lure, the way he stacked cash and junk, his unconscious cataloging of every year's leftovers. Now she knew her father by what he couldn't do. Just the week before, Heath had nodded out on the stairs; Robin had found him sprawled three steps from the top.

"What do you think?" Heath asked.

Robin flung her arms around his neck. How horrible it was to pity your own father. How horrible.

Heath kissed her forehead. "I knew you'd be happy," he said.

∽

Who worked hard? Who was industrious, toiling, not afraid to roll up her sleeves and get down to business? Who knew better than anyone how to get what she wanted?

There had been many times over the past three years and even now, during the summer following her junior year of high school, when Robin felt as if she'd found the answer to a vital, life-altering question her grandmother and father had neglected to ask. Instead of, I want that and what do I have to do to get it, Goldie and Heath just forged ahead, blind, deaf, even stupid in their desires. If calculation didn't come naturally, then they didn't bother with it; they couldn't manufacture manipulation, they couldn't plan. But Robin, somewhere inside her friendship with Kitty, after her failed union with Freddie, and during the first two and a half years of lurking and watching in the Lilac High hallways, realized that she could tackle desire in the same way she attacked her schoolwork or her bedroom closet: calmly, confidently, with a glowing end point, a prize, sitting at the center of her mind like the volatile core of the earth. This was the secret: you never let desire grow cold, you just made it a silent, red-hot partner in everything you did and said.

For a year now, Robin had directed her silent desire toward Lynn Nielsen, the perfect girl of her dream. Every day after classes at Lilac High School, Robin appeared at Lynn's locker, smiling, joking, a smart ass, a warrior: the best friend a high school beauty could have. The chosen one, perhaps Lynn's own glowing end point.

You had to make adjustments, though. Lynn and her friends, all of them boys, engaged in daily bacchanalia. Pot, beer, speed, MDA, hallucinogens: no matter what drugs Robin took, no matter how hard she tried to silence her thoughts, the steady drumbeat of her desire never quit. Perhaps this thump was what kept her father alive.

Robin also had to all but give up Freddie. Their friendship lingered, but it was sidelined, too far beyond the school-defined parameters of relationships between boys and girls for others to understand. Robin and Freddie met at night, in the Simonsen garage, where Robin cleaned and sorted, or in Freddie's backyard, where he kept one eye open for his parents. They whispered, heads together, stringing out all they'd saved up, all they couldn't say during the day. Robin thought Freddie was excessively romantic, sighing and mooning over different boys, all of them impossible, out of reach. Robin was stunned by Freddie's blazing desire: he had no idea how to shape it, direct it, use it, consume it before it consumed him. For Freddie, there were boys everywhere, distant and therefore more tempting; for Robin, there was one girl, the burning core.

"Tim Shoblom," Freddie said one night that summer. "We're going to be in senior band next year."

Invariably, Freddie's crushes were other horn players, boys with bad skin and an air of quiet anxiety. "The guy who wears his night brace to school?" Robin asked.

"So what?" Freddie said, his eyes alight. "He's different. It's weird. And he picked the band locker next to mine."

"Jesus," Robin said, shaking her head. "Nobody else likes him, Fred," she added. They were under the Eakinses' cottonwood tree; the air smelled of the damp earth in the garden, the stars shimmered beyond the tree branches, and Robin could hear Antoinette chattering while her parents put her to bed. It could have been a night from their childhood, just a few years ago, when they would have talked about books or their families or, maybe, if Freddie felt safe, they would have talked about what someone said to his father at work or how somebody turned over their garbage can or kept calling the house and hanging up. They would have talked until Robin convinced herself that even the Eakinses' perfect family and clean house full of food was a construction, a creation—the threats made Freddie's life look that thin. Perhaps, Robin thought, the threats were what made Freddie so sturdy now.

"Maybe Tim Shoblom likes me," Freddie said.

He knew better. Robin knew better. Everybody knew how hard Freddie worked to be unassailable, flawless, trustworthy, close to any Lilacian's idea of what a white boy with a black face should be. As soon as Robin had latched on to Lynn, Freddie had fallen in with a group of friendless, homely girls who, like him, studied during lunch, played in the orchestra, and populated the Lilac Public Library on Friday nights until the lights flickered. Robin wondered what these girls' parents thought of their daughters' friendships with Freddie. His camouflage may have been successful after all: sometimes Freddie seemed to squeak he was so clean, so tight, so tense; the only part of him that moved freely was his heart, which he poured out, breathlessly and endlessly, to Robin.

Freddie talked about Tim Shoblom's clothes, his smile, what he ate for lunch, his French horn prowess. Robin nodded. When she thought of Lynn she thought of her body, long and smooth, and her waist-length blond hair, her magazine smile and blue eyes like Goldie's and Heath's. She thought of the other unworldly elements of Lynn's beauty: curves like a grown woman, slim legs, and a smattering of light freckles, which kept Lynn's appearance from seeming so perfect as to be artificial. Only Robin—as Lynn's best friend and confidant—had seen the girl's few physical idiosyncrasies, like the egg-shaped red birthmark on her left butt cheek, or the fact that any kind of stress gave Lynn a pink rash across her stomach. Every day was another step toward her. Robin didn't wallow, like Freddie did, but then she felt she couldn't afford to. For a year now, her house, Heath and Goldie, her whole life, had trembled like a building about to collapse. Get out now, she kept thinking. Move fast.

"What are you going to do about Tim?" Robin asked Freddie that night. "He doesn't know anything."

Freddie's face fell. "Well, *I* know, Rob. God. Lynn Nielsen doesn't know about you."

"Freddie," Mrs. Eakins called, "are you out there?"

"I gotta go," Freddie said, turning.

"At least I'm doing *something*," Robin said. "I am."

"Yeah, sure," Freddie said, opening the back door.

∽

Every weekend, Robin went to parties filled with kids she'd never seen in Lilac High School. Some of them had dropped out, graduated years before, or had babies and left. Robin had never realized how much time other kids spent getting drunk or stoned and then milling around in some weird approximation of an adult cocktail party. Being wasted left you open to possibilities. But some nights, after attending what seemed like a victory party for stupidity and irresponsibility, Robin's impatience would drive her bang out of whatever house she and Lynn and the boys were holed up in, and she'd walk home to read a book. It was her deepest rebellion.

In August, at a late-night blowout before school started, Robin found herself backed up against a living room wall by a boy named Simon Furton. Despite the fact that he wasn't in Lynn's group and despite the fact that he didn't seem to have any friends, Simon was famous at Lilac High. He had dropped out early in his junior year and traveled around the country, sending select Lilac High dopers brief letters from the Macon, Georgia, jail and from a hospital room in Malibu, California. His parents were from England, and they believed he should see the world. He was back, Simon now told Robin, living at home, studying for his GED, and learning to play the banjo. His mother, Simon said, made him tea every day at four o'clock.

He stepped closer to Robin. She slid away from him, her back to the wall. His face was flushed, and he kept licking his lips. He sipped a Coke. Up in his bedroom at home, Simon whispered, he was learning to make acid.

"Acid comes from a fungus on rye," Robin said. "At least that's how it was discovered." A couple lounged on the dirty carpet at Robin's feet, making out with deep concentration.

"Yeah, but now you can make it yourself," Simon added quickly.

Robin smirked. Boys never liked the fact that she knew anything.

"I'm getting the ingredients," Simon said, "and I'm going to have a lab in my room."

"Won't your parents love that?" Robin said. She was watching Lynn on the other side of the living room, laughing in the middle of a group of guys that Robin's love for Lynn forced her to associate with: rich kid Steve Stansell, Billy Tree, whose house they were in, and a hanger-on, some ex–football player from Lilac High who had been ruined, people said, by his love of Quaaludes.

She liked Billy Tree's house. His family lived exactly as they should, in a converted doublewide trailer across Lilac from Robin's own irrelevant neighborhood. Like the Simonsens, everyone in Tree's area had old cars in their yards. Inside the house, Tree's mother had hung framed pieces of embroidered fabric cut from what looked like a tablecloth. They were rags pressed between glass, oddly endearing. The Trees were out of town with their VFW pals. Billy's father expected him to go into the service once he turned eighteen, graduation or—in Billy's case—no graduation. Robin hated the thought of the boy's mass of ashy blond curls falling under the Marines' electric razor.

"Try this windowpane," Simon was saying. "I got it from a guy in Elgin. It's my prototype." He pulled a tiny envelope out of his pocket.

"I've done it," Robin said. "Once. And I lost half of it cutting it up in my bedroom. It popped under the razor blade and was gone onto my rug."

"That's a shame," Simon said. "I'm doing some now."

"No shit," Robin said. A few years ago, acid had been one of Heath's favorite drugs. He did it only on the weekends, preparing for it as if it were a medical procedure, staying off alcohol for two days prior and then making sure he had no deals to run and plenty of drinks and food up in his bedroom. His visitors proceeded silently upstairs, as if to the lair of a meditating guru. On Monday, Heath would be back at the breakfast table with a slight sniffle, his forehead broad and shiny and empty as a blank notebook page. Tabula rasa: Robin had read that somewhere. It could mean open, or it could mean void.

"So you've probably read Baba Ram Dass," Simon was saying. "*Be Here Now.*"

Across the room, Lynn laughed and fell into Steve Stansell's shoulder. A flicker of pleasure crossed his face. "I've heard of the guy," Robin said to Simon.

"Then you know he did the Indian thing," Simon said. "He used to be this big-time psychologist, Harvard and all that, and then he dropped a couple of tabs and saw the light."

"What light?" Robin asked. Lynn sucked on a pipe the football player had passed her. The boys watched her every move.

"The light that showed him the foolishness of everyday American life," Simon said.

Right now, Simon seemed to be examining a corner of the coffee table. The Simonsens believed that nobody changed overnight without ten different kinds of incentives, most of them financial.

"You know, my dad does drugs," Robin said.

"Everybody knows that," Simon said.

"My point is," Robin said, "*he's* not getting enlightened from them. So how did Baba get that way?"

"You have to be looking for a certain thing," Simon said.

Across the room, Steve Stansell had pulled up the back of Lynn's top and was crawling his fingers up her spine.

"Now take that," Simon said.

"Take what?" Robin asked.

"Miss Nielsen, the goddess of Lilac High."

"What about her?" Robin asked.

"I can feel you throwing shit her way. With acid, desire becomes transparent."

"It is anyway," Robin said sharply. Who was this guy but a younger, more pretentious version of her father? Less dissolute, but on his way down that path just the same.

"Desire is a distraction, it's illusory," Simon continued. "It keeps you on this earth."

"I like it here," Robin said.

"You know what I mean," Simon said. His eyes roamed over Robin's features, as if they formed a map. "What you want is written all over your face, and that shows you're not really paying attention to what's important."

"What if what I want *is?*" Robin said. "The only thing that *is* important?" Simon shrugged.

Robin studied a picture on Billy's Tree's living room wall. This wasn't a framed rag but a real painting, right out of a cheap motel. It showed a man and a woman sitting in a horse carriage in front of blooming trees, the whole thing in shades of pink and gray. Here was the absence of desire. Or the mocking of it. Robin could no sooner mock desire than see it as illusion. She savored desire; it left a dormant taste in her mouth that she could taste with just one smack of her lips.

"The self is really all in the mind and spirit," Simon said. "Everything around us is illusion. Even the body. Sex, everything connected to it, it's all an illusion."

Robin laughed. Why, even that ugly painting was an illusion! Who was this guy kidding? That foolish everyday life that Baba Ram Dass was trying to escape, all of it was about getting some. The Simonsen house hummed with urges. Getting some was in every junk transaction, in every trip up the stairs by Heath's customers, in every one of his infrequent trips beyond the driveway. Getting some was in the very timbre of Goldie's laugh. *That* was noticing things. Calling them what they were. Calling for what you wanted.

Simon's face looked like it had been scrubbed with a hot, dry towel. His glasses were rimless, held in place by thin, gold temple pieces. "I was talking to you," he said. "No wonder you lost that acid. You weren't paying attention. It's not a party drug, you know."

"Oh, really?" Robin asked.

"I was saying," Simon continued, "first chakra, second, third: those are the Western points, the ones that get us in trouble."

"What are you talking about?" Robin asked. Steve Stansell slipped his hand under Lynn's hair and held the back of her neck.

"Keep up," Simon said, shaking his head. "Survival, sex, power—that's what those chakras represent. That's why they're bad."

Robin finished her beer and set the empty on the floor. "Did your parents support you while you wandered around the country, learning this shit?" she asked.

"You have to move into the higher chakras, all the way to the seventh, in order to really understand. To see."

"What's your job now?" Robin asked. "I mean, besides the banjo and the acid."

Simon took the envelope out of his pocket again, opened it, and showed Robin several tiny squares. "I'm working it so I can stay on one constant trip," he said. "Baba Ram Dass said: Don't just get rid of your desire. Know it and let it go. Free it from itself." A small smile appeared between his flushed cheeks.

The couple beneath Robin's feet rolled over, nearly crushing her toes. She noticed it, she ignored it. Lynn reappeared and entered Billy's brightly lit kitchen, the boys at her tail. What Simon didn't understand, nor Baba, nor anyone besides her, was that desire was all about your own power, not the power of what or whom you wanted. You were desire's only cause, so you had control over it; you named it. The only problem with Robin's desire for Lynn was that, if she expressed it, it ceased being transparent. It would appear instead as a stain on Lynn's skin, an all-over birthmark. You could take away the greatest beauty with what you desired.

"Give me some," she said, turning to Simon and grabbing his arm. "Give me what you have on you. I'll pay you later."

Robin took half a tab of acid and put the other half in the pocket of her jeans. She left Simon sipping his warm Coke and plunged into the party. In the kitchen, she found Lynn pressed up against the counter by the boys.

"Honey, honey, honey!" Lynn said, opening her arms. Robin blushed.

"Where have you *been*?" Lynn asked. "I've been trying to catch your attention."

Robin wished Lynn would discriminate, but she was like a gregarious movie star, confident in her status, friendly to everyone. Robin often found greeting cards from Lynn in her school locker, kittens smiling under straw hats, fat, bold flowers above the words BEST FRIEND! or FRIENDSHIP! CHERISH IT! When the two girls were together, Lynn literally hung on Robin, exuding her unique odor of orange and mint, and she dragged Robin around, presenting her as a kind of prize, proof of her powers of friendship. The fact that Robin never knew if she herself inspired Lynn's ardor or whether Lynn wanted any one girl to hang around with sometimes made Robin feel anonymous when they were together, just a girl named Friend.

"Listen, Robin," Lynn whispered. "Don't make me be the only girl. Come with. Steve wants to take us all to the quarry to swim. In the dark."

"There's a full moon," Robin said. "It won't really be all that dark."

"Okay," Lynn said. "But will you come? Please?"

Robin looked behind her. The boys' faces had flattened, like one face divided into three parts. She looked at them and thought, male. A species. Was there a male chakra? Robin thought, I'm thinking, and then her thoughts were stamped inside her head.

"Please, please, please," Lynn said.

"I've got to go," Robin said. "Really. Like now."

"Are you okay, sweetie?" Lynn asked, slinging her arm tight around Robin's neck. Orange blossom and spearmint, to be exact. If you crushed a flower or the leaf of a plant, you released more of its scent.

"I'll call you," Robin said, backing toward the living room. "I'm going to call you, later," she said. She avoided the boys' faces. She knew what would happen: Steve Stansell, Billy Tree, all the others—they would form a huge puddle, and Lynn would drown in it, calling out for Robin as she sank. But Robin couldn't save her tonight. In the living room, Simon Furton stood in front of the hideous pink and gray painting, which now throbbed like a weak heart. Robin rushed past him and burst from the house.

Outside in the inky dark, the lights from Billy's cast a weak glow on the front stoop. More silent trailers took shape, then some scattered bungalows and a shotgun shack. Robin started down the road, walking in the direction of uptown Lilac.

The ground rolled slowly under her feet like a conveyor belt, but she decided to ignore it. She also chose to keep her eyes away from the street lamps because their globes swung wildly every time she looked at them. Already, Simon was wrong: acid threw you off when you focused on one small thing; its real power lay in the sizzling trail it forged from idea to object.

People in Lilac wanted a house from an advertisement, square and clean and without a past or visible wear. An anonymous house, just like the ones Robin passed now, as she crossed from Billy Tree's neighborhood to genteel Merchant Street. Here were sidewalks, thick green lawns, and the blind fronts of the oldest houses in Lilac, with their insistent charm. Robin knew a kid on Merchant Street who sold PCP at Lilac High. One night with Lynn and her crew of boys, Robin had stopped at his house, a three-story Victorian with gingerbread trim and two broken windows on the second floor, and waited for him to come out with folded tin foil. In another house, further down Merchant Street, Robin's father knew a family that ran a car-stripping operation. Insects drummed in the big shade trees. The title of Baba's book was *Be Here Now*, and it was all about time like a long necklace that you fingered, one link per second.

The old Merchant Street homes gave way to uptown, the small business section of Lilac. Here were more streetlights, with tubs of petunias and trash baskets between each one. Old brick buildings, none more than three stories, lined the street. Dry cleaner, appliance store, cafe, jeweler: Robin ran her hand along their plate-glass faces. She crossed the railroad tracks. Lynn's lawyer father went to Chicago every day on the train, along with other men in suits and ties. Robin stopped in front of Larry Pike's store. Behind the window stood shelves of newspapers and periodicals. Further back in the shop were the magazines "just for gents," Larry said. Fronting the sales counter sat the collar of candy shelves. After a while, Larry had caught on to Robin and the magazines, so as soon as he saw her, he sent her out of the store with a free candy bar.

The commercial section of Merchant Street ended and Robin passed a few blocks of large houses; these were flimsy, but still grand, some with three-car garages. When Robin was very young, small bungalows lined these streets, simple, one-story houses made of brick with detached garages and patches of perfect lawn, inhabited for the most part by elderly Lilac natives. Sometime in grade school, Robin had seen the homes disappear, the larger split-levels going up in their place. Once when she was riding past the development with her father, he opened the window of his truck and spit at a construction site.

She came to Finster Road, the cutoff point. Her father used to call it the "money line." Even at night, a car or two cruised down Finster, usually someone driving to an early shift. Robin hesitated, then raced across the four lanes, crossing the path of distant headlights and bursting through a hedge into someone's backyard. There was a curfew in Lilac for anyone under eighteen, and Finster was the cops' favorite territory.

The house Robin hid behind was one of the original bungalows from the larger tract that had once extended across Finster and beyond, to Merchant Street. This house was meticulous, gray brick with white aluminum awnings. But the small rectangle of grass Robin looked out on was covered with building materials, broken toys, overflowing garbage cans, machinery, several lawn mowers, a motorcycle. It was a miniature version of her own yard. Sitting in front of the tableau of trash was a small black and white cat. Robin could hear it purring.

She ran out of the yard and kept running, not caring which streets she crossed, only aware that she was moving in the general direction of Highland. Each house she passed presented one face to the street and another to itself. At least her family didn't care: they were the same no matter where you looked.

She ran faster, the faces of the houses flashing past like huge photographic slides. The wind whined in her ears. She was four blocks from Highland. The sky was white in the east. A sparrow chirped on a branch.

Robin imagined Lynn at home, asleep—a fantasy, she knew. If Robin was being honest, she liked Lynn at rest. She liked to hold her as a glowing nugget in the center of her consciousness, a quiet beauty, an invalid in her tri-level house with her parents and her twin sisters, who were already stunning at age ten. Robin crossed the street into her own neighborhood. Under the lightening sky, a wall of bird sound rose up, as if on cue. Lynn and her family stayed quiet in Robin's mind, swaddled in their central air conditioning and shag carpeting, matching living room furniture and carefully archived china sets. Everything worked at the Nielsen house; all the family needed to be truly alive was someone like Robin to come in blazing with the full force of her devotion.

Robin turned down Highland just as the sun broke over the horizon. All the houses were dark except for the Corners'. Through their picture window, Robin could see the tops of two white heads; in the background, blue faces moved on a TV screen.

Heath's truck was missing, as was Goldie's Cadillac. The house had its own shuttered quality. The bus was black and quiet.

Inside, the house was sweltering; the air gripped her. The junk lurked, neglected and patient. Robin got herself a Coke and sat at the kitchen table. Goldie and her guests had left a litter of empties and overflowing ashtrays, dead matchbooks, a Kmart circular, and the movie magazines. The print wouldn't stand still, but Robin didn't need words to understand the stories; they were written for a worldly infant. She plumbed the profound depths of Elizabeth Taylor's diamonds and Joan Crawford's face-lift. Michele Phillips from the Mamas and the Papas was an actress now, and here she was dating Jack Nicholson. Far away in Los Angeles, a whole city of people got what they wanted without a second thought. Maybe the only difference was money; with that, desires became indulgences instead of greed. Poor people just grasped. The sky in the backyard turned a pale blue, and a flock of starlings descended onto what grass remained between the cars. A jay scolded from the sumacs. After some time, Robin heard her father's truck rattle into the driveway.

"We both had a late night, huh, kiddo?" Heath said when he came in. He opened the refrigerator and peeled a piece of bologna from the package.

"You seem happy about it," Robin said.

"No, not really," her father said.

Heath's face shifted, the skin now wrinkling, now smoothing out. His eyes were bloodshot but a startling blue. Impossibly, his hair was still spectacular. Beneath the ruin, Robin thought, her father was a handsome man.

He stared at her. He can tell about me, she thought. But he doesn't care. Soon enough, Heath turned his attention to the backyard. As usual, there was nothing for Robin to resist. It was exhausting making up all your own goals and limitations; you didn't know where you began and ended, what was possible or what your family ignored.

Heath and Robin sat in silence until sunlight dried on the grass. Then Goldie came home, scratching her lumpy hairdo and complaining about the Bogdanas men and warming up yesterday's coffee. For the first time, Robin asked for a cup, and her grandmother mixed her a concoction with lots of milk and sugar.

"It goes down better that way," Goldie said. She sat at the table with Robin and Heath and fired up a cigarette, and all three of them waited while the sun grew brighter and filled the house.

∼

The Thunderbird was easier than Robin had thought.

When she first got the car from her father, it was his sick birthday joke, another slip in his already precarious sense of what was right. She would never touch it. But then Robin saw the possibilities: the car's hide restored to its original luster, its motor quietly idling, chrome polished—this was a car to drive a girl around in. And it was a car that no other girl in Lilac would have, the kind in which she could carry the most beautiful girl in the world, someone like Lynn.

Despite getting pummeled for years by junk moved into and out of the garage, the Thunderbird was structurally sound. When Robin took off the tarps and parachute silk and opened the doors, she found old candy wrappers, used condoms, Jehovah's Witness pamphlets, a red shirt with no buttons, and, in the back seat, a pile of feathers and tufts of fur, as if game had been torn apart and eaten there. Under the hood, though, she found a solid-looking engine, plus some evidence that her father had cannibalized the car over the years.

Larry Pike found Robin an old Chilton's manual that included repair specifications for a 1956 Thunderbird, and late that summer she began examining and cleaning and replacing parts, first the generator and regulator, then the plugs and points. Some evenings, Goldie's men friends ventured out to the garage to sip their drinks and stand over oil spills with burning cigarettes and cigars. They gave bad advice, which Robin ignored. If they stayed too long, Grandma came clacking out to hover in the garage doorway until the men followed her back inside. "You come in, too," she'd say, pointing her cigarette at Robin. "There's some snacks with your name on it."

Robin would forget to eat, though, and would stay under the arc light, slowly dismantling a part to inspect it. Already thin, she lost more weight that summer; soon she could see the sharp outline of her muscles under her skin. Her face narrowed, like a cat's, and her collarbones stuck out. She had inherited her father's and grandmother's rich hair, though hers was long and straight like her mother's, and coffee-colored.

"You need to put some meat on," Goldie said to her that summer. "A girl's got to be just shy of hefty. Men are looking for round. Nobody wants a bag of bones."

One night before school started, Freddie came over to the garage and sat on an inverted clothes barrel with an old copy of *Look* magazine he'd found under the workbench. Eisenhower gestured from the cover. "When the car's done, can I have a ride?" he asked.

"Jesus, of course," Robin said.

"It was a rhetorical question," Freddie said. "Hey, what did you think of that article in the *Tribune*?"

Robin smiled. Freddie knew she'd read the whole paper that day, knew she'd read the right article on black history, knew she'd have an opinion. It was exciting, the purest sign of friendship. "Listen, Freddie," she said, "you don't think they're going to let anyone teach that kind of history at Lilac High. I mean, nobody here even pretends they want to talk about the history of blacks or race or the Panthers or whatever. I mean, I wish."

Freddie didn't respond. He often brought up something about race, let Robin make a hopeless comment, a sad truth, and then dropped the subject. Robin didn't know why he did this. It was the same with boys Freddie liked: Robin could say the words, paint the picture of what she and Freddie were really talking about, just so Freddie could turn away; he couldn't create the scene himself.

Robin opened the auto manual. The starter was one of the few parts missing from the Thunderbird, and it had taken two weeks of Tommy Boy's calls and visits to other junkyards to find one that fit. Now Robin looked back and forth from the manual to the car, trying to determine how to hook up the part. She felt awkward, even foolish and stupid: Freddie wanted something, but, more important, she couldn't reach Lynn, even after several phone calls. Robin didn't want to imagine where she was.

Freddie flipped pages in the magazine. He was a man, Robin thought, only no one, including Freddie, wanted to admit it. He had large eyes, dimples, and smooth skin, and a mischievous grin that even his measured life couldn't diminish. Mr. Eakins still wouldn't let him grow an Afro or carry a hair pick or, in general, appear to be fussing in any way with his hair, so Freddie kept it clipped close to his head. He wore the same clothes as other smart boys: khakis or nice jeans, button-down shirts, hard shoes. He stood in contrast to the disarray of Robin in her ripped jeans, with her oily hands, smeared face, her tough, muscled arms and hair in a messy ponytail. No matter how much Freddie wanted to be the best boy at Lilac High, and no matter how close he came to that goal, he was still a kid like Robin who knew how to sit on his desires. How long Freddie would wait to act, how long he would yearn in silence, Robin couldn't predict. She was through waiting. You couldn't control blank air.

"Everything is so fucked up," Robin said suddenly.

"What's the matter?" Freddie asked.

"We've got to get out of here," Robin said.

"We're too young," he replied, looking down at his magazine.

The page was open to an ad for Campbell's soup. Two little white kids smiled up from their steaming bowls. Freddie could turn every page of the magazine and not find a photo or drawing of anyone who looked like him. But what about Robin? Where was she in the magazine, dirty and lean, rocked to sleep by the thought of her mouth on a blond girl's breast?

"We could go to Chicago," Robin said.

"I know too many people there." Freddie slid off the barrel.

"You know what I'm talking about," Robin said. "We need to meet people."

"You're going to drop that wrench if you keep twirling it around," Freddie said. "You're not very careful with tools. Is that a Craftsman?"

"Fred." Robin wanted him to *do* something. She didn't want to be in charge of who they were, where they were. He had secrets, but he couldn't even put them together. He was a man! His shoulders were broad, his arms thick. He tried to be a small boy, though, nonthreatening and ageless. She wondered where he had room to keep Tim Shoblom; she wondered where Freddie's desire lived.

Freddie peered down into the Thunderbird, keeping the lower half of his body clear of the dusty side panels. "I'm going to college," he said.

"I might go, too," Robin said. But she knew she couldn't leave home, leave her father. It would be like abandoning someone by the side of the road. "No matter what, Fred," Robin said, "when my car's done we'll get away. We'll leave Lilac and go live in Chicago, or even somewhere else. We'll go away to college. Okay?"

"There's my parents and Antoinette," Freddie said.

"For Christ's sake, we'll come back and visit them. I'll visit my dad, too, or he'll come to us."

"Oh, no," Freddie said, rolling his eyes.

"Listen," Robin said, "my dad can't do what he's doing forever."

"Maybe he'll get arrested," Freddie said, with a sharp nod of his head. "Or he'll die."

"Fred! No, he'll just get too old. You can't deal when you're old. No one buys from you after a certain age. It's too creepy."

"I don't know where you get your information," Freddie said.

"We could furnish our own apartment from just this garage," Robin said.

"No, thank you," Freddie said.

"We could do what we want in Chicago."

Freddie looked around the garage while he brushed dust off of his hands.

"How's Romeo?" Robin asked, pulling in the real subject of the conversation.

"Work on your car," Freddie said, but he smiled.

"Really," Robin said. "Can't you tell me?" Her eyes ached with tears. The thought of Freddie abandoning her along with her desires—it left her breathless.

Freddie scowled. "I'm trying not to think about him," he said.

"What happened?"

"Nothing. It's just like, why bother."

"You should help me with this car, man." Robin stepped closer and smiled into Freddie's face. Give me just one thing, she thought. Tell me I'm not alone in here, trying to fix it so I can love Lynn.

"I have to go," Freddie said.

"Remember, though, we have a pact," Robin said.

"Pact," Freddie said.

"Look at me, Fred. Listen, we have a pact to go away. We'll take the car and we'll start living someplace else." He wouldn't look at her.

Robin knew what to do. She held her arms and oil-stained hands behind her and leaned forward. Freddie was so much taller now, not the same skinny boy Robin had seen naked under the leaves. She touched her lips to Freddie's. He tasted and smelled different. Older, wiser, more like a man, more like someone who could look over her head and beyond.

chapter eight

∼

"I'm a sociopath," Heath said. He leaned back in the easy chair and spread his legs. He smiled.

"No you're not, Dad. God, cut it out." Robin stood between her father and the older police officer. The younger one, not a friendly Roger Dodger, but some kid who looked serious about his crew cut and muscles, was out in the squad car in the driveway. Robin could hear the police radio buzzing, carrying news of her father all around Lilac, all around DuPage County.

"Get up, Mr. Simonsen," the older cop said. "I've asked you once, and I've asked you nice."

"Don't be a pain in the ass, Heath," Goldie called from the kitchen. Larry Pike shushed her. "*Well*," Grandma said. Lately, Goldie watched her son's decline as if it were a TV drama. She talked at him but never to him.

"He doesn't feel well," Robin said. "Right, Dad?" She'd come home from a trip to Rush Street with Steve Stansell, Lynn, and Billy Tree, her hair was twisted like a gorgon's from riding in Stansell's convertible, and her brain was simply a gathering place for thoughts as flimsy as chiffon. Ideas tried to scratch themselves out of her head. Stansell had given them all PCP, a horse tranquilizer. Pretend you never heard of it, Robin told herself, as she stood between her father and the cop. She wanted water; she wanted to sit down.

"What's the charge, officer?" Heath said, laughing. His hairline, his bare chest, his thin, pale face, shone with sweat.

The officer shifted on his feet, his belt creaking. They had no charge, that was clear, but Robin couldn't figure out how they'd gotten into the house. Now the younger cop came in, eager and smiling, primed for a big bust that would make his suburban career. He looked no older than Robin, yet here he was, ready to take down Lilac's big dealer.

"You know you guys could be out there making the streets safer for my daughter," Heath said. He opened his legs wider, exposing the ripped inseam of his jeans and the fact that he wasn't wearing any underwear.

"If you don't have a charge," Robin said, "you can go."

"Aren't you the mature thing," the young cop said.

"Somebody's got to be," Heath said.

"Speaking of," the young cop continued. He put his hand on his holstered gun as he nodded in Robin's direction. "How old is your daughter? Lilac has a curfew for kids under eighteen and here it is three A.M."

"My daughter is very smart," Heath said.

"Goodbye," Robin said to the cops.

"They caught him driving bad," Goldie called from the kitchen. "What a shock," she added.

Robin tried to make the PCP into something else, an aid to clarity, like Simon Furton's acid. She pulled an idea through her brain. "Who let you in here?" she asked.

The cops looked at each other, then back at Heath.

"Did you guys?" Robin asked, walking to the kitchen. She used the back of the easy chair to support herself.

"God, look at your hair," Goldie said.

Robin gripped the chair. "Dad," she said loudly, "did you tell the police they could come in?"

Heath tilted his head back to look at Robin. His face engaged in several mighty efforts to form an expression, but each attempt failed. Robin barely recognized him. He was flushed and wan at the same time, the last of his health surging forth to mask his decline. At least his arms were covered. Heath's face gave up and then he said, "Give me a break."

Sentences rubbed up against the inside of Robin's head. She saw them, written out in newspaper type, speeding toward her and then getting smaller, like cars she was trying to flag down. "You have no legal right to be here," she said. "Leave now."

The older cop started to say something, but the younger one put a hand on his arm. "Let's go," he said.

It was the young officer who turned back at the door and gave Robin a questioning look. He sees, Robin thought. He sees my father's face in mine, and he'll have my wrist in a minute. But the cop just shook his head and left.

Heath rose from the chair, but then he stumbled forward onto the couch, which was covered with bundled clothes and two grocery bags full of old bakery bread.

"Dad! Listen!" Robin approached her father, but then she, too, tipped over, landing on top of him. The two of them wrestled to get upright.

"Kiddo," Heath said. "Time for bed now."

"Don't ever make me do that again!" Robin yelled. There was a burr inside her thoughts. She heard cicadas screeching—were they outside? The more she writhed with her father on the couch, the angrier she became. "What is *wrong* with you?" she yelled.

"Whoa," her father said, rising from the couch and displacing Robin from his back. He got up but then fell again, sinking to the floor, like a man repeatedly fainting and then coming to. He was laughing so hard that tears mixed with his sweat.

"You're all that's left," Robin said, grabbing desperately for a handful of her father's hair, a grip of his dirty clothes.

"What's going on in there?" Goldie asked. "Cookie, are you drunk?"

"Don't be so stupid all the time," Robin said. She lunged for her father. His zippered sweatshirt flapped open over his broad chest, his hair cascaded over his eyes. He was barefoot. "Dad," Robin said, "don't be dumb and throw me away."

"Jesus," her father said, still laughing.

Robin surprised herself by pushing her father back onto the couch. "Just stop," she said, breathing heavily. She grabbed the front of her father's sweatshirt and started pulling at him. "I don't have time, Dad," she yelled, "to save your goddamn life."

At that point, Goldie and Larry bustled into the living room. The two of them gently embraced Robin and pulled her away from her father.

"Ah, sweet pie," Grandma said.

They sat Robin in the easy chair and petted her shoulders, but it was a good half hour before she could stop crying. Heath passed out on the bread. Several bags had broken open during the wrestling, and a yeasty smell filled the living room. At dawn, clucking and sighing, Goldie worked through Robin's tortured hair with her teasing comb.

∽

That whole summer of 1976, and well into the first weeks of Robin's senior year, people came and went from the house on Highland. All day, most of the night, at any time, from anywhere. There were a few folks Robin recognized—a guy named Keith, who would show up every day for a few weeks, then disappear; Tom McAfee, of course, who always came in from the bus for some free drugs—but most of the men and women looked more destitute than the people in years past who had bought junk or kept Heath company. These newer folks were truly desperate; Robin could tell by the way they trudged up the back stairs with the last of their natural energy, the way they hammered on the front door or just walked in, wind-blown on a calm day, sweating on a cool one, shivering even when the temperature topped eighty-five. Chakras in crisis, Simon Furton would say; all seven chakras, blown out.

Then Freddie made Robin walk home with him during the first week of school just so he could tell her—hand on her arm, voice in her ear—that his father had heard from a friend of his uncle down in Harvey that there was some dealer out in Lilac who ran the whole show from a trash pit he called his house.

"That's your dad, right?" Freddie asked. "It's got to be."

They were standing on Highland in front of the Hazens' house. Mrs. Hazen trimmed old flower stalks while ancient Strudel stood barking at the head of the driveway. Robin could feel Mrs. Hazen's eyes on them. Freddie stood before Robin, a tall, well-built young man, handsome like his father, even-tempered like his mother, a balanced composition.

"My dad knows some guy in Harvey?" Robin asked. It wasn't the thing to say, especially under a hard blue sky and in such buttery sunlight, and especially since Harvey meant black and they both knew it. But she'd decided to treat the subject of her father like a piece of fiction from her new honors English class: symbol, allusion, metaphor; she would read Heath and his behavior from the same two steps backward, as if his life were full of layered meanings stretched over the less enticing reality of drugs and money.

"Rob, your daddy's *known*," Freddie said. "That's not good, right? What are you going to do?"

Robin took a deep breath. What wasn't she doing? Just the week before, she'd sold the last of the furniture from the spare bedroom, several cases of dented cans of peas, an antique lace dress she'd found folded in a box in the garage, and she'd put a new oil filter in the car. She'd also read *Hamlet* for English honors, completed a score of trigonometry problems, learned from Goldie how to cut a man's hair, practiced her new skill on Tommy Boy, and she'd talked Lynn out of going with Stansell to a party in Chicago. Robin had even stood at the bottom of the stairs, after not having seen her father for three days, and called up to him, whispering first, then screaming, until he stumbled out of his room and lunged down to the first landing. "What?" he'd asked, as Robin, disgusted, walked away and left him. She squinted at Freddie. He didn't look at her, didn't see her anymore.

"I gotta go," Freddie said. "I thought you'd want to know what I heard."

"Thanks, Fred," Robin said. "But I'm not sure what—"

Freddie started to walk up the hill, waving goodbye behind his head. He left Robin alone in the street.

In *Hamlet,* characters deceived with every word they uttered, though Robin's teacher, Mrs. Kopopolous, said that what we thought was deceit might really have been atmosphere, Shakespeare's enrichment of the surface action. In other words, it was hard to tell the difference between what the created character might really do and what the author wanted him to do. Who was creating, Mrs. Kopopolous asked, the character, with a life of his own; the author, with his intentions; or us, because when we read something we also make it? Were we all fabulists? Robin had looked up the word. A fabulist invented, spun tales. If her father was a character, or, better yet, a whole play, she could shape his life, move him, shake him until he took the form of someone she wanted. What she wanted was a father who cried uncle, admitted defeat instead of embracing it. Hamlet held back and lied; Robin loved him for it.

Strudel barked and barked at the head of the driveway. Mrs. Hazen in her Chinese straw hat glared. Martha had graduated from college and was gone, like the character in a play whose absence twists the other characters' lives, upsetting the balance they strive at all costs to maintain. Greek plays, which Mrs. Kopopolous said they would read later, had choruses, voices from above which set things straight. "Enough!" Mrs. Hazen yelled, and Strudel ceased barking.

∼

When your father was notorious, it wasn't clear whether you should acknowledge his reputation and his questionable deeds, or whether you should keep quiet and simply let your silence communicate your regret.

The problem was, Robin couldn't do either. She loved her father with a fury that increased with every one of his transgressions, but when it really came down to it, when she'd spent a good three hours in her darkened bedroom in the middle of the night, flat on her back and sleepless, wondering if the lights would go on if she flipped the switch or if the Simonsens had lost power once again—under those circumstances, the closest Robin could get to judging her father was to feel an overwhelming and almost paralyzing pity. The problem was, pity didn't do anything; pity didn't move. Desire did.

Lynn Nielsen had a pink bedroom—walls, curtains, carpeting, coverlet on the canopied bed—in a new tri-level home on the better side of Lilac. Because Lynn's room promised privacy and proximity, Robin tolerated it, but she also found the space vaguely disturbing. The plush surfaces, the rose hue: being in the room was like being inside a body part. So Robin winced when Lynn's father, a lawyer, entered her sanctum one day.

Mr. Nielsen was tall, slim, and handsome, with a full head of dark blond hair and an air of something better to do; he was home, in the middle of a late-summer day, wearing a crisp gray suit and taking the time to meet his daughter's friend. He shook Robin's hand. Lynn sprawled across her canopied bed.

"Simonsen," Mr. Nielsen said. "Why do I think your family has something to do with the hardware store uptown?"

"We don't," Robin said. "But we sell stuff."

"Antiques," Mr. Nielsen said.

"Sure," Robin said.

"Daddy, stop!" Lynn said, laughing. "Leave her alone."

They both looked over. Lynn lay like pale nougat in her pink candy box of a bed, gently colored, firm, yet pliable. The waistband of her jeans cut below her navel. Her golden hair shone. Robin began to cough.

"What kind of lawyer are you?" she asked Mr. Nielsen.

"Defense," he said. "Criminal. I try to keep people out of jail." Mr. Nielsen smiled around at Lynn's Peter Frampton posters, her closet jammed with clothes, her white and gold desk bereft of books and papers.

"Why?" Robin asked.

"I beg your pardon?" Mr. Nielsen asked.

"Robin's the smartest girl in school," Lynn said. "She knows everything."

"That's quite a burden," Mr. Nielsen said.

"Don't you think," Robin said, "that sometimes people *should* go to prison? It's like the regular world is too free for some people."

"That's the point of being out, though," Mr. Nielsen said. "Freedom."

"But some people just keep doing what they're not supposed to, so what good is freedom. They keep fucking up."

"Excuse me?"

Now he was looking at her. Something about Mr. Nielsen reminded Robin of the principal at Lilac High, or Steve Stansell's rich father, or some customers from out of town who came to the junkyard looking for treasures: you had to work to get them to really see you; you had to wait until their attention clicked into place because they could talk forever without thinking of you.

"Okay," Robin said, "so what do you do about repeat criminals?"

"We don't use curse words in this house," Mr. Nielsen said.

"You do, Daddy!" Lynn said.

"I'm just asking. I'm curious." Robin stood straight and folded her arms.

Mr. Nielsen sighed. "Well, if you must know, repeat offenses are not my concern. My job is to get my client off on the current charge, period. What he does after that I don't even think about. I'm not hired to keep the public peace. That's a district attorney's job. You see the difference?"

"Sure."

"My loyalty is to that one person, my client. What he needs, I do. He needs to stay out of jail."

"We're going swimming," Lynn said. "Steve's coming for us in a minute."

"Are you thinking about going to law school?" Mr. Nielsen asked Robin. He looked her up and down.

"No," Robin said. "I'm just interested in laws. I mean, doesn't it really matter more *which* laws people break than whether people break laws in general? Personal or public laws, like those in your house or outside in the world."

"Search and seizure?" Mr. Nielsen asked. "Illegal entry? Is that what you're talking about when you say inside or outside the house? Should the police come in?"

"The police should never come in," Robin said. A thin strand of Mr. Nielsen's hair blew across his forehead. Was that all the reaction she could get out of this guy? "I'm saying you have to compare. How badly are people being hurt by somebody breaking this law or that law? I think that if you're breaking a law on your own, then who the hell cares?" Mr. Nielsen frowned at her again. "Something's illegal only if it goes out of the house and hurts somebody."

"The law is an abstraction. On paper it doesn't allow for these differences. It's absolute."

"I know times when it's not," Robin said.

"Do you have your suit with you, sweetie?" Lynn asked Robin. "We're going soon."

Mr. Nielsen squinted at Robin. "I think we're talking about two different issues," he said. "You want some people in prison no matter what, but then you seem to think that some laws are more necessary than others. You can't have it both ways with that argument."

"I don't know," Robin said. "I guess I'm just saying that if people are miserable in the outside world, and they keep messing up, then how hard can it be in jail? Maybe they'll recover better then."

"Recover from what?" Mr. Nielsen asked. Outside, someone honked.

"That's Steven," Lynn said, rolling off the bed. "Let's go."

"Please be home at a decent hour," Mr. Nielsen said to Lynn, as she and Robin pounded down the stairs. "Try. Humor your mother and me."

Steve Stansell had a 1966 Ford Fairlane GT convertible, total cherry. Steve's father, Big Steve, owner of Stansell Ford in Addison, had forced the service guys at the dealership to work up the car two years earlier for his son's sixteenth birthday. More than once Robin had seen the mechanics give Stansell the finger. He didn't care. Stansell lived in a kind of Lucite cube: you could see in, he could see out, but he thrived in his sequestered air, perfumed by the green and inky smell of money. As Lynn ducked into the back seat, Steve smiled at her, then tried to pull away before Robin could get in. Led Zeppelin wailed from the stereo.

Stansell, bathing Lynn, Robin, and Billy Tree in a stream of chatter and cigarette ash raced over to the car lot on Lake Street for his weekly hassle with Big Steve. Stansell Ford sat on a vast spread of land; it was the largest Ford dealership in the country. You could see it from the highway. People from Chicago came out, sure they were getting a deal, and farmers drove all the way from Iowa for new pickups, dickering over prices in their soft accents. Inside the dealership that day, behind the line of LTDs and Grand Marquises and Monarchs and the smell of rubber and oil and car upholstery, the showroom crawled with salesmen in horrifying leisure suits and comb-overs. Big Steve, hair coiffed, skin caramelized, emerged from behind a bank of receptionists and secretaries and began yelling at his son at the same time he pulled him back into his office. Minutes later, Steve was back, all smiles, leading them out under the fluttering plastic flags while he counted cash and pocketed a pack of cigarettes he had charmed out of a receptionist. The Fairlane waited, gassed up for free.

Uptown, near Bogdanas Hardware, Stansell picked up a new guy, Marqueese, who hunched up in the back seat next to Robin like a dark spot on the upholstery, his rumpled, patchy goatee shuddering in the wind every time he glanced over at her, which was too often. The boy was a damp weight against her side. She moved an inch closer to Lynn.

If Marqueese had any sense, Robin thought, he would have been looking at Lynn. She sat smiling in her bikini top, this one black and white gingham printed with daisies, her golden hair caught in a ponytail; she wore tiny daisy earrings that trembled in the wind. Her only other clothes were short black cutoffs. One day last spring, Stansell had announced to everyone assembled in the high school smoking area that Lynn Nielsen was "the only girl in Lilac High with an honest-to-god cleavage." Lynn grabbed Robin's knee and shook it, shooting her eyes in Marqueese's direction.

"Go get him," she mouthed.

"Ugh," Robin said loudly.

At a red light, Stansell pulled the Fairlane up to the bumper of a Lilac police car, gunning his engine and laughing. Roger Dodger stuck his head out and waved. Hanging out with Stansell was like keeping company with the mob, like Robin's grandmother dating wiseguys in Vegas. Nothing touched you when you were with them, Goldie said. And always scads of cash. Stansell revved the engine again, creeping up to gently tap the cop's bumper. There were two cases of beer and an ounce of sinsemilla in the Fairlane's trunk.

Marqueese's narrow frame, his look of discombobulation—he reminded Robin of Stansell's drug connections, those lost boys. Every few weeks Stansell drove them all out to some claptrap apartment complexes in Hanover Park or Elgin or Aurora. Stansell's connections, those fierce partiers, all of them recent graduates or dropouts from local high schools, were scrappy, nervous young men, their prospects plummeting even at age nineteen, their adolescent acne leaving behind ugly, permanent sores thanks to their constant diet of amphetamines and doughnuts. The lost boys scared Robin so much that she always stayed in the car and read a book while everyone else went in to get high.

Marqueese ran his finger down the side of Robin's thigh.

"Knock it off," she said. Marqueese smiled, revealing a mouth full of jammed teeth. Hanover Park, for sure. Marqueese was Heath, minus the brains and kindness. Or Heath was Marqueese, with age and better genes on his side. Either way, this boy operated on Heath's frequency, transmitting first a leering, friendly vibe, then turning it off to become a stranger you didn't want to know. Lately, though, Robin's father didn't have energy for a flicker; a withered shape in a bathrobe, he could only drag himself downstairs.

The trip to Stansell's was like a pilgrimage to a king. Steve drove them all past the Lilac strip malls, past the high school, and through uptown Lilac, then he turned onto the leafy streets of the toniest section of town. The Stansells' house, at the head of a cul-de-sac, was the largest home Robin had ever been in. It had an intercom system, a wet bar in its cavernous basement, and a team of house cleaners that came in twice a week. It rivaled the most grandiose piles out in Wayne and Geneva, two fancy villages to the west of Lilac, and it dwarfed all of its neighbors on the street, which had once been lined with huge elms, and where children never ran or played.

As they climbed out of the car, the double front doors burst open and Marilyn, Stansell's mother, appeared, followed by a barking pile of fur that soon separated into three cocker spaniels. They sniffed around the Fairlane and peed on the tires.

"Well, look who's here," Marilyn said, cigarette bobbing between her lips as she searched her purse, "the future of America right at my doorstep."

Mrs. Stansell was Robin's favorite among all her friends' parents, but she hadn't admitted it to anyone—and she wouldn't, until she figured out why she liked Marilyn so much.

"Steven," Marilyn said.

"Mother," Stansell said, pausing on the front porch. He lit a cigarette.

"If you or one of your friends finds the need to relieve himself or to upchuck, please use the bathroom. Last time you children were here, the cleaning crew had a hell of a time getting the vomit out of the carpeting. Louisa was fit to be tied and I had to pay them all extra."

"Right-o," Stansell called over his shoulder. Robin lingered after everyone else had entered the house.

"Goddammit to hell!" Marilyn yelled. "Moe, Larry, Curly, get your butts in the car! Now!" The dogs left off digging under the shrubs and galloped toward Marilyn, tongues askew and collars jingling. She held open the door of her Mercedes sports car and the dogs leapt into the back. According to Stansell, his mother and Big Steve got into a screaming fight the day she bought the Mercedes. Big Steve said it was inappropriate for a Ford dealer's wife to drive anything other than the Lincoln Town Car he would have been happy to order for her in any color. Marilyn told Big Steve to fuck off, which shut him right up, Stansell reported. Robin thought he had a grudging admiration for his mother.

Mrs. Stansell took a deep breath. "And how are you, Robin?" she asked, looking her up and down.

This was why Robin stayed and why she didn't mind coming to Stansell's house, despite the fact that she hated his guts. It was these moments with Mrs. Stansell, who could look at a person and see no one else, whose every sentence seemed a distillation of thousands of words into a mere ten, all politeness and bullshit carved off. Robin tapped on the Mercedes' window to draw the spaniels. The sun was warm, the breeze high in the maples that marked the property line of the Stansells' half-acre yard. Robin looked self-consciously toward the street, as if she were expecting someone. The front lawn bristled with dog shit.

"Why don't you come to the club with me?" Mrs. Stansell asked. Then she laughed and took a quick drag on her cigarette.

Marilyn golfed in almost any weather, or she stayed at home with the dogs, but that was about it. Last winter, whenever Robin came crashing into Stansell's with everyone else, she would find Steve's mother in the TV room watching some old movie and chain smoking, a drink next to her, the dogs snoring at her feet, Big Steve nowhere to be seen. But in better weather, Marilyn put her golf bag into the Mercedes and drove to the Butterfield Country Club, the car's back windows smeared with dog nose prints, Larry, Curly, and Moe barking desperately from inside the cloud of cigarette smoke.

"I don't know how to golf," Robin said. She surreptitiously examined Mrs. Stansell. Only an inch or two taller than Robin, with freckles covering her dish-shaped face and her coppery hair cut into a pixie, Marilyn was the picture of vigorous affluence. Today she had on green plaid shorts, a green polo shirt, and Keds with pompon socks. Marilyn had golf-tanned legs, short, stocky, and strong, with a thin layer of cellulite that shimmered when she inserted a leg into her car. She looked ready to mount a horse. Robin stopped her gaze at Marilyn's small, hard-looking breasts, and then she looked away.

She could visit this woman sometime, like she'd visit a friend, when no one else was home. She could sit with Marilyn in the paneled TV room and impress her with the movie knowledge she'd acquired over the years from Goldie: for example, how many hours it took to put on Gloria Swanson's makeup for *Sunset Boulevard*, which toupee maker in Vegas crafted Charlton Heston's rugs, why Busby Berkeley liked to hire underage boys for his dance extravaganzas. Robin could make Marilyn laugh. Right now, that seemed like urgent business.

"Don't you ever get tired of all that?" Mrs. Stansell asked, jabbing her cigarette toward the front door. "You know, don't you, that spending time with my boy is just fiddling while Rome burns."

Robin laughed. "I guess," she said.

Marilyn sighed. "Don't guess, Robin," she said. "Jesus H. Find out the facts, then act on them. Cut *out* the rest." She touched her hair and frowned. "I could always *teach* you to golf, you know," she said, getting into the car with a sad smile. "And I would," she said, closing the door.

Marilyn didn't even wave goodbye, but just started up the Mercedes and screeched off. Moe, Larry, and Curly crowded the back window, barking and lunging at Robin as if they'd never seen her before.

∽

Lynn's black gingham bikini, which had one huge daisy printed on each breast and each butt cheek, almost made a joke of her beauty, highlighting what was already alluring, but, oddly, Robin found the ridiculous suit and Lynn in it all the more desirable. Lynn stretched out on the lounge chair she had pushed next to Robin's. Her nails were pink, and she wore a silver toe ring.

"I don't know why you don't like that suit," Lynn said, her eyes closed, her hair hanging in a golden sheet over the back of the lounge chair. The boys practiced backward somersaults off the diving board. Robin was on her second beer.

"Because I look like a guy in it," Robin said, staring down at her small breasts and narrow hips encased in a sheath of black Lycra. "I look like a guy no matter what."

"That's crazy, honey," Lynn said. "You've got the long, thick, dark hair. All the boys love it."

"I don't give a shit what the boys love," Robin said quickly. She was watching a bead of sweat slide between Lynn's breasts. A daisy earring shivered.

The truth was, she felt that all the other girls her age, and especially Lynn, had gone on without her, growing into the kind of shapely women Goldie liked so much. Robin's body remained stuck in early adolescence, at the cusp of puberty, as if it wanted to get it right before moving on. She blamed her father's genes for this stasis: if he could keep Robin young, she'd stay around to take care of him.

"I think that Marqueese guy likes you," Lynn said.

Robin didn't respond. Stansell approached. He was big for seventeen, already six feet tall, with wide shoulders and hammy thighs. The pimples on his cheekbones looked angry and sore in the harsh sunlight. Stansell's hair was the color of mushrooms.

"Ladies," Stansell said. He bent over Lynn's chair and shook his wet head. She shrieked and tried to kick him.

"I have a proposition," Stansell said, dodging Lynn's foot. "My friend Marqueese—"

"Who is he, anyway?" Lynn asked, shading her eyes and looking over at the diving board. Marqueese looked back.

"Business acquaintance," Stansell said.

"Please," Robin said, falling back. The sunlight seemed to sizzle behind her eyelids.

"Listen, Marqueese has prepared some fine joints for our perusal."

"Enjoyment," Robin said. "Delectation, maybe. Perusal means we look at them." She knew without opening her eyes that Stansell was giving her the finger. She smiled.

"My proposition," Stansell continued, "is that we set up a competition. You two get a joint and a six-pack to share. We boys get a joint apiece and a six-pack each, seeing as we're larger human beings. Whoever stays conscious the longest, wins."

"What do we win, Steven?" Lynn asked.

"That's a surprise, baby," he said.

All three of them laughed, a rare shared joke, the theme of which was, "Why pretend?" They all knew what the prize was: Lynn.

Steve had already rolled the joint, so he gave it to the girls and left. Robin lit it and she and Lynn smoked and talked of classes and teachers and people Lynn didn't like. Marqueese sat like a gargoyle by the diving board, his eyes burning at Robin.

"What do you think of Mr. Tomasini?" Lynn asked. She lounged with her eyes closed and one knee bent.

Mr. Tomasini taught Humanities, the cool kids' English requirement that Robin was taking for extra credits, just to be near Lynn. She didn't like the teacher, in part because of his self-congratulatory visits to the student smoking area and his penchant for calling students by their last names. In Humanities, he made students look at slides and watch dance films and listen to jazz and even examine Chicago architecture. Somehow, Mr. Tomasini made it desirable to know who Martha Graham was or what kind of sax John Coltrane played, yet there was something about her teacher that nagged Robin. Maybe it was Mr. Tomasini's two-tone thrift store shoes and baggy trousers and vests. Or the hipster sunglasses he wore even on cloudy days, or his porkpie hat or slick black hair and baby face. Mr. Tomasini was too well constructed, too planned, just like one of the Mies van der Rohe buildings they had studied during architecture week.

"I'm going to have trouble with that class, I just know it," Lynn said.

"I'll help you," Robin said.

"Oh, god, I didn't tell you!" Lynn said. "Colleen McIlhenny is pregnant."

"You're kidding." Robin opened another beer. Across the pool, Billy Tree looked as if he'd already passed out. His head lolled off the lounge chair.

"Lisa Gimino told me," Lynn said. "Colleen told her. She's going to get out of gym, but her parents are letting her stay at home to have the kid."

"That makes—what?—four girls from our gym class last year

who've gotten pregnant? God," Robin said. Just as the girls' bellies had begun to protrude, preventing them from dribbling a basketball or stepping up on the balance beam, they'd disappeared from school.

"Colleen won't tell who the guy is," Lynn said, stretching her arms over her head.

Stansell and Marqueese talked, their heads close together. "It doesn't matter for boys," Robin said. "If they're dads or not." Even Heath assumed that Robin would go on as always, while he took his time wasting away.

"You know," Lynn said, "you see all these girls sitting in the nurse's office at school, and you're like, I know *you're* not waiting for aspirin. They're puking or whatever, or they don't even know what's happened to them, and the nurse is about to tell them. Can you imagine? The nurse? She's the one who really knows everything in school. Definitely not the teachers."

"Except maybe Mr. Tomasini," Robin said.

"Maybe." Lynn yawned. "I bet there's only like twenty kids in the whole school who haven't had sex."

"Shit, more than that!" Robin laughed. "There's three thousand kids at Lilac High!"

"How do you know how many are virgins?" Lynn asked. "Did you do a poll or something?"

"No, it's just, I think, well, that's too small a number. What about band kids and math club and all those kind of people?"

"Oh, god, you'd be surprised," Lynn said.

Of course, all boys were after Lynn, not just the freaks and stoners. Her desirability crossed all boundaries at Lilac High. At the same time, Robin had never heard Lynn utter a word of covetousness, a single desire, or ever mention one boy she liked. She didn't have to: everything came to her.

"You're so lucky you never have to worry about what would happen if you got pregnant, with your dad and grandma. Your dad probably *wants* you to have sex, right?"

"Sex with who?" Robin asked.

"I never thought about that," Lynn said.

"And besides, my dad doesn't *want* me to do anything," Robin said. "He never has. Grandma doesn't either. They just think—well, nothing, I guess. There's a big difference between encouraging someone to do something and just ignoring them so there's this big space for you to do whatever you want."

"That's profound," Lynn said.

"You shouldn't make fun of me."

"Are you sure you and that Freddie guy aren't doing it?"

"Oh, come on. You think Freddie wants a bunch of black eyes?"

"From you?" Lynn asked. "Or you mean from the football team?"

"Did you know the coach tried to get Freddie to join again?" Robin asked. "He's never played football in his life. He hates it. It's just because he's black." Lynn wasn't listening. She was laughing, as she leaned closer and closer to Robin's ear.

"You know what they say about black guys," Lynn whispered.

"You're wasted," Robin said. "And we don't want to lose Stansell's bet." She had to distract Lynn. Every time Freddie's name came up, somebody put up their dukes: he was too smart, too big, too much a man. "If we can stay awake," Robin said, "we can beat these guys. They're brain-dead anyway."

"You have no idea," Lynn said, leaning back. "Maybe you do. But, okay, you have no idea what it's like when a guy's over you and then inside and there's nothing else around but you."

Lynn rolled her head back and forth on the lounge chair. Oranges and mint. "I have some ideas," Robin said. "Sure I do."

"Let me tell you something," Lynn said. "You know, like women's liberation?"

"What about it?" Robin asked. Whenever that subject came up at home, Goldie said, "Please, they're just some gals whose biggest problem is they don't know how to dress. End of story."

"Women's lib makes sex a big secret, like it's no good for you," Lynn said. "There's so much nobody tells you! Just at that second, when you're with a guy? You can lie there, not moving, not doing anything, and then the guy just changes. It's like in a fairy tale when the prince goes blind at the biggest moment. It's like the guy's not really human anymore."

"You're kidding," Robin said. "That's awful."

Lynn sat up. "But, no, that's the best thing, honey. That is the exact moment you become the most beautiful girl in the world."

Robin put a palm on Lynn's back to steady her. Was that Lynn's blood surging in her veins?

"And you know what you can do then?" Lynn asked, her eyelids drooping. "You can make that guy do any, any, any, anything you ever wanted."

Dusk came and went, and then it was dark, only Robin had neglected to notice. She and Lynn had finished off everything that Stansell had given them. Now Lynn was snoring. One corkscrew of pubic hair stuck up from the leg band of her bikini.

Across the pool, the boys sat talking in a close circle of lawn chairs. Marqueese had the skinniest legs Robin had ever seen, as if he'd been sick as a kid, or crippled. They worked well enough—he'd jumped off the diving board with the biggest bounce—but he looked fragile. Those dark eyes, too, sneaking looks at Robin: they were consumptive. Who was it Mrs. Kopopolous had mentioned? Kafka. Tuberculosis. You burn up inside and cough blood and suffer in a kind of flushed and elegant way.

Robin drank down the last of her beer and got slowly to her feet. The concrete patio swayed like a wave-tossed ship. "Yeow," she said, steadying herself on the back of the lounge chair. She ignored the boys and headed for the back door.

Lights blazed in Stansell's kitchen; hot air puffed through the screen door even while air conditioning blasted from the registers. Everything in the room was white, table, chairs, counters, even the phone. It looked like no one had ever cooked a meal here. A laminated phone list lay on the table. Gino's Pizza, Susan at school, Dealership—Service, Dealership—Office, Dealership—Fleet, Maxi Maids, Ray's Pool Service, Williams Liquors, Marshall Field's, Lord and Taylor, Lilac Savings and Loan, Butterfield Country Club. There was no phone list in the Simonsen house, not even a phone book—that had somehow been incinerated: one night last year, Robin had noticed singed sections of the Yellow Pages floating out of the burn barrel. If Goldie or Heath wanted to find a phone number, they called the operator.

Robin padded through the silent dining room and living room, negotiating an obstacle course of heavy upholstered furniture. She passed under the huge chandelier in the foyer and continued up the stairs.

Robin stopped in the dark hallway on the second floor. Here the carpeting and walls seemed to hold their breath. A family's home was like this: an invitation, a curse, a promise. Door number one was Marilyn's bedroom; number two was Big Steve's. They were the only couple Robin had ever met who slept in separate rooms. When Robin told Goldie about it, her grandmother had said, "I could have predicted it. A guy with a head of hair like that and all that dough."

Door number three belonged to Susan Stansell, Steve's sister. She was away at college, at Radcliffe, of all places, majoring in politics. Very early one Sunday morning, after a night of drinking and loud music, Stansell had looked at his Rolex and announced that if Susan had been home she would have been the only family member to, as he put it, "answer the call of the church bells."

Don't snoop, Robin thought. Have a purpose. She decided she had ventured upstairs in order to change the music. Hendrix had been playing on Stansell's stereo for hours. Now that Robin had survived the bet, she wanted a victory song. "Whipping Post" maybe, or "Misty Mountain Hop"—something noisy that churned.

The odor in Steve's room was so strong it was almost visible, a mix of sweat, bong water, cigarettes, and the same citrusy cologne Big Steve wore. In addition to an oak stereo cabinet containing his Bang & Olufsen, Stansell had four huge speakers—two of which pointed out the windows to the patio—a queen-size bed, a tall dresser with clothes caught in all the drawers, a black bean bag chair, and a bedside table covered in ashes that held a small lamp with a red scarf over its shade. Two feathered roach clips clung to the scarf. Robin sat down on Stansell's crumpled sheets to examine the record albums that carpeted the floor in front of the stereo cabinet.

While she was looking through the albums—Cheap Trick, Styx, Zeppelin, the Allman Brothers Band, and, inexplicably, Laura Nyro—she spotted a stack of books under the bedside table. She pulled them out: *Darkness at Noon, The Trial, Death in Venice, Slouching Towards Bethlehem, All the President's Men,* and *I'm OK, You're OK*—the binding cracked on that one when Robin opened it. Inside the front cover, written in tiny, cramped handwriting, was "To My Boy. Love from Your Mother."

During their junior year, Stansell had almost gotten into a fistfight with his English teacher, Mr. Bielewski, a soft-spoken hard grader who always looked sadly out the window while he lectured. Stansell had also tracked lower than Robin. And since Robin had become friends with Lynn, Stansell had given her constant grief about her good grades, her reading, her attention to school. Egghead, brain, nerd, good girl, even narc, he'd called her, as if being smart meant you were out to get kids who got high, as if Robin's own using was a cover. The books had to be a joke. Stansell had no right to read them. And when did he have time? In between hits on his bong, after fucking some little freshman girl, or before he got into his car with a six-pack and Billy Tree and headed off to the city to make some trouble? It was too exhausting, the thought of rearranging her idea of Stansell. Hendrix ground on at top volume. She would let it play.

Robin fell back onto the bed and closed her eyes. The stale odor of Stansell's sheets rose around her. She felt sour, betrayed yet again by a boy she had never trusted. Or betrayed, really, by her own belief that she was unique. Maybe she was just a junkman's daughter who studied too hard.

Robin felt a shift in the air, and then fingers pressed down on her collarbone. It was Marqueese, his red eyes barely open, his ghostly goatee flattened and smashed over to one side. He reeked of beer and Stansell's high-grade pot.

"Whoa!" Robin said, trying to sit up, but before she could raise her shoulders, Marqueese crushed her mouth with his lips. She tried to spit him out, but he pressed harder.

Marqueese stuck his hand inside Robin's bathing suit and snaked his fingers over her breast. She began to push him off and then she almost laughed, his hand felt so clumsy. Lynn had said sex could make men inhuman, render them harmless, just creatures in the clutch of desires—a kind of trick only women and girls knew. Robin could tell Lynn about this, their heads together whispering, she could even get Marqueese to do what she wanted. But she wanted nothing from him. Maybe that was the point: not the things, the privileges a woman could get from a man, but the fact that you could get them at all; this was her grandmother's philosophy. Marqueese shook her, as if he knew she wasn't paying attention. Robin relaxed her body, but she kept a hand on Marqueese's shoulder, ready to push him off. This was the power of a queen, Robin thought, the power of all rulers, confined to the bed.

Marqueese pulled off Robin's bathing suit. Then he reared up and pulled off his shorts. Robin looked down at his thick and tangled patch of black pubic hair and tried not to laugh. This was it? Skin, hair, smells—no surprises at all.

"Okay," Marqueese whispered. He grabbed his penis and aimed it at Robin's crotch. Hendrix stopped singing, the arm of the player lifted, and the record started again. Robin put her hands on top of

Marqueese's head, over his thin, dark hair, and he slid his dick inside her. There was a slight hesitation, some pressure, and then he seemed to be working around in the middle of her stomach, like a finger in a baseball glove. Once, smiling, her grandmother had whispered to her: all the boys want just one thing.

Marqueese picked up speed. Wopp, wopp, went Hendrix's guitar. One afternoon, years ago, Robin and Kitty had hidden in the sumac that ringed the edge of the Simonsens' property and touched each other. Now, Robin couldn't remember Kitty's fingers on her, or her voice. What she did recollect was that it had been fall and the sumac had turned red, and she and Kitty had been together under a line of flames. "Uh," Marqueese said. Then: "Uh. Uh. Uh." On the eastern edge of the Simonsen property, behind the bus, ran a trickle of water that sometimes became a creek of melted snow or storm water. When the creek was high, Robin and Kitty would wade side by side looking for leeches and for the sick goldfish dumped upstream, which sailed down the current on beds of leaves and twigs and candy wrappers.

She had forgotten Marqueese again, and here he was on her breasts. First one nipple, then the other. Lynn's breasts were lightly freckled, with tiny pink nipples. Robin saw her own mouth, her small teeth parted, come down on Lynn's breast. She put her hands on the sides of Marqueese's head. He pushed harder inside of her. What did girls do? Freddie had once asked Robin. The two of them had found Kinsey in the library: girls sucked, girls kissed and knelt before each other and buried their heads in the dark and wet and the scent. Kinsey had asked women about kinds of acts, frequency, duration. Each woman was a model for those who read about them. Robin pushed up with her hips. Marqueese rose up on his hands and drove into her, his eyes closed, his bony chest in front of Robin's face. He chuffed like a steam engine. Lynn's pubic hair was light brown and curly. Robin could drag her palm down the crack of Lynn's ass—she could see herself do it, right now—and then under and to the front, right up to that patch of hair. Robin could grab it without causing pain. If you pulled up in the right spot. If you put the heel of your hand down on the point where everything grew moist and warm, the fevered place, and then you pulled up.

Marqueese smiled, opened his eyes, put his arms under Robin's back, and turned them both. She sat astride, impressed. Marqueese's bony legs were covered in dark hair. He pushed himself up until he was sitting against Stansell's headboard, then he gripped Robin's hips and bounced her. She swallowed her laughter, tried not to smile. Tribadism, that was it: in Kinsey that was what most women did. Rubbing, the dictionary had said. Mutual stimulation. The rituals of a secret tribe. To cover Lynn with her own body, as some kind of protection, to be the one to make the girl's eyelids flutter and open to blue, to make the girl smile up into her own face. Robin fell forward onto Marqueese, her head on his neck, her mouth by his ear. She gathered his wispy hair and hung on while he humped her. Lynn's hair, a shower in her hands.

"Ah," Marqueese said. And then: "Ah shit ah shit ah shit." Marqueese grabbed Robin's hips and bounced her up high and then brought her down hard on his pubic bone. "Ah," he said. His tongue probed her mouth while he held her face, then he pulled back and looked at her. What did his expression mean? He looked like Stansell cutting up a big weed delivery into smaller bags; he looked like Heath used to, the moment before he opened the door and let in a date; he looked like Freddie when Freddie and Robin studied in the bleachers and watched the football team work out.

"Shit, girl," Marqueese said, twisting his torso to look over the side of the bed. "Steve didn't warn me near enough." He picked up his shorts and dug through the pockets, then popped a cigarette between his lips.

Robin pulled off of him and paused on her hands and knees. There was nothing to keep her there. A new smell glazed over Stansell's bong water, cologne, and dirty laundry. Hendrix sang "Purple Haze" for the hundredth time that night.

Robin stood up on Stansell's bed, one foot on either side of Marqueese's hips, while he lit his cigarette. She looked over the speakers to the patio outside, where Stansell leaned laughing over Lynn's body, and she let what was inside of her trickle out onto the boy below.

chapter nine

Steve Stansell liked to drive them all into Chicago for various reasons—food, booze, drugs, mayhem. One night he took them to a motel on North Avenue and made everyone get out and stand in the motel's tiny courtyard. "Watch this," he said, stepping forward. Then he screamed, "I'm looking for the guy who's in there fucking my wife!" Nearly every window of the motel lit up, and Stansell collapsed into fits of laughter.

That was all right, Robin thought, just Stansell being sleazy, but then he would take them at night to Grant Park, or, if it was warm, to Oak Street Beach, so he could hustle wasted people for money. One time he got a fat roll of bills off of some smalltime dealer who had passed out in a vacant lot on the North Side. Another time, when he took a junkie's wallet, Robin wrestled it out of his hands and threw it into Lake Michigan.

Finally, though, she gave up. Stansell would do what he wished, like Heath and like Goldie. And Lynn didn't seem to mind. She laughed off the worst of Stansell's behavior. When Robin asked her how she could put up with him, Lynn simply said that you had to expect those things from guys, especially guys like Stansell. Robin was never sure what kind of guy Stansell was.

As a child, Robin had been all over Chicago with her father, especially its poorer parts, buying and selling junk. Some of Heath's junk territory and some of Stansell's bad-behavior territory overlapped, but Stansell also drove the Fairlane to parts of Chicago that Robin only saw on the news or read about in the paper. These were neighborhoods with no white people, and war-torn houses. This was where Martha Hazen was working, according to Goldie, the place where her parents had truly lost her. On trips to these neighborhoods, Robin tried to shield her face, not from what was outside the car windows but from the people looking in, from their frowns and curses and from their awareness that Stansell was a mere tourist, a sightseer of poverty.

In October, on a crisp autumn evening that made Robin think of German beer fests, rye bread, apples, heavy cheeses—things she knew about from magazine ads—Stansell drove everyone to the South Side in order to "cop something good, the real shit." Before they left Lilac, he pulled out a roll of cash and gave it to Robin.

"Why me?" she asked.

"Because, Simonsen, believe it or not, you're honest."

"She is!" Lynn said, pinching Robin's cheek.

Stansell drove with the top up and the windows down, despite the fall temperature. The last of the sunlight warmed the backs of their heads as they drove the Eisenhower into Chicago. Robin pocketed the roll of bills and pushed closer to Lynn. She was forever stuck between her and Marqueese in the back seat. Whenever the car started, the maneuvering began, Marqueese trying to fondle Robin, and her sneakered foot mashing his boot and then Robin shoving Lynn over to the side so Robin could wallow in her exciting proximity. She felt like a shuttlecock.

On the highway, Stansell lit a joint. It got to Robin just as the car passed under the Post Office and over the Chicago River. This had been Robin's favorite part of the trip when she was younger. A building you could drive through, followed by tires growling over the bridge grating, more evidence of Chicago's power to break open structures and span rivers. Stansell turned south on State Street just as the streetlights were going on. Billy Tree slept in the front seat, his cheeks red from the cold, his mass of hair flattened against the seat back.

"There's not enough of anything in the world to keep me warm," Lynn said.

"Really," Robin said.

"Pass that back here," Marqueese yelled to Stansell, reaching for the joint.

"My dad gave me some kind of lecture at dinner last night," Lynn said. "He's like, 'ethics this and ethics that.' I don't know what the hell he's talking about."

"He's a lawyer," Robin said.

"I guess," Lynn said. "Sit closer, for god's sake—it's freezing. Here. Okay. So my dad makes me look up 'ethics' at the dinner table, and my mom's over in the corner kind of frowning at me. This was all for my benefit, but I don't know why."

"Maybe your dad knows what you're doing. He's a lawyer, after all."

"You keep saying that. He's just my dad."

"But dads have their own ideas," Robin said. She rested her head on Lynn's shoulder. Marqueese put his head on Robin's shoulder, but she shoved it off, sending him banging into the door.

"I can't hear you, Lynnie," Stansell called from the front seat. He drove fifty miles per hour down State Street. The buildings got smaller, the houses crumbled, as they traveled south.

"My dad's hassling me," Lynn said. "At least, I think he is."

"He's just trying to tell you something," Robin said. "Like straighten up and fly right."

"I don't want to know," Lynn said.

"Get him high," Stansell said.

"He's a lawyer," Robin said.

"Oh, and I'm sure no lawyers get high," Stansell said.

"Let's get back to my problem," Lynn said.

"You're not grounded, are you?" Robin asked.

"No, but my dad's like, 'blah, blah, Lynn, behave with good intentions and think about the consequences of your actions.'"

"What actions?" Stansell asked.

"'Blah, blah, no one has ethics anymore,'" Lynn said.

"It's a way of him telling you to be mature about stuff," Robin said. "To think about what you do."

"'Blah, blah, blah, think about others and not just yourself, blah, blah, who do you want to be as an adult.'"

"Okay, so he knows what you're up to, hanging around Stansell and all," Robin said. "You better quit."

"Very fucking funny," Stansell said.

"I'm not joking," Robin said.

"Will you guys cut it out, please?" Lynn said. "So my dad's been snooping in my room, then."

"Maybe," Robin said. "Or he just knows. He feels it."

"He can't even remember my birthday," Lynn said. "He's not feeling anything."

"Hey," Marqueese said, "that looked like a hooker back there."

"Where?" Stansell said, slowing the car.

"I'd be careful," Robin said to Lynn. "Parents know stuff, no matter what we think. I'm good with parents. We'll do stuff to make your dad forget about what he thinks you're doing."

"And here I go in Chicago," Lynn said, grabbing Robin's hand, "den of inquiry."

"Iniquity," Robin said, wind-blown, happy, as her small hand nestled in Lynn's larger one.

"That was definitely a hooker," Marqueese said.

From State Street, Stansell took 46th Street over to Cottage Grove. Here again, no white people except the young fools in the speeding Fairlane. Every time Stansell took them to these neighborhoods, Robin tried to reverse the chronology of Freddie's life, but she had to stop before she got to the South Side, before she got to Freddie and his life before Lilac had built up fear, insecurity, and confusion inside him. They were all tourists.

The street numbers grew: 98th, 103rd, 109th. Stansell drove faster, dodging in and out of the traffic. He produced another joint and lit it. His hands shook.

"Now I'm hungry," Lynn said.

"I have some gum," Marqueese said, digging in his pocket. "Somewhere."

"That's okay," Lynn said, rolling her eyes at Robin.

Marqueese grinned at the girls. Robin thought he had a Charles Manson look, his eyes wobbly, his smile too big and toothy for his head. "Robin stole the gum from my pocket, I bet," he said.

"Oh, stop, for god's sake." Robin laughed.

The ragged houses petered out into acres of cyclone fencing and weedy lots full of trash. Sulfur lights glowed orange. When they reached an area devoid of buildings or people, Stansell stopped the car.

"Okay, man," Billy Tree said, yawning. "Where the fuck are we?"

"Robin," Stansell said, reaching a hand into the back. She gave him the roll of bills and he began counting. He smiled.

"I thought you trusted me," Robin said.

"I think there's snakes around here," Marqueese said, looking out at the tall weeds and scattered, sickly sumac. "I hate snakes."

"We're going to put this money back into circulation," Stansell said. He put the car's top down and looked at his watch.

"What does that mean?" Billy Tree asked.

Robin saw two figures far down the road, walking toward the car. "It means another deal," she said.

Stansell responded by getting out of the car and stepping on his cigarette.

"Do you know these guys?" Billy asked.

"Let's stay here," Marqueese said, sinking down in his seat.

"I feel like Dorothy in *The Wizard of Oz*," Lynn said. "This is outer space."

The advancing figures walked a dip in the road; they were somewhat obscured, despite the sulfur lights. Robin remembered Stansell turning off of Cottage Grove and onto a service road. She could hear air brakes and mufflers on a nearby highway. "Move over, Lynn," Robin said, "I'm getting out."

"What for? Stay here with me."

Stansell stood on the side of the road, conversing with the two men. They were his height, but broader, and they stood not in an arrogant pose, like Stansell, but in comfortable slouches, like this was part of their daily business, meeting stupid suburban boys in the dark. Robin sniffed the air. On bad days the Prairie Path in Lilac smelled like this: acrid, humid, intimately human and carnal. Stansell had driven south and then turned east: they were at the sewage treatment plant, the one on the far South Side. Years ago, Heath had pointed it out when he and Robin were looking for a junkyard. Robin remembered the poor houses in the neighborhoods beyond, the kids on the stoops, the fact that you'd smell shit every day of your life.

Robin walked toward Stansell and the men. They all stood with their hands in their pockets, Stansell pretending cool in his expensive boots and suede jacket.

"Hey!" one of the guys called. "Who's that?"

Stansell turned. "Simonsen, get in the car!" he yelled.

"Why?" Robin asked, walking up to the group. The two men were black, with close-cropped Afros. One of them had a neatly trimmed beard. The other man wore a black bow tie and black pants, a uniform, maybe.

"Yeah," the guy with the beard said to Stansell. "So."

"I want a taste," Stansell said.

"These the kind of little girls you're going to sell to?" the guy with the beard asked. "I'm Kendall, honey," he said, nodding at Robin. "This Ronald."

Robin put her hands in her pockets, too. The lining of her coat had ripped, so she fingered the belt on her jeans.

"Are you done?" Stansell asked her. "I'm trying to do business here."

"Go ahead, big shot," Robin said, sending Kendall and Ronald into peals of laughter.

Stansell sighed. "Let me see it," he said.

Kendall turned slightly and took a large baggie of white powder from under his jacket.

"Where you from?" Ronald asked Robin.

"Lilac," Robin said.

"Lilac? That in Illinois?"

"It's west of downtown? You know, like, past Maywood, Melrose, way past that," Robin said, mentioning suburbs closer to the city.

"Don't know it," Ronald said.

"You go, okay, Elmhurst, Villa Park, then there's Lilac. It's by Wheaton and those towns. DuPage County?"

"You're talking about the moon now. I never been past the West Side or so and then down here and up by Gary."

Stansell's and Kendall's voices rose. Robin looked back at the car, but all she could see was the silhouette of Billy Tree's bushy head. A truck downshifted on the highway.

"I have a friend from the South Side," Robin said.

Ronald was silent for a moment. "You know somebody from around here. Now you're bullshitting me," he said.

"No, I'm not," Robin said, smiling. "Really! Freddie Eakins. He's my neighbor!"

"In this town you live in?" Ronald said. "I see it now."

"He's a lot younger than you," Robin said. She felt herself blush.

"How old do you think I am?" Ronald asked.

Kendall turned to Ronald. "Ronnie," he said, "seems you miscalculated."

"What miscalculated?" Ronald asked. "There's nothing wrong with my equipment, man," he said to Stansell.

Stansell lit another cigarette in reply. Robin watched sweat trickle down his neck and into the collar of his suede jacket.

"You didn't answer my question," Ronald said, turning back to Robin.

She said the first number she thought of. "Twenty-two."

Ronald guffawed. "Girl, I'm eighteen next week. That's all."

"Jesus," Robin said, "that's my age practically."

"There you go," Ronald said.

How could she and Ronald be the same age? Freddie did say that all his South Side cousins put on five years for every one of his. "What are you wearing?" Robin asked.

"This shit is for banquet waiter," Ronald said, fingering his bow tie. "Weddings, anniversary parties, like that. I came right from it to see your boy here."

Kendall raised his voice and Stansell backed up a few steps toward the car.

Robin backed up with him, and Ronald followed. "You must make a lot of money," she said.

"I'm saving for college," Ronald said. "And I see you looking at Kendall and your boy. But this is just a sideline. Kendall's letting me in on it for a while. I don't really go for this."

"Simonsen!" Stansell said. He started to run. "Let's go!"

"You think because of your dad," Stansell said, panting, when Robin caught up to him.

"Well, yeah, I do," Robin said. "It didn't matter anyway."

"Just get in the fucking car. We've got to get out of here."

"Why are you in such a hurry?" Robin asked, sliding into the back seat next to Lynn, who had been dozing. Robin made her sit in the middle.

"Hey," Marqueese said, "those dudes look like they're coming back this way."

Over the top of the windshield, Robin saw the two heads bobbing, growing in size as they came closer. Stansell started the car.

"Hang on," Billy Tree said, "they're trying to say something."

Stansell put the car into gear.

"Don't you move, stupid!" Kendall yelled.

"Stop!" Robin cried, putting her hand on Stansell's shoulder.

"What's going on?" Lynn asked, sitting up. "I was about to have a dream. It was going to be good, too."

"Stansell, stop the car!" Robin cried. She leaned over the front seat and threw her arms around his neck.

"Get the fuck off of me!" Stansell yelled.

Ronald and Kendall caught up to the car. "We've got a problem here," Kendall said.

"Oh, yes, we do," Ronald said, his chest heaving.

The Fairlane's engine, timed and torqued by the best at Stansell Ford, just hummed. Robin sat back down next to Lynn.

"You're short, man," Kendall said.

"Look at all these folks," Ronald said. "Hey."

"Hey!" Lynn said.

"My, my," Ronald said.

Stansell looked over his shoulder as if he were going to back up.

"Hold on, man," Kendall said. "I told you nice."

"Stansell," Robin said quietly. He put the car in park.

"You're about a hundred short, slick," Kendall said.

"That's impossible," Stansell said.

"It's very possible," Ronald said. "Now Henry said go ahead and do business with the dude. He's a repeat customer and all. Remember Henry, Steve?"

"Of course I remember Henry."

"All right. You don't want to make him out a liar, do you?"

"Look, I gave you what he said I should," Stansell said impatiently. "We've got to go."

"You know, Steve," Kendall said, "we're not even the man Henry is. Not even. Henry might not have bothered chasing you down. So you're coming up lucky here."

Kendall sat on the car's hood. Ronald joined him. Then Kendall started counting out bills on the car's hood. When he got to one hundred he pushed the pile over to Ronald.

"Hold that down for me," he said.

Ronald reached into his jacket, and Stansell gave a little yelp and cringed. When Ronald pulled out a fat wallet and placed it on top of the pile of bills, Stansell rolled his neck as if trying to get the kinks out.

"What'd you say your name was?" Ronald said, nodding toward Lynn.

"I didn't. Lynn."

"Who's these other dudes?"

"I'm Ralph," Marqueese said. "That's Bob."

"Don't be a jerk, Marqueese," Robin said.

"Two hundred," Kendall said, pushing over another pile.

Ronald was watching Stansell's face. "Boo!" he said, lunging at the windshield.

"Watch out, Ronnie!" Kendall said. "That money'll fly."

"This dude's thinking, I'm in the city, I better watch my back," Ronald said. "Right, man?"

"Get off my car, asshole!" Stansell said.

Kendall continued counting. "Maybe I looked in the wrong pocket," Ronald said. "Maybe I've got the thing you're looking for right in my other one. This dude's thinking, where'd that brother hide his gun? You know he's got a gun. He's a South Side boy!" He smirked at Stansell. "You more an idiot than I first thought."

One of Mr. Tomasini's favorite words in Humanities class was "context." Paintings had context, so did music, and especially books. Robin thought of context as a kind of womb, a place to transmit DNA, a place where things acquired full dimension. The context for the business on the car hood was the shit-smelling neighborhood and the fact that Robin and Heath had found not one but five junkyards when they'd been here years ago. But mostly the context was Stansell's ignorance, which he'd covered up so far by staying put in Lilac.

"Three hundred," Kendall said. Another pile.

"This is taking too long," Lynn said. "I'm getting cold."

"Now don't tell me," Ronald said. "You're the prom queen."

"Hardly," Lynn said, laughing.

"She could be," Robin said. "But it's not her thing."

"I went to prom once," Marqueese said.

"What is your thing?" Ronald asked Lynn.

"She doesn't have a *thing*," Billy said. "Nobody here has a *thing*."

"I'm not talking to you, am I?" Ronald said.

Everyone looked jaundiced under the glow of the sulfur lights.

"I'm just a girl from Lilac," Lynn said. "Along for the ride."

"That's what your friend here tells me," Ronald said.

"My name's Robin," Robin said. Stansell's shoulders were shaking.

"Four hundred," Kendall said. "We got a little bit more," he added, looking at Stansell, who hadn't moved his hands from the steering wheel.

Context was a combination of who was telling the tale and where the tale was told. What could a person do with, one, a weedy berm outside a sewage treatment plant on Chicago's South Side, two, a couple of black guys from the city, three, a white kid from the suburbs, and four, that same white kid's *Late Late Show* nightmare?

"And change," Kendall said, slapping a few tens down on the Fairlane.

Ronald swept up the tens with the other bills and placed his hand over the staggering pile.

"Either I can't add or you can't add, and I got a A in math," Kendall said. "And I already know you're stupid for pulling this shit in the first place."

"Really," Ronald said. "The money's basic, man. This is baby stuff."

"I didn't know," Stansell said.

"Didn't know you were simple or didn't know you were wrong?" Ronald asked.

"We'll make it up," Robin said. "The difference." It seemed only polite. Context here was a car full of helpful people with wallets.

"That's right," Kendall said. "And then you don't come back."

"That's right," Ronald said. "And we have a talk with Henry."

"Who's got money?" Stansell said. The back of his neck glistened in the orange light. His hands remained on the steering wheel.

"I do," Lynn said, digging through her suede purse.

Billy Tree and Marqueese went to their pockets.

"What about you?" Ronald asked Robin.

"Nothing," Robin said. "Sorry."

Everyone piled money on the dash except for Stansell.

"Don't tell me there's nothing in your pockets," Kendall said.

"Afraid not," Stansell said.

Ronald reached over the windshield and took the cash. "I see about forty-three," he said.

Kendall squinted into the car. "What's that?" he asked, pointing at Stansell's white-knuckled hand.

"What?" Stansell croaked out. "Nothing."

"We'll take the watch," Ronald said.

"It's a fucking Rolex!" Stansell yelled.

"Hold on, slick, hold on," Kendall said.

"It's worth way more than, what, seventy dollars!" Stansell said.

"That's the point, man," Ronald said.

"Stansell," Robin said "give them the watch."

"It's your fault I'm in this," Stansell said, turning around. "Stupid bitch," he added.

"Whoa!" Ronald said.

"How do you figure it's her fault?" Marqueese said, sitting up.

"Shut up, every single one of you!" Billy Tree yelled. He leaned over and unclasped Stansell's watch. Stansell resisted, and they wrestled over his wrist.

"I don't believe this," Kendall said.

"Here," Billy Tree said. Stansell rubbed his bare skin. "Take the fucking thing."

Kendall put the Rolex in his pocket, then he and Ronald turned and slowly walked away.

"Let's go, Stansell," Robin said.

Stansell turned the wheel and roared away, the tires spitting gravel. He got them back onto Cottage Grove in no time, running through two stop signs and a light. The odor from the sewage plant dissipated.

"That was close," Lynn said, "but I wasn't really worried too much."

"Those guys could have killed me without even thinking about it," Stansell said to himself. "So don't tell me they didn't have a gun. No way. These people are crazy. Fucking. Crazy."

Robin watched the boxy houses rush by, this one with a limbless tree in the front yard, that one with two young men on the front steps who could have been Kendall and Ronald or Freddie in a different future or any number of young men whom Robin knew absolutely nothing about.

∼

Heath smelled like Magic Markers. Robin circled the kitchen table, traveling from the phone by the window—Lynn wasn't home—to the bookcase on the opposite wall—her father had asked for a pack of Panatelas—and never once took her eyes off of him. Heath had soaked in the downstairs tub for an hour, but the chemical smell remained. It clung to his damp hair, his whiskers—Robin leaned down to kiss her father's cheek—even to his breath. He was rotting from the inside.

"I think I'm losing my hair," Robin's father said. "Look." He pulled up his forelock to show the roots, far back on his forehead. Heath's smell reminded Robin of grade school days, teachers using markers to letter bulletin boards or to write equations on a big tablet at the front of the room.

"Do you need your clothes washed?" Robin asked, sitting down across from him. He could have just returned from the hospital after an operation. Or come home from the war. Here was the tender reunion with the daughter.

"Done," Heath said. The washer under the stairs knocked into its spin cycle.

"You threw up last night," Robin said. She tried to compose an expression that showed neither too much love nor any sign of judgment.

"That I did," her father said. His beautiful face sagged. He lit a Panatela, then put it in the ashtray.

Grandma had gone off with Old Man Bogdanas; Robin had seen his Chrysler waiting in the driveway when she came home from school. This year, her senior year, she had vowed not to worry so much about the careening lives of her father and grandmother. Already, work on the car progressed. Mr. Tomasini had started a unit on dance, and the class watched films of Balanchine's ballets. "They're all about the foot," Mr. Tomasini had said, pacing the back of the classroom in his porkpie hat and zoot suit. Robin got an A on a trigonometry test. Then last week she came home from school to find three large strangers at the kitchen table laying out cash and pocketing small velvet bags. Yesterday, after a late party at Stansell's house, she found Goldie in the kitchen wearing new diamond earrings. She and her men were drinking Bombay gin and eating shrimp that Larry Pike had boiled on the stove in a big kettle. This morning before school, Robin checked the cash box behind the washer and found a neat stack of hundred-dollar bills. She took one, carried it all day like a secret reward, and now she could feel it folded up in her pocket. She had meant to steal it from her father, but, against her wishes, she'd seen him, and now any joy in her crime disappeared.

It was cold outside. Heath had been quiet in his room for a week, only calling down to ask Robin to leave water outside his door. Every time Goldie heard his voice, she flapped her hand behind her head and said, "Aw, enough already." But Robin went up with glass after glass. Finally, she washed out an old bucket and filled that and brought it up with a plastic measuring cup. Tonight, while her father was in the bathtub, she had snuck upstairs and found the empty bucket outside his door.

Heath shivered. He had sores around his mouth and on his neck. "Can you get me some dry toast?" he whispered.

"Orange juice?" Robin asked.

"Just toast," her father said.

"I can make coffee."

"Toast," Heath said, nodding slowly. "Please."

Robin stuck a slice of bread into the toaster. She examined her father from behind. His cigar smoked in the ashtray. He turned his bleary eyes to the outside, where it was gray and windy, the weather gearing up for something big.

"I have to take a trip," Heath said, as Robin placed the toast in front of him.

"A trip?" Her father hadn't traveled anywhere in months. Something had happened over a year ago during one of his visits to Champaign to see Martha Hazen, and since then, as far as Robin knew, her father had barely left the county. "Where are you going?" Robin asked.

"I'm not sure yet," her father said.

"What do you mean?" Robin asked. "Did you get busted, Dad?"

Heath approximated a laugh. "Busted. That would be a neat trick. From my bed even."

"Well, I'm not here all the time," Robin said. "I don't know what you do."

"Where's Fred these days?" her father asked, slowly examining the kitchen, as if Robin's friend were part of the household junk. "And that foxy girlfriend of yours? What's her name?"

"Lynn. Dad, I don't think this is a good time to go away."

"Why not?"

"Well, I'm going to graduate in June."

"Kiddo, for god's sake, it's a short trip. This is still fall."

"What if you don't get back? For some reason."

Heath sighed. "I'm just letting you know that I'm going. There's money in the box, and Grandma knows where there's more. So ask her if you need anything." Heath picked up his toast and put it down again.

"Maybe you should make out a will while you're at it," Robin said.

"Don't be a smartass," her father said. "Not now, please. I'm very aware of your cleverness. In fact, I don't even know how you got to be my daughter." Heath looked genuinely sad. Regretful.

"Maybe I'm more like Mom," Robin said.

Heath dipped his head and tried again with the toast. He lifted it to his mouth with shaking hands. "We don't really know what your mom would have been like, do we?" he said, giving up on the food.

Of course: Patricia's aging had stopped with her death, when she was still a very young woman. And Robin's memory of her mother had remained static. When Patricia died, she hadn't been ten years older than Robin was now. An unformed woman. Unknowing.

Heath reached out and touched the sleeve of Robin's flannel shirt. "Aw, now, Rob, don't cry."

"You don't even think about her, Dad. Really, you don't."

Heath nodded. "Every day, I do. Yep."

Robin remembered her mother's brawny and straightforward approach to Heath, her winning approach. Patricia always made Robin's father think about the meaning of his actions, just like Lynn's father, the lawyer, did for Lynn. The best Robin could do was to read consequences, like a fortuneteller read cards, and sit back and watch helplessly as events unfolded.

"If you thought about Mom," Robin said, "you wouldn't do what you do."

Heath had pulled back his hair and braided it. A long, damp plait hung down his back, the dry part of his hair frizzing and curling about his face like a lion's disheveled mane. Even at his most destitute, Heath was handsome, in a ruined way.

"You're wasted all the time, Dad," Robin said. "And you've got a kid in the house."

"Meaning you? And let's not be hypocritical, Robin."

There was silence while they looked at each other. Robin's mother might have tread more carefully, more slowly, but Robin couldn't. The words spilled from her mouth.

"At least I'm not a junkie," she said.

"I don't think it's appropriate for you to tell me how to raise you."

"Raise me? Come on."

There were too many versions of Patricia for Robin to know which one to turn to. Heath wanted one Patricia, Robin another; Goldie probably had her own idea of her daughter-in-law, based on the slim college girl she'd met just once, after the Vegas wedding.

"Dad, you know I know everything," Robin said. "The heroin, selling it, and Grandma and the guys, with illegal stuff."

"Fenced," her father said.

"What?"

"It's called 'fenced' goods, the kind of stuff you sell that's been stolen. But listen, honey, your grandmother and I never hide anything from you. Do we? We don't pretend to be anyone else or to do things differently. You and I have talked about this."

"But you know, Dad, there shouldn't have to be anything to hide. I mean, you're so proud, like you're so honest, but not hiding something against the law doesn't all of a sudden make it a good thing."

"When did you get so righteous?"

Heath's cheeks flared pink. It was the first color Robin had seen in his face for months. A zombie, coming back to life. She hadn't planned it—she hadn't planned any of this confrontation—but here was the reward: her father, feeling.

"What I'm saying," Robin continued in a soft voice, "is that sometimes there's a reason to pass a judgment. Not everything means the same, or is the same weight."

"I'm not sure about that." Heath leaned his grizzled cheek on his hand and tried to smile.

"Couldn't you have just been sad when Mom died? Couldn't you have just cried or something, instead of taking everything you could get your hands on and going out with like every woman in DuPage County?" The return of her tears made Robin angrier. "Couldn't you, and Grandma, too, just for once thought, maybe not, that's not a good idea, or whatever? About anything? You never said 'stop,' Dad. Not once."

"I'm really tired, honey. Really, really."

"You're always tired now."

"Kiddo, the thing I hate most is lying. And pretending. Okay, two things." Heath relit his Panatela, then left it in the ashtray.

It wasn't lost on Robin that her father was exhibiting unprecedented restraint, a restraint he neither desired nor controlled. There was no greater pity than that of a child for her father.

"Sometimes, Dad," Robin said, "I wish you would lie."

"Telling you the truth is how I show respect. I think you're adult enough to know things."

"But wanting me to be that way doesn't mean I am. Maybe I don't want that respect, or I can't take it, or whatever. Technically, Dad, I'm still a kid."

"Those age markers are arbitrary," Heath said. "What does it matter if you're seventeen, eighteen?" he asked. "You can be ten and be more mature than some adults."

"Yeah, but why should you be? Who wants to be?"

"If that's the way you feel, Robin, then I guess I'll keep everything to myself." Heath shrugged.

"God, Dad, like there's anything I don't already know."

Her father gazed silently out at the gunmetal sky. Robin missed him, fiercely. A network of thick, raised veins covered his knuckles, as if tiny animals had been burrowing inside his hands.

"You think I'm sick, I know," Heath said. "But I'm really made of indestructible material. Like Skylab." He tried smiling again; it looked painful for him to part his lips.

"Just don't crash to earth," Robin said, laughing.

Robin's father looked somber now, his shaky hands clasped, his bloodshot eyes on her face. "Listen, kiddo," he said, "I loved your mother like crazy. I would have done anything for her. I did, too."

"I know," Robin said. Someone had scratched the name "Rosie" in the Formica tabletop. One of her dad's dates, probably. If every one of Heath's women had taken a knife to the table's surface, there'd be a sea of letters, a new language for her father's sex life.

"Your mom was just bones, lying there," Heath said. "She wasn't Patricia anymore. Even she didn't think so. All her brains and prettiness gone. And so much pain! Christ. I'd go out to work and then come home and then she'd start begging me to finish everything already."

"What are you saying?" Robin asked. Her father's eyes had absorbed drops of the liquidy sky. They glinted, overflowed.

Heath rubbed his hand under his nose. "It was so fucked," he said. "Really fucked. But what could I have done? You know? She was already on morphine, she said okay. That's what happened. We both knew about it, nothing secret or sneaky. I hate lying. Okay?"

The furnace banged on. "You gave Mom morphine?" Robin asked.

"The doctor said he'd never seen anyone so full of cancer. Full. Like a glass of contaminated water."

Robin saw her mother in the big bed, her hair, face, bones—all of her, sliding away. She had died, conveniently, while Robin was at school. "Oh, no, Dad," Robin whispered.

"She asked!" Heath said. "Like I said. Honey, she was right near the end. She'd suffered like, I don't know how bad or how long."

"So you helped *kill* her?" Robin asked. She watched as her father took in her hair, the same color as Patricia's, as he took in her anger and disbelief and sorrow.

"Didn't you listen?" Heath said. "Christ, what should I have done? There's a difference between murdering someone and helping them escape a kind of torture. At their request, too, kiddo—at your mom's request."

"I understand the distinction, Dad." Robin felt oddly calm, as if knowing where she stood required only this further proof of her father's haplessness. His ignorance and fear of blame made everything clearer: she really was alone, and he'd had a hand in making her so. "You just happened to have extra morphine," Robin said.

Heath scanned the wall behind her head. "They don't give you that much at one time," he said. "There was a nurse, and she'd come and give it every day. I got extra."

"And the needles."

"The kits, yeah. I got those, too."

"From the nurse."

"Not then. From a different one. You remember her, don't you? Janie? She used to come around after your mother died."

"'Come around,'" Robin said. "Dad, what a euphemism. You were fucking her."

Her father winced. "Jesus, honey," he said.

This was a plan only a couple could have worked out. Heath and Patricia hadn't even considered Robin.

But her mother never would have asked her father to break the law. "How did Mom think you were going to get the morphine?" Robin asked.

Heath looked out the window again. It could rain, or even snow. "Robin," her father said, "your mom was a very smart girl. She knew everything I did for a living. Everything I would do."

A parent is so powerful, almost mythical, a god instead of a human, even in his ability to do wrong, to fail. In Robin's myth, Heath sold drugs out of some kind of misery, out of lingering grief over Patricia's death, and over the years his grief got buried under his selfishness and pursuit of desire, and then even that got buried under addiction, which was desire for desire's sake.

Robin got up from the table and kissed her father's head, in a kind of blessing. She was breathless, almost stumbling. She went to her room and lay on her bed. Soon she heard her father banging around upstairs doing his junkman's version of packing. She didn't think of him, or of her mother, but of Lynn. You put yourself together, she thought. After you realized you had the power to create yourself, after you jettisoned as much of the bad as possible, the useless traits of your father and all the weaknesses of your grandmother, after you put yourself together and then presented yourself to someone, all shiny and ready to be taken: then what? She heard Heath start up his truck. Now there was no time to say to Lynn, I'm not who I thought I was. Let me start over.

Larry Pike knew a guy who had a cousin who used to work for Earl Scheib in Chicago but had to quit because of the black lung he got from years in the painting bays at Scheib's, and this guy had the most exotic car repair machinery just sitting in his backyard in Cicero. Robin ordered a hoist. It came to the house late one Sunday night in the back of a paneled truck, and after she and Larry and the nameless guy driving the truck rolled the hoist on its dolly into the garage, Robin noticed that the serial number had been scratched off. "Not again," she said. The hoist joined the company of the other equipment and appliances—TVs, washers and dryers, chainsaws, nail guns—languishing on the Simonsen property. All of it was untraceable, as if created in some vacuum, junk without a past and, at the Simonsens', without a future. The cousin of the guy Larry knew never wanted to see the hoist again.

Robin prepared to pull the Thunderbird's engine on Thanksgiving, against the advice of Goldie's kibitzers. She set up a listing space heater next to the car and opened the garage door about a foot. She didn't need to pull the engine—it was in good condition—but she wanted to see how it worked, the plan and layout of the whole thing. Disconnecting the engine required an endless series of detachments: heater hoses, generator wires, fuel tank line, even her own expectations. She broke at dark and she and Grandma, Tommy, and Larry had turkey sandwiches for Thanksgiving dinner. Robin didn't know where her father was, and she tried not to care. She thought of him as a fugitive, post-confession, on the lam from his conscience.

Lynn came over the next night in a white rabbit-fur jacket, trailing Stansell and Marqueese. Robin felt self-conscious about her dirty hair, pulled back in a rubber band, and her oil-stained tee shirt and work boots, her skinny arms, and the fact that she wasn't wearing a bra and didn't need one. As always, next to Lynn, Robin looked like a starter woman, a tiny, underdeveloped example of womanhood that would never grow any larger. Lynn stood far away from the car and the rest of the junk and beamed at Robin and called her honey and played with the leather belt on her jacket. Stansell hopped up onto the workbench along the back wall and threw wing nuts at Lynn, then rolled a joint and smoked most of it himself. The space heater smelled like a pot of boiling motor oil. No one had ever spoken directly about the bad buy in Chicago, but Stansell let everyone know he had unloaded the coke in record time.

Marqueese stood off to Robin's side, reeking of cigarettes and beer. "Do you want something?" she finally asked.

"You got to drain the cooling system and oil," Marqueese said.

"I'm getting to that," Robin said.

"Maybe Marqueese can help you," Lynn said.

"I could do the draining while you work on the flywheel," Marqueese said.

Robin sighed, but gave him the tools. She ignored him while she continued to work on the engine.

They all talked of school. The day before Thanksgiving, Mr. Tomasini had shown them a slide of Frank Stella's *The Marriage of Reason and Squalor:* two seemingly identical halves of the same painting of black, nested rectangles, extending from the center out to the edges, narrow to wide, all of them edged in white; a long white line down the middle of the painting separated the two sides. "Is it the same? Is it different?" Mr. Tomasini kept asking, as he strode around the room. He wore his porkpie hat; the top of his Marlboro pack peeked over the edge of his shirt pocket. Robin had looked, pondered, while Charlie Parker played "Cherokee" from a record player next to the slide projector. Finally, Robin shot up her hand and said loudly, "Different!" but before Mr. Tomasini could do more than confirm her answer, the bell rang. Later, he had waved to Robin in the parking lot. His car went with the rest of him. He had a dented Volvo sedan with a Grateful Dead sticker on the bumper, and one side of the license plate was attached to the car by a pink shoelace. Mr. Tomasini out-grooved even Heath Simonsen in his better years.

"Where's your old man?" Stansell asked, as Robin looked at the engine.

"Why?" Robin asked. Stansell shrugged.

"I think your dad's cute," Lynn said.

"Please." Robin snorted. She pulled at the motor mount nuts, pinching her finger in the wrench. "Shit!" she said. Then, without thinking, she said: "What's so cute about a junkie?"

Roger Daltry, Robert Plant, Jimi Hendrix—all the rock boys—jeered from their posters and album covers on the back wall. There were dirty cobwebs over Mick Jagger's face.

"Happy Thanksgiving," Stansell said, pulling a silver flask of whiskey out of the pocket of his suede jacket. He wore a new Rolex.

"Here," Marqueese said, holding his hand out to Stansell.

"Do you have any of that old speed left?" Lynn asked. "Give some to Robin and she'll have this stupid car done in like a day. I'm getting bored with the whole thing. I want a ride."

Robin had a reoccurring fantasy of necking with Lynn in the front seat of the Thunderbird, the upholstery creaking, the radio playing some of Mr. Tomasini's bebop, just like an old date movie come to life.

"That speed's long gone, baby," Stansell said, shaking his head. He tapped his cigarette ashes onto his jeans and rubbed them into the fabric. "That didn't last more than a day or two. Remember? I told you the other night."

Robin had convinced herself that Stansell was a convenience for Lynn, just as he was for her. He was a guy with money, a car, an agenda. Lynn swore she and Steve had never dated or slept together, but that he'd tried several times to get her into bed. They made out once, Lynn told Robin, during a party sophomore year, but this confession conjured up such disturbing images that Robin couldn't sleep for several nights. The years that Lynn had lived without knowing Robin seemed to Robin like the swirling, eternal time of an epoch, the period before the coming of the savior prince or the end of the plagues or the resurrection of the princess's honor.

"What color are you going to paint this?" Marqueese asked.

"I don't know if I will," Robin said.

"So it's just going to be the old white and primer and some Bondo?" Stansell asked. "That's stupid."

"I think it's so cool you're doing it," Lynn said. "I don't know any other girls who work on cars." Lynn took off her rabbit jacket, revealing a red, V-neck angora sweater. The garage fell silent.

While Robin worked, Stansell told a long story about how the mechanics at the dealership wanted to restore his Fairlane one way, but how he insisted they do it another way that took longer but that kept the original spirit of the car and how Big Steve said he was right all along, and how Stansell himself had helped preserve the car and increase its value.

"Grab a wrench and let's go," Robin said, interrupting him.

"I don't do the dirty work," Stansell said, holding up his hands. "Somebody's got to supervise."

"I don't see a supervisor in here," Robin said.

"Don't you?" Stansell said. He paused. "Anyway, that's the way of the world, somebody in charge and somebody doing the heavy lifting. That's what it's going to be when we're out of school."

"Same as now. I'm out anyway," Marqueese said.

"Oh, don't talk about it," Lynn said. "You're like my father. Maybe I'll just travel with Robin. Right, honey?"

Robin blushed and kept working. "I can't say," she said, her face in the car's engine.

"If I'm going to take over the dealership someday," Stansell said, "I've got to learn how to run things."

"Into the ground," Robin said.

"Shut up. Management," Stansell said. "You've got to do the job you were born for. Like, I'm not buying anymore."

"That'll be the day," Lynn said.

"No, listen," Stansell said. "I'm not buying, but I am selling. I'll front the money, but someone else can go get the stuff. They can live with the hassles, and I'll give them a piece and some product for all their trouble."

"A middleman," Robin said.

"Yeah. I already have somebody in mind, too." Stansell laughed. "Somebody who needs me more than I need him."

Marqueese, Robin thought, and he was too stupid to say no. Kendall and Ronald had scared the shit out of Stansell, and that was the truth behind this plan. The Simonsen way was no middleman, no meddling. You did the whole job yourself, and you pocketed all the profits. You got all the problems, too, but when you created them, you could figure out how to solve them.

"Robin," said a voice from outside the garage.

A pair of desert boots appeared in the gap under the garage door. Corduroy pants fell in perfect pleats to the tops of the shoes.

"Freddie?" Robin asked. "What are you doing? It's freezing." She rolled up the door. Freddie stood smiling on the driveway in a watch cap and red plaid jacket and huge black snowmobile gloves.

"It's late, Fred," Robin said. No one else greeted him.

"You're not going to believe this," Freddie said, his face alight. He ignored the people in the garage.

"What's wrong?" Robin said, wiping her hands. The sweat dried on her skin. "Get in here so I can close the door."

Now Freddie looked. "Naw, I'll wait out here," he said. "Robin," he whispered, "I got early admissions."

"What are you talking about?" Robin whispered back.

"What'd he say?" Stansell called.

"Shut up," Robin yelled over her shoulder.

"I got accepted to Yale, Rob," Freddie said. "Yale University. You know, in the East."

"Like New York?"

"Near there. Do you believe it? They called my guidance counselor the day before Thanksgiving."

"When did you apply?" Robin asked.

"Where's he going?" Lynn whispered.

"I didn't apply," Freddie said. "I inquired and I guess they found out my test scores or something."

"So how can they say you're in?" Robin asked.

"I don't know," Freddie said, shrugging. "They just did."

"I don't believe this," Robin said. "We were maybe going to apply to Northwestern or Wisconsin."

"I know." Freddie was silent for a moment. "But then you didn't do anything about it."

"You mean you went ahead without me?" Robin asked. "God, Fred."

"I didn't go ahead on anything," Freddie said. His nose was running. "It just happened. Anyway, my parents are all excited. Even Antoinette is crying and she doesn't know why."

Robin could feel her future behind her, clinging to the back of her head like a bat, breathing hard in her ear. She was embarrassed again by her stains and sweat and muscles. In Stansell's world she'd be a plow horse.

"Maybe I can apply to Yale University at the regular time," Robin said.

Freddie paused. "Sure," he said. "You'd probably get in."

"What do you mean?" Robin asked, stepping closer to Freddie. Her bony shoulders felt like metal hinges under the thin cotton of her tee shirt. The warmth of the garage leaked out onto her legs. Freddie towered over Robin, handsome and anxious and brainy and separate. She'd kissed this boy, she'd loved him since they were both the same size. "What do you mean, Freddie?" Robin asked. "We have the same grades. Of course I'd get in."

"It's other stuff, too."

"Like what?"

"Come on, Rob," Freddie said. "You didn't take the test yet. My counselor said there aren't many black kids with grades like mine. And in a place like Lilac."

On the same day, at the same time, Freddie could be both knocked down and lauded for the same characteristic. Right and left, people could make you who they wanted you to be—a mean, opportunistic black kid or an unthreatening scholarship boy. Robin was a smart poor kid and what else? A lecherous lover of girls. None of that translated to college. Robin hid her hands in her armpits. They were cut up and stained with grease.

"Thanks for telling me, Fred," Robin said, turning away. "Congratulations. Now you don't have to do all that application shit."

"Okay," Freddie said. He paused.

Robin ducked under the garage door and returned to the engine. She started to remove the valve rocker cover.

"Okay," Freddie called. He pulled down the garage door, then adjusted it. Finally, his soft footsteps receded.

"Yale? Jesus," Stansell said, sliding off the workbench.

You were born for it, and she had landed in the wrong family. Robin picked up her tools, but when she turned back to the Thunderbird she saw a hundred scattered parts. She had no idea what to do with them.

chapter ten

∼

Robin had a soft spot for the Duaneiacs, five gentle, music-besotted boys who hung out only with one another and who never bothered Lynn Nielsen except on the day during their junior year when she came to school wearing a halter top made out of a car chamois. Lynn's sudden appearance as biker chick and Southern swamp goddess all rolled into one sent them into near paroxysms of desire out in the Lilac High School smoking area.

To the Duaneiacs, the great Duane Allman and his guitar lived on. To them, he'd never died in a motorcycle accident, and the strings of his Les Paul still vibrated in the ether. In homage, the Duaneiacs grew their hair into long, lanky, uneven sheets that hung down below their jawlines. They stood in a bad-postured clump in the hallways, wearing low jeans and long-underwear shirts, their mouths ajar in imitation of either stoned distraction or guitar-playing orgasmic release. They tried to grow whiskers. The Duaneiacs even took turns wearing a metal guitar slide, which they treated like some kind of prosthetic talisman.

But on this cold December evening, all five Duaneiacs huddled in the snow-bedecked shrubbery of Post Park, grinning at Steve Stansell. The park was the first stop on Stansell's tour of Lilac's drug-using spots. He was diving into the trade, apparently with his new middleman, while Heath was coming out of it. He'd been back for a week, and in that time Robin had noticed her father's cold breeziness, his friendliness without affection. She saw no trace of the destroyed man who had helped her mother die. Her father's revelation now seemed false, as if his former self would confess to crimes he'd never committed just to further his deterioration. Not now. Heath was clean, smooth-cheeked, with trimmed hair, but oddly, Robin now thought, her father and the Duaneiacs seemed to share the same bright, sniffing look. The boys stood in a group in the frigid dark, merrily answering the questions Stansell yelled through the window of the Fairlane.

Robin leaned out the window and waved. She'd had a memorable debate with the Duaneiacs about whether Dicky Betts should even be allowed to *play* the late Duane's parts.

But now the boys looked aghast at Robin, as if she'd just cursed them. "It's me!" she called. "I know them, you know," she said, sitting back in her seat.

"They don't seem the same," Lynn said.

Maybe it was the nature of Stansell's business. Everywhere they went that night—into Post Park, the high school grounds, Fairview Park, where Stansell cruised past the empty swimming pool—they found shivering groups of high school kids, happily talking and chatting as if they were at a cocktail party and greeting Stansell with shouts. He was like a rancher visiting his scattered herd in the fields.

"Aren't these people freezing?" Robin asked. It was below zero, the snow hard and crunchy under the tires.

"They're feeling no pain," Stansell said happily. Robin had never seen him so even-tempered, so matter-of-fact. She didn't like it. He turned down Church Street.

Starting from the north end of the street were the Episcopal, Methodist, Lutheran, Baptist, and Presbyterian churches; on the four corners of Church and Stanley were Immaculate Conception, Visitation, another Lutheran, and Christian Scientist. Goldie refused to drive down Church Street, and once, years ago, Robin and Heath got caught in the snarl of Sunday traffic, which sent Heath into a flood of swearing, all with the truck window open.

As they passed Evangelical Lutheran, a group of kids came out the front doors. Stansell slowed down. Heading the group was Kitty Paint, hand in hand with a boy. Kitty was as tall as Lynn now, though she'd kept the same childish round face and flyaway brown hair. Her hips were outlined by her tight jeans. This was Kitty's real body, the one that had been straining for years to get out. And the boy: the fact that the Paints had put Kitty and David back into parochial school hadn't kept Kitty from her Jesus Freak friends, including Perry Flaygell, Lilac High's inveterate smiler, who held Kitty's hand.

Robin and Kitty saw each other. Robin put her hand to the window to wipe it clean, and Kitty mistakenly waved in response, happy and full, Robin imagined, of Perry's devotion to both Jesus and Kitty, in that order. Kitty seemed genuinely happy to see Robin's face, and she continued waving even after the car had passed. She had become pretty.

Stansell finished his rounds and drove Robin and Lynn to his house, where they were met by Billy Tree and Marqueese, two folded-up scarecrows on the front steps.

"Stansell's mom said we couldn't come in unless Stevie was here," Billy Tree said.

"I don't think she likes me," Marqueese said.

And no wonder, Robin thought: he looked like Rasputin, dark and devilish in his navy blue parka and watch cap.

"Hey, babe," he said to Robin.

Billy and Marqueese were also more chipper, sniffling and smiling. Something in the air, something in the water, maybe Christmas cheer: no, Stansell's drugs, no doubt about it. Perhaps he was administering anti-psychotic medicine to people who weren't crazy, pumping them up when they didn't really need it.

"You should put Marky out of his misery," Lynn whispered to Robin as they entered the house.

Robin was following Lynn toward the basement stairs when she heard someone call her name. She turned back, stopping in the doorway to the TV room. Mrs. Stansell sat in her chair, the three dogs in a ring around her feet. They lifted their wrinkled, sleepy faces, but as soon as they saw Robin, they lay their muzzles back on their paws and closed their eyes.

"*Touch of Evil*," Mrs. Stansell said. "A classic."

"Orson Welles, like, huge," Robin said. "And Marlene Dietrich, Charlton Heston, and Janet Leigh."

"Meow," Mrs. Stansell said.

Robin laughed. "Nineteen fifty-eight," she said.

"Okay, now that that's established," Marilyn said. "I'm halfway through. Watch the rest with me."

The room stunk of cigarettes and dog. Marilyn wore an old pair of jeans and a polo shirt. Her coppery hair stuck up all over her head. "Come on," she said, shaking the ice in her glass.

The room smelled, but it was also dark and confining—embracing. A matching green armchair sat next to Marilyn.

"Just a sec," Robin said.

When she told Stansell she was going to watch TV with his mother instead of party in the basement, he stopped in the middle of rolling a joint and accompanied her back upstairs.

"Mother," he said, hanging from the doorjamb, "is this true?" The dogs lifted their heads again and kept their muzzles pointed at Stansell, sniffing him.

"Steven, really," Marilyn said. "Go about your business. Sit down," she said to Robin, "it's coming back on."

Stansell gave Robin a warning look, as if she were being entrusted with a child.

"This idiot," Marilyn said, pointing her cigarette at the TV, "left our poor Janet—that's Heston's wife—in this motel. Now here comes trouble." A carload of partiers drove into the motel parking lot, jacked-up desert versions of Stansell and the rest of them, cruising Lilac.

"I know it," Robin said. "My grandma and I watched this a couple of times. It's been on a lot."

There followed several minutes of the interlopers turning up the music in their motel room and of Janet Leigh trying to find peace.

A commercial came on, but Marilyn continued to stare at the screen. "Steven's father and I are Republicans," she suddenly said. "Do you want something to drink? You can have a beer. I say, why fight it."

"No, thanks," Robin said. The thought of getting tipsy with Mrs. Stansell gave her butterflies. She imagined making all sorts of confessions, about Lynn, about her family, as gifts to Marilyn. "My dad's an anarchist," Robin said. "At least he says he is. He might be a socialist now."

"How is your father?" Marilyn asked, picking up a bottle of scotch from the floor and pouring some into her glass. "Feeling better?"

"What?"

"Cleaned up? Cleaned out? What do they call it?"

"How did you know about my dad?" Robin asked. Jesus, were there notices in the Lilac paper about addicts? Billboards featuring local junkies?

"You think I don't know what's going on with you kids," Marilyn said, sipping her drink. "For god's sake, I read the news. I know what you all are doing down there, how much it costs, even where my son gets it."

"Okay," Robin said. This was about Steve, after all. Marilyn probably thought Heath was responsible for corrupting him. Robin shifted in her chair, furious. All she'd wanted was an ear. And if Robin felt close to confession, maybe Marilyn did, too. She winced, imagining some whispered details about why the Stansells slept in separate bedrooms.

"You probably think, what *kind* of mother is this woman." Marilyn laughed. "But for crying out loud, I could scream and throw fits and either nothing would happen or I'd be out a son. Even part of something or someone you love is worth it. Steve is half here, at least, taking up some kind of space." Marilyn looked around the room. "This is a big house," she said.

The movie had started again. "And, just for the record," Marilyn continued, talking over the TV, "I think it's my *son's* fault for leading you down that rotten road. I don't blame you at all. Even Steven tells me what a good student you are."

Stansell talked about her? Thought about her? Heath had been right years ago when he said intelligence more than anything else really got under people's skin.

"Now here's trouble come to the door," Marilyn said, pointing her cigarette at the TV.

In *Touch of Evil*, the partiers had broken into Janet Leigh's motel room. Some of them held her down, others circled her bed.

"There, see? See?" Mrs. Stansell asked. "That's Mercedes McCambridge, dressed like a boy. A woman dressed like a boy! Strange, huh?"

The partiers looked at Janet Leigh as if they wanted to swallow her whole. Mrs. Stansell watched avidly. Robin got out of her chair.

"It's not over yet," Mrs. Stansell said. "Where are you going?"

"I should really go downstairs," Robin said, backing up toward the door.

Mrs. Stansell just shrugged. "You won't find any surprises there."

But Marilyn was wrong. Stansell had taken the big Budweiser mirror from over the wet bar and covered it with what Robin assumed was cocaine. It was the first time Stansell had brought it out; before tonight Robin had thought about cocaine as a rumor, nothing solid.

"Hold on," Robin said, steadying Lynn's hand. "You're going to blow it all over."

It was Stansell's hundred-dollar bill, of course, rolled into a tight tube to snake along the mirror. Lynn chased the white powder across the glass; it looked like a flood moving in reverse. Robin held Lynn's hair.

"Good shit," Marqueese said.

Robin bent to the ritual. Marqueese reached to hold her hair back and she swatted him away. After she was done, she sat up, and then her nose seemed to rear back and begin to run.

"You guys," Tree said, "it's my birthday."

"Happy happy," Stansell said, chopping the coke on the mirror.

Lynn squealed and gave Billy a hug. Then she touched her forehead. "Whoa!" she cried. "Now I really feel it."

"How much does this cost?" Robin asked.

"What do you care?" Stansell asked.

"I'm just curious." She'd read about cocaine in *Time* magazine, in the *Tribune,* even in the Lilac newspaper. The press had jumped all over what they thought was a new drug. Some kind of mysterious market forces had made it popular again. Feelings of confidence, even arrogance, flooded Robin's body. This was a drug for people who wanted to be winners.

Stansell's basement had the bar, two couches and a cocktail table, rejected exercise equipment, and four complete sets of expensive-looking golf clubs. A LeRoy Neiman painting of someone taking a golf swing hung next to the bar. Now, though, Robin saw the room for what it was: a dumping ground. Despite the bar, the expensive wood trim around the doors, the discreet exits and entrances to the laundry room and the furnace room, and all the other separate rooms rich people needed, this was a straining, overly optimistic space. This was where you put stuff nobody wanted or played with anymore; it was where you let your son break the law while you sat above him. This was the way it was with rich people: if you didn't see it, it didn't exist.

"God, huh?" Robin whispered to Lynn. She sniffed. The denim of her jeans seemed softer; Tree looked almost innocent; Marqueese's lust was suddenly so palpable that it clicked into Robin's veins.

"Hmm," was all Lynn would say. She sniffed. She sat with her usual perfect posture, back erect, breasts high, her hair streaming.

There was the phalanx of boys, always the boys. That's what they were, too, just boys, not men-in-training, not Heath, not flattened males like Tom McAfee. Just boys. Robin could see their assumptions, their assurance, their rock-solid belief that what they wanted and what they could get was the same thing. Robin felt their desire; all of the boys' energy, all of their yearning, was directed at Lynn. But not this Lynn, another Lynn. What distinguished Robin's desire was that she was in love with the particular, not the general. If you knew this, if you looked hard enough, the boys lost some of their threat. Stansell chattered away, snorting up the fattest lines. It was only fair: he had found it, he had bought it, he was teaching them all how to appreciate the drug. "Some of the guys on my dad's lot are doing coke," he said. "And like stockbrokers and actors do it, people who can get the best." This *boy*, Robin thought: *I'm Okay, You're Okay* under his bed, with an inscription from his mother, who sat each night in palpable loneliness. This *boy:* You are small, Robin thought, smaller than you want to be. Stansell's wide shoulders filled his denim shirt. Robin saw a child in a large body, a blustering boy, stamping his feet.

Robin stroked Lynn's back, her hand grazing the fabric of her sweater. Here was a true beauty, the girl picked to receive the full power of all Robin's sexual desires, which waited inside her like a tight flower bud. She felt certain that if she could only lay hands on Lynn, hands that spoke of all her desperation and devotion, the two of them would be together. In the summer sun that was coming—Robin could feel the earth tilt to the south, ever so slightly—Lynn would sit next to her in the Thunderbird, the capsule that would take them purring and smiling into their life together.

"This is great," Robin said loudly, interrupting Stansell. "This is really great."

"Honey," Lynn said, laughing, her own eyes shiny and farseeing. She knew, Robin thought. She saw it all, too.

"The best part is," Stansell said, "it's money in the bank. Lots and lots and lots of money in the bank."

∼

She decided to crank it up. Why not? Everyone else was. Cocaine was a revelation, a drug finally worthy of a whole book and a philosophy like Baba Ram Dass's *Be Here Now*. Only cocaine's book would be called *Be Do Go*. Robin wanted to find Simon Furton to tell him, to encourage him to convert, but Stansell said Simon had sold a load of his homemade acid and split to India. He had his own pursuit; Robin had hers. Stansell talked endlessly about the great setup he had, how with just a small investment, he and his middleman were rolling in dough. "I sit here, he goes out, the money comes in for both of us," Stansell said. A parasite, Robin thought, looking at Marqueese, who never betrayed anything. A sap. A poor kid who wants the easy life Stansell has, but who doesn't realize that Stansell's ease comes at his expense. Stansell, the benevolent papa, gave everyone in their small group gold metal straws he'd had specially made which were closed on the top, with a side vent you could hold against the inside of your nostril. The best part about coke was that you never needed to want it. It came along, you sniffed it up, then you felt your resolve, your strength, your very personality, rise effortlessly to meet it.

Since his return in late December from wherever, and his new, more groomed look, Heath Simonsen had undertaken no less than a vast restructuring and remodeling of the family home and life. This movement seemed to require new and more stuff, a simple transition from junk and others' castoffs to brand-new goods. Robin didn't see the house's clutter reduced, merely prettified.

In January, Heath bought a 1976 Ford truck. A week later, Grandma got a new washer and dryer and a ring with an emerald chip in it. A few days after that, Larry came over with boxes of the cleanest T-Bird parts Robin had ever seen, insisting he'd gotten them from some relative; she didn't need any of them, but they looked good. Then Robin came home to find men up on ladders, hammering. For the first time in memory, Heath had hired someone to work on the house, in this case to put siding on the second floor. No more tar paper and plywood and plastic crackling in the wind. The paneled trucks still backed up to the garage at least once a week, sometimes displacing Robin as she worked on the Thunderbird. She tried not to notice the unmarked boxes of whatever Tommy, Larry, and Heath pushed into a corner. Tommy Boy supervised, claiming a war injury kept him from lifting and hauling. "Prison fight," Goldie whispered to Robin.

At first, Robin sat through these additions and changes and revelations like the still point in a piece of speeded-up film, incredulous, suspicious, full of dread, her head barely able to keep up with the bustle that money seemed to bring. She was used to the frantic push to acquire things, but it took a lot of energy to spend so much cash, especially when you were in a hurry to get rid of it, as her father and grandmother seemed to be.

"Lookit, sweetie," Goldie said one day. She pointed to the kitchen island where a new, shiny toaster stood. "I'm afraid to use it," she added.

That same week Grandma came home from Oakbrook with a nutria jacket. The brown pelts drooped; Goldie's coat still didn't look as nice as Lynn's bunny jacket. Grandma's nutria had huge brass buttons, too, with a rhinestone in the center of each one. She called up Rex and in Norwegian described the coat, stroking the fur as she did.

Heath's customers were more single-minded than ever. His own reform seemed to have inspired his clientele, or else he was attracting a different class of people. Robin really did see "class" in them, too: some attempt to project a certain style, a certain way of thinking, a kind of careless freedom that never risked deterioration or debauchery. These customers belonged to a new kind of caste system. They drove good cars, wore neater clothes, charged up the back stairs as if taking exercise, and they didn't linger. They seemed to have jobs.

Heath responded like a psychologist instead of a dealer. He had turned down the volume of both his voice and the music he played upstairs. Robin heard a mild bumping through her ceiling. On the phone Heath was ingratiating, expansive, generous. He told Robin that selling drugs was like giving gifts. Desperation was a thing of the past. You took money, but the product was so intimate, like granting someone a new personality or outlook or temperament. Afterward, nothing was left for the user except a memory of feeling better. Heath told Robin selling drugs was like creating a cult. Bring the dealer money and he grants you wisdom. Robin's father was responsible not for others' well-being, but for others' ability to distill the meaning and beauty of themselves into one dose. I make people happier, better, he told Robin. Heath Simonsen as Baba Ram Dass.

Heath was trimmer, tighter. Still, there was his beautiful hair, rippling about his shoulders. Robin thought there was something perverse about the fact that her father's hair had survived all the years of abuse that his body couldn't hide. It was like the new siding the workers had hammered over the crappy construction on the second floor. Heath began leaving Robin gifts of clothes, envelopes of cash, books. He didn't know what to do with his money: soon they all had new TVs in their bedrooms, the living room hi-fi was replaced with Heath's old Bang & Olufsen; he got a new one. One day, Robin watched her father pull into the driveway in a brand-new Pontiac Grand Prix. A few weeks later came a new bedroom set for Goldie. Then Grandma bought a short, sequined dress and diminutive pearl earrings that got lost in her hair, got out her good crocodile handbag, the one Rex had bought for her years ago in the Sands gift shop, and wore the whole outfit to a club in Chicago, accompanied by young George.

Another day, while Robin was in the kitchen doing her homework, the back door burst open, and three of her father's derelict friends plus Tom McAfee pulled in a huge blue sofa, which they then propelled up the back stairs. The next day this same crew wrestled in a new television set.

Under Goldie's direction, a team of men from Sears shampooed the living room carpet. When the material disintegrated under their cleaning machines, Grandma ordered new brown shag.

Tommy Boy bought a new Mercury from the Stansell lot and drove Robin around in it so she could hear the stereo and feel the air conditioning, which he fired full blast on her thighs, ignoring the late-winter cold outside. Robin powered down the window and hung her head out like a dog, but when Tommy coasted home down the Highland Street hill, she had trouble recognizing her own house.

"I always thought it would be cool to have a real home," Robin said, standing with Freddie one day in the middle of Highland. They watched a group of men, some of them Heath's old customers, haul brush and chop down dried weeds in the snow-patched backyard. "I mean, now our place looks more like yours," she said.

"I guess," Freddie said. "There's still the bus."

Tom McAfee, a wraith on the steps, watched Robin and Freddie watch the workers. Heath's fortunes had risen, but Tom stayed the same, an old fence post in mud.

"But, I don't know," Robin said, "you just get used to your life the way it is. Now when Grandma's friends come over, they're like, where do I sit down? The old kitchen table's gone, and now there's this wood dinette set, and the whole room smells like a Swiss cottage or something. Larry Pike brought over an old cuckoo clock, but it's broken already."

Freddie laughed. A long-haired man in overalls swung a scythe through the tall grass, his figure framed in the space between the house and the garage. "Jesus," Robin said. "Where am I?" She'd been surprised to see these same guys at Stansell's house the week before, shoveling snow and moving rock. Clearly, her father hadn't brought any of his old friends up with him; instead, they had to farm themselves out to rich people.

Freddie ignored her. She caught him staring at a short man with a cigarette stuck between his lips who was dragging several big maple branches into the front yard. Up the hill, Freddie's family was already preparing for his departure to Yale. Freddie said his grandmother had sent him a set of cardboard suitcases that his grandfather had used when he came up from South Carolina to Chicago. His aunts gave him handkerchiefs embroidered with his initials. A great-uncle who was a mortician in Gary set up a bank account for Freddie in New Haven, depositing the first fifty dollars. Mrs. Eakins compulsively bought shirts at Sears. Robin was already worried that when Freddie got to Yale he'd no longer be Freddie, that his whole being would alter, like her father's had. In its place would be a refined Freddie, an upright version of Heath's tonier customers, a young man sitting and reading in a swanky, wood-paneled dorm room, but with another boy, someone like him. Robin knew this boy, he was out there, waiting for Freddie, packing his suitcases for Yale full of Oxford shirts and khaki pants, and books, dozens of books.

"My adviser says I might not be valedictorian," Freddie said. He'd taken off his jacket and rolled up the sleeves of his shirt.

"Those look like bruises," Robin said.

"They said Susan Nagler is like one tenth of a grade point better than I am," Freddie said. "They have to go by the rules, by the points."

"Did you hurt yourself in gym?" Robin asked. For years, Freddie had worked on excuses to get out of gym class: colds, sprained ankles, possible asthma. The P.E. teachers would park him in a folding chair on the sidelines, the pages of the book he was always reading ruffling in the breezes the other kids made as they ran up and down the floor.

Freddie looked down at his arm. "It's not gym." When he raised his head again, his eyes were wet.

"Jesus, what's wrong?" Robin lowered her voice to a whisper, looking to make sure that the yard workers didn't hear her.

"It's a guy," Freddie whispered, his voice shaking.

"Tim!"

"Not Tim."

"Who?" Freddie had never mentioned another boy.

"I can't say."

"Freddie, Jesus." The bruises circled his forearms, as if someone had been holding him. "What's this guy doing to you?"

Freddie shook his head. "No, not what you think. No way. It's just he's strong and I'm strong, and it happens."

"What happens?" The guy with the cigarette had stopped working and was watching them.

Freddie looked shocked, as if she'd got a wrong answer. "Well, I'm not going to *explain* it, Robin! It's just such a huge secret. Nobody can know anything."

"But *I* don't know anything," Robin said. She imagined one of Stansell's hangers-on shoving Freddie up against the locker, while another jerk held his arms.

"He even says he loves me," Freddie whispered.

A different kind of shoving, then. Different holding. Where could Freddie be doing this? How? "Oh, my god, Fred," Robin said. "Who is this guy?"

"I told you, it's too huge. What do you think is going to happen if I tell?"

"When?" Robin asked. "When?"

"I have to go," Freddie said, looking at his wrist. The bruises circled the bone like another watchband. "I want you to stop worrying about me all the time," he said, looking sternly at Robin. "Really. Stop worrying."

"You can't go to Yale," Robin said.

"My parents are already planning a graduation party. You're coming."

"Fred." But he had turned to walk up the hill. Robin watched him stride away, but she didn't see him as he was, tall, broad-shouldered, with a thick head of hair; instead she saw him at twelve, under the shifting sunlight, embarrassed at the sight of someone he loved but could never want.

The yard workers loaded their equipment and debris into an ancient truck. Robin gave a start: it was her father's old Ford. The workers got into the truck and started it up. The familiar rattle of the Ford engine was like the voice of a dead person. Robin felt stunned, bereft. She turned, but Freddie had already crested the hill. On her way into the house, Robin noticed the willow tree reflected as clearly and sharply in the picture window as if it were a photograph. As she came closer, she could see the new living room set inside, the new curtains, even the new television in its wooden cabinet. Someone had cleaned the glass.

～

Every morning while she ate her cereal, Robin watched her father's impassive face. Every day, Heath got up on Robin's schedule, showered and dressed in a shirt and nice jeans, sometimes even pants, and pulled his long hair into a tight ponytail. He wore a watch, a thick, expensive-looking model that worked underwater. Robin was too taken by the fact that her father now had to keep track of time to wonder why he'd have to do so while swimming—or drowning. Heath left the house after his toast and coffee, his old mailbag replaced by what he called a "vintage" satchel with a stranger's initials stamped on it, and he drove off to work his magic from his office, which was the Grand Prix.

Robin hated the change. Her father was brittle, crisp, almost efficient, reminding her of an officious husband, one of the characters parodied on *Mary Hartman, Mary Hartman,* Grandma's favorite new TV show. Robin was glad to see the return of her father's prodigious energy and twitchiness, but now he channeled it into the pursuit of desires instead of the desires themselves. The chase defined the want. Heath was dating again, after a dry spell of nearly a year, except now he took women to Chicago, to clubs and movies, and to concerts at Arie Crown and the Amphitheater. These women were coiffed and better dressed than Heath's past dates, women with money, and they shared Heath's clipped attitude, walking quickly as if something were nipping at their heels.

Robin worked at school as if she too were going to Yale, and she matched her scholastic efforts with the final repairs on the Thunderbird. It would never be a show car, but she had fixed it herself and it suited her: it held some family history, but also her fingerprints. Robin didn't want a prettified life. She wanted things *as they were:* love, work, even possessions.

Robin wrote a long term paper for her economics elective in which she analyzed the budget of the Lilac Police Department and divided its spending on particular types of crimes. Money for drug busts won out over spending on assaults and robberies, a fact that Robin criticized in her paper. Mr. Palczek gave her an A, but he put a large question mark next to Robin's conclusion, in which she argued for the legalization of marijuana as a cost-cutting measure. Freddie, who was in the same class, also got an A for his project on the economic history of the Fox River, which came complete with a papier-mâché river barge, little straw-hatted figures waving from its bow. He and Robin barely talked to each other. Robin watched Freddie's locker, his trips through the hallways, but there was no boy at his side, only the good, sexless girls. Freddie's secret life must take place in another universe: that meant another town, not Lilac, a place where someone like Freddie could be naked and—at that point Robin couldn't imagine anymore. Freddie's success, no matter how painful, was her failure with Lynn. What would it be like to stop yearning?

The spring arrived glorious, the days warm and the nights cool, and every evening the sun struck up a lemon and lavender sky that sent even Goldie and the men and Heath outside to watch the sinking, glowing orb. The Hazens came out, too, Strudel sniffing the air. On the other side of the Simonsens, the Corners struggled outside just so they could turn their shaky heads toward the sunset.

One night the whole Bogat family appeared, having risen up still chewing from the dinner table; they stood on the front lawn clutching their napkins.

"Jesus," Heath said, "maybe it's the end of the world."

chapter eleven

~

She had to be a new kind of daughter. There was no other way to figure it. Before, Heath and Goldie had stumbled ahead, dragging Robin along with them, but never looking back to see if she was keeping up. Now they merely glanced up as she raced by. New possessions fueled them; they didn't order their lives, they were the same mess of desires, they still had no thought of turning their attention to Robin. Robin thought she'd exceeded their expectations of her, if they'd ever had any. After all, if she could organize twenty years of junk, if she could refurbish a car, then she could do anything, even be an adult. Overnight, Robin acquired a new status: she was the family's well-oiled machine, the generator that ran without a sound, and she was also the family bulldog—the protector.

Robin's grandfather, Rex Simonsen, the restaurateur down in Corpus Christi, Texas, had never been more than a photograph of a strapping Westerner in dark-framed glasses, with a huge stack of white hair and a mustache, or a gravelly, slightly accented voice on the phone asking for Goldie. Rex never talked to Robin or Heath. Long ago, Grandma explained that her husband never really wanted a family life, so as soon as Goldie got pregnant, Rex left Las Vegas for Texas and became a name on monthly checks and on the title of each year's new Cadillac. Rex kept Grandma afloat. So when Robin came home from school one day in April and found her grandmother sobbing over Rex's portrait, she thought he had died.

"Your—grandfather." Goldie struggled to get the words out. "The goddamn bastard."

Rex had finally sunk her. The money was gone.

"I wish he was dead!" Grandma yelled, shedding fresh tears.

Tommy Boy pulled into the driveway at top speed. He and Larry got out of the car and ran for the front door.

"What happened?" Robin asked her grandmother. "Where's Dad?"

Goldie's chest heaved under strings of plastic beads. She poked at her eyes with a tissue. "Your *grandfather*," she said. "Here!" she cried, handing a snapshot to Robin.

It had been creased and then flattened out. In the picture was a craggier and thinner Rex with his arm around a much younger woman with long brown hair and honey-colored skin. Her smile was a perfect V. In the woman's arms lay a newborn baby dressed in a blue sleeper. He had a full head of spiky brown hair and deep blue eyes.

"That's your grandfather!" Goldie cried. "And that's Pinky."

The men barged in. "We got your call," Larry said, breathless. "Don't do nothing rash, Goldie," he added.

"Who is Pinky?" Robin asked.

Grandma sniffed and sat up straight. "Pinky Bacho is Rex's paramour. She was just the hostess at your grandfather's restaurant until she got her claws into him."

"So who's the baby?" Robin asked. He was so big, he bowed Pinky's skinny arms.

"That *child*," Goldie said, "belongs to your grandfather."

"Holy shit!" Larry cried.

"Aw, honey," Tommy said, patting Goldie's arm.

"Wait a minute," Robin said, "you mean I'm related to this baby?"

"The little bastard *and* the big bastard," Goldie said.

"Now he's just a baby, Goldie," Larry said. "He can't help it."

"He's my uncle!" Robin cried. "Isn't he?"

"Half," Goldie said. "*Half* uncle, if he's anything. Bastard."

"Again," Larry said, "just a baby."

"Does Dad know?" Robin asked.

"You see, honey," Tommy said to Robin, "this Pinky is Mexican, so she's got a different idea about having babies and whatnot. She saw a good thing in your grandpa, so she hung on, marriage or no marriage. He's a cute little thing, though, in' he?"

Grandma wailed and tried to hit Tommy.

"Where's Dad?"

"Your father is upstairs," Grandma said. "Can't you hear him?" She blew her nose.

All Robin heard was Sinatra cooing from the living room. She grabbed the photo and ran up the back steps, calling for her father.

"Don't come in!" he said.

Robin stopped at the top of the stairs. "Dad, listen!"

"Just a second, honey." Robin heard clothes rustling, then a zipper. "Okay," her father said.

"Dad, is somebody there?" Once, several years ago, Robin had run into her father's room to find a woman sleeping in his bed, a sheet across her middle, the rest of her nude.

"Nope," Heath said. "Come on."

"Guess what?" Robin asked, running in and flopping down on her father's bed.

Heath was standing in the middle of his room wearing just a pair of jeans. The dresser mirror still stood opposite the bed. On the floor lay a barbell and dumbbell with several weights attached.

"What is it, Robin?" Heath asked. His face was flushed.

"Listen, Grandma got a letter and a picture from Grandpa in Texas, and he's got a *baby*! See?"

"You're shitting me!" Heath laughed. He wouldn't take the photo. "Who with?" he asked.

"Somebody named Pinky."

"Jesus, he's been with her since she was a girl practically. That old bastard."

"That's what Grandma said."

"I bet she did."

"Dad, the baby's my *uncle*."

"I guess you're right."

"And, Dad, listen, that baby's your *brother*."

"Well, not really," her father said, crossing his arms.

Robin tried not to see her father's skin. Soon after Heath had returned from wherever, she had walked in on him sleeping in the bathtub. His body had looked remarkably pale and old, and his chest and arms, even his stomach, were dotted with small scabs, as if he'd worked over dozens of mosquito bites. The scars were still there, though Heath was starting to fill out.

"Isn't that cool, Dad?" Robin asked. "It's like a new family."

"Let's go talk to your grandmother," Heath said, pulling on a tee shirt. He had sharper muscles, less bulk than when he had been hauling junk. Now his body looked stringy and strong.

Goldie was still dabbing at her eyes. Tommy had poured drinks for everyone.

"Heath," Grandma said. "Do you believe?"

"So is the old man going to cut you off now?"

"Well, no. He didn't say that."

"What did he say?"

"That he'd keep up the payments."

"Then what's your beef?" Heath asked. He lit a cigar.

"It's the principle," Goldie said.

"Ma, may I remind you that you're jumping generations yourself. Or humping, as the case may be. You've been as busy as Rex. Busier."

"Your mother's suffering here," Tommy said.

"Listen, don't you guys hold your breath waiting for her," Heath said. He pointed to Tommy and Larry. "Neither of you: don't hold your breath."

Grandma started crying again. "You never did have any sympathy for anybody," she said. Heath pulled an Old Style out of the refrigerator. "You probably like it that you've got a little bastard for a brother," Grandma said.

"I feel no pain, Ma," Heath said. He left the house.

Goldie rubbed her eyes with the tissue and sighed. "This happened to a gal I danced with for a couple of years," she said. "Bitsy. We called her Little Bitsy because she couldn't have been over five five, and that was short for a dancer." Grandma sipped her drink. "Anyway, Bitsy married this good-luck fellow who always had a marker to pay at the casinos, and then his real wife shows up towing two kids to one of our shows and I have to keep Bitsy from kicking the witch in the chops from the stage. You know, make it look like a little whoopsee because the witch doesn't know about Bitsy, and what does the good-timer care. What was *that* bastard's name? I don't recall. This guy, he's telling Bitsy he's in import-export and all when he's really a beer distributor from Logan, Utah, and how much money are you going to make carting beer all over a Mormon state? After those kids and the mother showed up, Bitsy sold his ring and forgot him, and in a week or two she was all over the floor manager, who was married, too. I had to fill in for her for a few days. We had these costumes made us look like little fishies, and then the opening singer would come out with a line and a hook and a net. It was pretty cute. The fins were this long . . ."

"Grandma, that's not the same thing at all," Robin said.

There was a pounding on the front door.

"Yeah!" Grandma yelled.

A slab-shaped man appeared in the kitchen. He wore a toupee and a chain bracelet. Parrots ran riot over his shirt.

"Who are you?" Robin asked.

"Are you Otelia Simonsen?" the man asked Goldie.

"Why?" she asked.

"Are you Otelia Simonsen?" the man said again. He had the labored breathing of a bulldog.

"Yes," Goldie said.

"You have been formally served," the man said, pulling a piece of paper from his shirt pocket and giving it to Goldie.

"Oh, no, you don't," she said. The man left. "Get back here!" she called.

"What now?" Tommy asked.

"This must be some business my son's dragged me into," Grandma said, reading the paper. Then she screamed.

Larry grabbed the paper. "Holy cow! Your granny's been named a correspondent in *two* divorce cases," he said to Robin. "Seems both the Misses Bogdanases are fighting mad."

"Ay, carumba," Tommy said, pulling his pint bottle from his jacket. Goldie beat her forehead against the table and cried.

Robin's muscles stiffened. Everyone she loved, including her new baby uncle, dangled from a thread at the edge of her life, ready to fall. She was furious; it was too much to be the one who knew where everything was, where it all belonged. It was too much to be in charge of people who were always in danger of disappearing. You couldn't just curve out your arm and scoop up every member of your family. She grabbed Tommy's pint bottle and ran from the house.

The man was backing out in his rusty station wagon, trying not to steer into the ditch near the road. Robin tore down the driveway, taking aim at the car.

"Stay away from us, you son-of-a-bitch!" she screamed, and fired the bottle at the wagon, neatly shattering the windshield just as the man pulled out and roared up Highland hill.

∽

Heath might as well have been mainlining Novocain. Not only could he be perversely cheery and generous, passing out money at the breakfast table—no food for him, thanks!—or organizing a crew of his old wasted buddies to blacktop the driveway, but the next minute the same cheeriness became a chilly disregard for other people's feelings or even for his own unhappiness.

Heath refused to look at the photograph of his father and his new half brother, Miguel. "Listen, kiddo," he said to Robin, after days of her beseeching him just to take a look, wasn't the baby cute? "Rex wasn't my dad when I was a kid, he's not my dad now, so I can't have any brothers by him. You can think what you like."

Robin kept the creased photograph, taping it to the wall next to her closet. She searched Miguel's face for any trace of her own features, but all she saw was a mammoth baby who could belong to anyone.

After Goldie calmed down, and once she'd had several rounds of drinks with the men and done a quick evaluation of the new finances, plus consulted with a lawyer Tommy Boy had heard of from some ex-con friend, she filed her own lawsuit against the Bogdanas women for defamation of character. In no time, the kitchen became the scene of strategy sessions.

For years, both Old Man Bogdanas and his son, George, had pretended that they didn't know the other was having an affair with Goldie. So when father and son came over the day of the subpoena and heard the news, they were obligated to get into a clinch in the driveway that then turned into grappling and wrestling and ended with Old Man giving George a black eye. George stood in the driveway crying and saying that he couldn't bring himself to hit his own father. The whole thing played out like a myth.

There was no Greek chorus though, just Tom McAfee like a statue barely alive, sentient enough to observe from the margins but never to respond. The kids who had once spent every afternoon on the bus with Tom had grown up and gone off, and for a while new recruits came. But as Tom deteriorated, more quickly and more severely than Heath, the kids stopped coming, and Robin only saw him when he sat alone on the bus steps or during his rare visits to the Simonsens' shower. Heath said he usually bathed out of the same bucket he washed his clothes in.

Still, Robin had come to think of Tom McAfee as a permanent fixture, a kind of gargoyle, so she was alarmed one Saturday afternoon when Stansell and Lynn dropped her off and she found Heath, dressed in black pants and a gray shirt, his hair back in a slick ponytail, yelling at Tom in the driveway. Tom looked as if he'd barely returned from the dead. His face was squinched up and his features blurred, his hair a wiry tangle, and his shirt buttoned wrong.

"How long and how much?" Heath was asking.

"I don't know what you're saying, man," Tom McAfee said. "Hey, Robin," he added, giving her a crooked smile.

"I give you a place to stay," Heath continued. "Rent free. You can come and go. You eat with us."

"When did I ever?" Tom asked. "I'm living on beer and crackers out here."

"So you steal from me," Heath said. "That's a great way to show gratitude, asshole."

Tom looked like a stomped-on version of Robin's father not eight months ago. Weary, wrecked, a racked and slat-limbed remnant of a different man. Tom also looked bewildered: how did the rules change in a house where there were none to begin with?

For the first time, though, Robin didn't hear Tom McAfee's second voice; she had no sense, despite his slack features and still-stuttering mouth, that he was really leaving something unsaid. Whatever had been behind all his words and gestures in the past had now been rubbed away. He was what he was: almost gone.

"Dad, Dad," Robin said. "This is old news. You don't remember, but I told you about Tom getting in the cash box a long time ago. A long time. But he stopped. Right, Tom? What's the point now?"

"Kiddo," her father said, "you don't know what's going on. I'm concerned with now. The cash box is empty. I checked today."

"Maybe Grandma took it for the lawyer," Robin said.

"Yeah, man," Tom said. "Ever think of that?"

Heath looked like he was going to relent, but then he took a deep breath and continued. "I'm getting rid of the bus, Tom," he said. "You're going to have to find other accommodations."

"Aw, come on, Heath," Tom said, his eyes cloudy. "I'm in no condition to move or anything. You know what I'm saying here. No condition."

Tom had fresh scabs on his forearms and neck. His teeth looked shriveled. Robin studied the bus, so she wouldn't look at him too hard; she felt her glance could topple him, crack his skull. He was Heath uncooked and soft, unsaved.

"Listen, Tom," Heath said, "I've got some phone numbers for you.

I just can't do this anymore, brother. You know. And not after the stealing."

"I didn't take any money!" Tom yelled, the violence of his outburst almost knocking him over. "At least not for years, man. Come on, I'm telling the truth here."

"But you did, Tom," Heath said evenly. "Robin just said so. It doesn't matter when you do a thing, that kind of act has reverberations."

"Repercussions," Robin couldn't help whispering.

Then her father looked at his underwater watch. "I'm having the bus towed away this weekend," he said. "Come in the house later, and I'll give you that information." With that he got into his Grand Prix and drove off.

"Jesus, man, oh, Jesus," Tom said, shaking his head. "Robin, talk to your dad. What's happened to him anyway? I don't even know the guy."

Who was her father now? He was driven, but he folded, he collapsed like Tom McAfee did on his weakest days, and only for one thing: a deep, abiding desire for money. Not enjoyment or oblivion—only greed, which had taken on a menacing, blind shape that was blinding Heath in turn.

Robin was dreaming that night when her father called her. His voice came out of the dark and grew louder, yet no figure ever appeared. Just his voice, insistent, demanding that Robin find him.

And then Heath's face was above hers and the darkness was her own room.

"Get up, honey," her father said.

"What's wrong?" Robin asked. "Grandma," she said.

"She's fine. In fact, she's not here. Come on."

Her father wore jeans and a tee shirt, but he was barefoot. He practically ran from the house. Robin put on some clothes and followed him outside.

The bus was ablaze with lights, a pile of garbage at the bottom of its stairs.

"Help me," her father said, as Robin climbed into the bus.

"What are you doing? Where's Tom?"

"He's already left," Heath said. He poured out the contents of a cardboard box. Rolling papers, file folders, a plastic baby doll, seeds, and a flannel shirt fell to the floor. "Help me clean," Heath said.

Robin's father looked at her with urgency. His face was a little flushed and he sniffled. His eyes were glassy, wide awake.

"What time is it?" Robin asked.

"I don't know," Heath said. "One, two, maybe three." He pulled the blankets off of the army cot and threw them on the floor. "I think some of our stuff is in here. This is what I'm saying, baby, he took it."

"What stuff? You're crazy, Dad." Crushed glass covered the floor in the corner; Robin watched her father's bare feet skirt the edge of it.

"Here," Heath said, pointing at a pile of blankets and boxes at the front of the bus. "Start there."

"What am I looking for?" Robin asked. She pulled two moth-eaten blankets off the pile; she recognized one of them as having been on her mother's sickbed. A box full of old baggies, cracker packages, assorted Maybelline makeup, a roach clip, a pipe, loose pot that you could tell by the smell was stale. "There's nothing here."

"Look," her father said, standing up. He held a framed photograph of Kim Novak. "This is Grandma's. See?"

"I'll take it," Robin said. Kim Novak looked worried. She looked worried in her movies, too, always set upon by men, too big to be elegant, just a curvy body, walking sex. She was one of Goldie's favorite actresses. "She's got that tragic face," Grandma always said, before she explained, for the umpteenth time, that Kim had been born a poor Polish girl and rose to stardom against everybody's predictions. The photograph was a bad print, flat and dull, a sample picture that came with the frame. The glass was crosshatched with scratches.

Heath worked furiously, pouring boxes of stuff onto the floor, kicking around the contents. Robin made her desultory way through a few piles. Almost everything she saw had once belonged to the Simonsens, as the junkiest of their junk. "Didn't Tom have any of his own stuff?" she asked.

"Aha!" her father cried, holding up a pruning saw.

Robin looked out the window, wondering where Tom might be. Was he lurking right outside, ready to burst in and gather up all his junk? Who would give him new things?

They worked for over an hour, until Robin heard the first bird chirp and saw an edge of light in the east.

Finally her father sank down into one of Tom's lawn chairs. His chest heaved. He lit a cigar and surveyed the wreckage.

"Are you happy?" Robin asked him. "You got an old picture and a saw. Big deal."

"It's the principle," Heath said. "And doesn't this look better now? I'll get rid of this pile of shit, inside and out." He paused. "Listen, kiddo, I wanted to talk to you anyway."

"In the middle of the night?"

"Sure. Rob, what are you going to do after school?"

"I want to go to college," Robin said.

"Well, yeah, but I mean, until you can do that."

"Get a job."

"But honey, I was thinking, you know, I'm making money now, and we've still got stuff that Grandma and her boys bring in, so money's okay for once. I was thinking, why not take our expertise, and time, which we have because of the money, and why not start an antique business?"

"You already did that," Robin said.

"High-end this time. The good stuff. Chippendale, Queen Anne. You'd be surprised the goodies these old farmers are hiding out in Kane and McHenry. And now that they're selling out to the new developers, they're willing to go cheap. We could clean up."

"You're asking me to sell furniture. We're going into business together?" Robin saw them in the Grand Prix, driving around the farmland with a map and a checkbook. No one in her family had ever had a checkbook.

"Grandma's still got her finger in some things, even though she's a little distracted at the moment."

"You could do the talking," Robin said. "I could fix up stuff. It's got to be easier than cars."

"It's so easy," Heath said. "Just act nice, be willing to bargain but stay hard-nosed, and you've got it made. People would love to sell and buy from a cute little thing like you."

This was going to be a solo effort; no father. "Freddie's going to Yale," Robin said.

"So you told me," Heath said.

"What are you going to do?" Robin asked. "While I'm driving all over buying furniture I don't know shit about."

"Listen," Heath began, then stopped. He reached into his jeans pockets and pulled out a tiny brown vial with a black cap. He shook the vial, and then he looked up at her coyly.

Of course she knew what he'd been doing, Robin told herself. It was just so hard sometimes to keep up. "Okay, Dad," she said, "I get it."

"No secrets," Heath said. "What do I always say? No lying."

"Right, Dad. Yeah, thanks. No lying." Robin pulled up another lawn chair and sat down. The bus looked as it had before Tom moved in. All he'd done for years was rearrange trash.

"Look at me!" her father cried. "Have I ever looked better?"

"Yes," Robin said. When her mother was alive, she wanted to say. Before her illness, when you poured all your desires into your wife and child.

"Notice I'm not asking what you do, where you go," Heath said. "Notice that I give you your own life, your own privacy. If you got into the antiques, we could incorporate, have a real business."

"Then you'd do it with me?" Robin asked. She was always stunned by her own hope, her stupid hope.

Heath sighed. "No, honey. You do that, we incorporate or something, we put out a sign and have cards printed and all. I do *this*. Grandma does her own shit, as always. But it looks like we have just the one business."

The curious thing about her father's glassy expression was how strong it made him look. He could roar at this moment, he could punch out a window on the bus. He was the dealer after all, now and forever; he was the guy with the real stuff.

"I might go to college after all, Dad," Robin said. "I might move, too."

"Uh-huh," her father said, clearly not listening. He dug in his pockets, then pulled out some change, an old tissue, a matchbook, the stub of a Panatela, and a piece of string. Finally he reached into his other pocket and drew out a short, gold metal straw that was closed at the top and had a hole, a kind of vent, in the side.

"Where did you get that?" Robin asked.

"This? Very new, very special," her father said. "You have to get them made."

"Who gave it to you?" Robin said.

"Customers give you stuff, honey. Who remembers?"

You were born for it, Stansell said. Everybody had a set job at birth. "Oh, Dad," Robin said. Stansell and his Rolex, Stansell and his cash: risk free, while every day Heath drove the Grand Prix into potential madness, gun fights, territory disputes. Stansell had hold of her father's life, and, right now, her father looked thankful for that fact.

"Honey, what's wrong?" Heath took out his vial.

Robin bolted. This was the first time her thoughts had been too much to bear, and she bolted. Down the bus stairs at high speed, into her bedroom for the car keys, and back out to the garage. Her father waved merrily to her from the bus window.

Robin rolled up the door. She hadn't even taken the car on a test drive. She didn't have a license. The Thunderbird started with a roar, its muffler coughing for a second before settling into a low growl. Someone besides Heath was responsible for his own degradation. There was no way for Robin to explain her fear or her outrage; there was no place, certainly not in Lilac, to go to relieve her father's suffering, a suffering he couldn't even feel. *Be Do Go.* Robin slowly pulled the car out of the garage, and, without putting on the headlights, turned out of the driveway and puttered up Highland. The car hesitated a few times, but then the engine caught a rhythm and steadily climbed the small hill. The street was quiet, the Bogats' and Hazens' and Corners' houses all dark, not even an outside light burning. It was the neighborhood, the collective wanting of the whole street, the whole town, the envy of the suburbs for Chicago: that had to be what made Heath so foolish as to throw in with Stansell. Desperation couldn't explain his actions because desperation was smarter, more focused. Her father had floundered around and Stansell had caught him.

Robin put on the headlights. The Thunderbird might as well have emerged from a hole in the sky, a blank space. It was too easy to make Heath, Goldie, even herself, invisible. It was too easy to squeeze them out of their tiny space in the town. Lilac would do almost anything to forget who lived in her neighborhood.

At Freddie's house, Robin stopped. Dark, of course; in this house people got up for work, looking good, thinking ahead. The apple tree in the front yard had finished blooming. One day, years ago, Robin had gone to Freddie's for lunch, and Mrs. Eakins had given them apple preserves. For Robin, who never had homegrown food, eating the preserves was like eating the earth itself, sweet and full of vitamins, the kind of food that made someone smart and kind because of its origin and purity. A few months ago, Freddie had come down the hill to show Robin a catalog from Yale; it was full of people who looked as if they'd been raised on backyard food. They had long limbs and effortless coordination, most likely from playing polo and skiing and sailing. The students in the catalog lounged on impossibly green lawns in front of gothic buildings; they sat with furrowed brows over books in a cathedral-like reading room. The Yale students all looked on the verge of something, biding their time until they stumbled on their true calling. No wonder Freddie was frightened. The catalog had given Robin a kind of vertigo and made her glad for her car, her vast yard, even for her hodgepodge house and scratchy family. Those kinds of smooth, even surfaces made her nervous. There was no way to enter perfection; there was nothing to fix or change or work against.

At the convenience store on Finster Road, Robin stopped to get a Coke. She was shaking when she got out of the car; her body couldn't reject the fear that there was something illegitimate about her driving around, aside from the lack of a license. Surely there was something wrong with having no destination in Lilac, no place that would take her in.

The boy working the register was someone Robin recognized from parties, a guy who used to sell speed in the boys' locker room after gym class but who dropped out his junior year and then continued on with the same friends and the same parties, living at home, and now, clearly, pulling the late shift at the store. This was life after high school, whether you finished or not.

"You're the first one in here for like two hours," the kid said, handing Robin her change.

"It's early, I guess," she added. Her hands shook as she tried to pop the top of her Coke.

"You babysitting your dad, maybe?" the guy asked, smiling.

Craig was the kid's name, Craig with the chronic cough. At Heath's lowest point, Robin had seen him at the house, a skinny, hacking shape rising up the back stairs. How could she have forgotten? No one else ever did. Her father had his own kind of fame.

Outside, the sky was still black above the glaring lights of the convenience store; in the east, the lights of Chicago created a huge parachute of pale color. Robin imagined that the city held an all-night party, just to spite the clock-watchers in the suburbs, with fireworks, carnivals, the klieg lights of movie premieres, anything to create that glow and to remind outsiders of what they were missing.

She could drive to Chicago. The car had new tires; she could try it on the Eisenhower, see what happened when the carburetor cleaned out, her foot smashed down on the gas pedal. Robin watched Craig pick a pimple and turn the pages of a magazine. Next to the cash register, hot dogs rose and fell in their warming ride. Robin started the car and pulled out. First the Simonsens' house, now Craig in his deadly job: soon all the dimmed lights in Lilac would blaze.

On the edge of Robin's neighborhood, hard up against Route 53 and before the development across the street with its sewer systems and garbage disposals and attached garages, sat two shacks, which over the years had begun to sink into the swampy earth that lay underneath most of northern Illinois. Years ago, Robin and Kitty had investigated the shacks and found a couple living in each one, old people who looked like pioneers, with overalls and flowered dresses and bad teeth and hair like animal nests. They'd chased Robin and Kitty off their property. Years later, when Robin and Freddie returned, the couples were still there, but now they had shriveled, and they watched from the shack windows as the kids hiked through skunk cabbage and horsetail and compass plants and trampled the overgrown remains of old vegetable gardens just to get close enough to see them. The last time Robin had checked, the shacks were deserted.

Route 53 was empty, so Robin drove slowly. She saw the first shack, the one that had the vegetable garden, but it was just a leaning pile of lumber. The next one, though, was standing, and there was a light in its window, yellow and flickering like a flame.

She stopped her car. The two front steps were almost completely obscured by tall castor bean trees, sumacs, and various saplings, but Robin could make out a seated figure. She strained to see. It was a man, and he was smoking; the red coal of a cigarette rose to his mouth.

"I knew you'd take it out sooner or later," the man said.

Robin put the car into park and slid over to the passenger's side. "Excuse me?" she asked.

"Fucker's running, isn't it?" the man said. "What more could a girl want?" he asked.

"Tom!" Robin cried. "What are you doing here?"

"Guy's got to live somewhere," he said. "I go around the corner, and here I am. It's got an address, so I can get my army check. Done deal."

"Are you all right?" Robin asked. She thought about offering Tom something—money, food, other comforts—but then again, he seemed to have taken a step up. Frogs peeped in the swampy area behind the shacks and a row of corn plants flourished in the side yard. The branches of gnarled apple trees cast their silhouettes against the moon. "Are you all right?" Robin asked again.

"I'm here," Tom said. "I'm living on nerves and that nasty juice. Speaking of, how's your daddy?"

"You don't want to know," Robin said.

"Come visit me sometime," Tom said, standing up and waving. "Now here comes a car, baby."

A short drive past Tom's, Robin turned off of Route 53 and headed toward Stansell's part of town, earth to the Pluto of where Tom lived now. The T-Bird puttered almost happily, as if it were glad to be put to rights, just like the tinny, fussy robot in *Star Wars*.

From the street, Robin could see only the top floor of Stansell's house, so she pulled a few yards into the driveway and then killed the headlights. You could never tell who was home at Stansell's because the family hid their cars in the huge garage. Lights were on in the TV room: Marilyn. The last time Robin had seen Stansell's mom, she'd ambushed Robin on her way to the kitchen for beers, asking her had she ever read Saul Bellow, had she ever seen *Bonnie and Clyde*, and why didn't she stay and watch a rerun of *A Face in the Crowd*. There was something assumed in Marilyn's TV room that had started to worry Robin, a right to leisure and relaxation, a determined effort to forget what bothered you. And Mrs. Stansell loved to fill the space left by worry with a kind of moist hectoring that made Robin laugh and run.

Robin put the car into neutral and let it drift out of Stansell's driveway. Then she put on the lights and drove on. The high school, a box of a place with reinforced windows, was lit around the perimeter with arc lights and burglar alarm fixtures—it looked like a prison. She turned around and drove to the old trailer park. Tree's house was dark, its screen door broken off and propped against the locust tree in the front yard. Robin didn't know where Marqueese was. She imagined he lived in Stansell's car, sleeping in the trunk like a huge haul of pot, inert and smelling of wood.

Robin turned around again and drove into a development with mature trees and lots big enough for small swimming pools. She took a right on Parkside, Lynn's winding street. The park of Parkside was a small patch of green two blocks from Lynn's house where three streets met. It held a bench, a sign warning dog walkers to pick up after their pets, and a concrete planter.

Robin stopped the car a half block from Lynn's house and turned off the engine. She'd called her earlier that evening, but no one had answered. Sometimes Robin thought Lynn only existed when Robin decided to create her, or when Stansell did, or any boy or man on the planet: desire was so powerful you could use it to make a person. Sometimes Robin thought her desire created her, just for misery and longing, just for emotions stretched as far as they could go. There was no light in Lynn's room, no lights anywhere in the house or even on the block. She was going to tell Lynn about her father, about Stansell. She had proof of Stansell's betrayal. An exploitation, she would tell Lynn. An enormous cottonwood tree shaded the Nielsens', a remnant of the prairie, which every spring rained fluff that caused Mr. Nielsen's sneezing fits. The breeze in the cottonwood leaves sounded like water running. Robin was almost asleep when headlight beams swept over her face. The car's engine rattled in a familiar way. A Volvo, Robin decided, closing her eyes again, an old one. Maybe diesel.

The rattling stopped, followed by the ticking of a cooling engine. When Robin opened her eyes, she saw that the car—it was a Volvo—had stopped a few doors past Lynn's house. It was dark inside the car, and the globe of the closest streetlight was smothered in the branches of a maple tree. The cottonwood leaves rushed overhead. After a few minutes, the passenger door of the car opened, and Lynn Nielsen ran across her front lawn, long hair swinging at her waist. The driver waited until Lynn was inside to start the car, pull into the nearest driveway, and back out. The Volvo coughed and then chugged past Robin's car. It had a dented rear door, a Grateful Dead bumper sticker, and its license place was attached at one end with a bright pink shoelace.

chapter twelve

First of all, Robin stopped everything: drugs, insomnia, constant partying, bad food, no food, alcohol, her hatred for Stansell. Everything but her father and Lynn Nielsen.

If you lived in a world of fools, you rose above them and showed them the way. There was such a thing as vanquishing a foe to help a loved one. This was Robin's legacy from her mother, no doubt about it. Only Patricia had suffered fools so long they wore her out.

In the old Westerns Goldie and Tommy Boy watched, when you saw the end coming, you sharpened your wits and you tightened your belt. You took your money out of the bank, you paid back your debts, you told the woman you loved that you loved her.

You lied and you betrayed.

Graduation was nothing, a dead piece of time. At the ceremony, Robin's guidance counselor asked her to sit in a special row of successful students, Freddie and Susan Nagler among them, but Robin refused. She preferred to sit out of alphabetical order with the common folk, next to Lynn. She had to keep an eye on her. Stansell had flunked math for the third time that final term, so he couldn't graduate until he passed a summer school class, which he vowed never to attend. Tree didn't graduate, to no one's surprise. Marqueese had perhaps graduated at some unspecified, earlier time; no one knew for sure. All three boys sat in the back row of the mass of chairs set up for family and friends and whistled and catcalled when Robin and Lynn crossed the stage. Neither Goldie nor Heath attended the ceremony: Heath was out of town, and Goldie had an all-day meeting in Chicago with her lawyer. The tough part, Grandma had said, was to figure out how to present herself as a woman wronged by the Bogdanas wives. The hard part was to make yourself lily white, Grandma had added, laughing.

After the ceremony, Stansell drove them all to Highland Street and waited in the car with Lynn and Tree and Marqueese for Robin to change her clothes. The house was dark, but when Robin turned on the kitchen light, she found Tommy Boy at the table with a pint and a glass of ice.

"Congratulations," he said sadly.

"What's wrong?" Robin asked.

"Change of seasons." He poured another glass.

"I'm going to some parties," Robin said, starting down the hall.

"Goldie turned down my proposal," Tommy said.

"Believe me, Tommy," Robin called from her bedroom, "you don't want to get involved with Grandma. Besides, she's already married."

"I didn't say marriage, did I?" Tommy said. "Your pop's hardly home, and I'm always here, so I say, let's move in together. No funny stuff either. She says no anyways."

Robin returned to the kitchen, tucking a black tee shirt into her jeans. "So you need a place to live, huh?" she said, smiling at Tommy.

"She graduates from high school and all of a sudden she thinks she knows everything about a person," Tommy said.

For two days, they went from party to party. At one point, Robin stopped at home for another set of clothes, and she found Goldie and the men outside in the screened room, the space thick with cigarette smoke. "Having fun, honey?" Goldie asked.

"I guess," Robin said.

"We was taking a poll," Larry Pike said. "And not a-one of us here ever graduated."

"Wished we had," Tommy said.

"No, you don't," Robin said.

"We're so proud of you, cupcake," said Goldie.

"We got together a little something for you," Larry said. "It's in the kitchen."

"Sorry it was so last-minute, baby," Tommy said.

Robin took the shopping bag of gifts to the car and distributed them as Stansell drove them to the next party: Billy Tree got two tickets to the Elks Club fish fry; Marqueese got a beer mug with Secretariat's face on it; Stansell got a pint of Jim Beam; and Lynn got a Jean Naté gift set. Robin kept the illegal Cuban cigar and lit it off of Marqueese's match.

"Take me a picture of that," Marqueese said, as Robin blew smoke out the window. "Please."

They navigated a series of backyards, parks, and train track berms under swooping swallows and darting bats. Nighthawks screeched and buzzed high above. Robin didn't sleep the whole time. Every so often, a parent would look out a back door at the sea of wasted teenagers, their long hair blowing about their faces, and then retreat into the darkness of his house. Lynn wore a white tube top and hip-huggers and red straw flip-flops, and her hair fell long and golden over her shoulders.

The two of them sat cross-legged on a picnic table in Post Park while Lynn drank an Old Style and talked into Robin's face with an ardor that took Robin's breath away. Lynn declared her love and her gratitude for Robin getting her through high school and her recognition of Robin's loyalty and cuteness and her sincere insistence that there would never be in the whole world a girl and a friend as wonderful as Robin Simonsen. Lynn cried; Robin knew why. Robin listened to every word and wondered why lovemaking had to be limited to the mouth, breasts, and genitals: Lynn had a tiny mole in her armpit. There was so much more.

Stansell tried to arm-wrestle Robin. He set up bets, all in dope, and he cleared off a card table some ill-advised parent had covered with cans of Coke and bowls of potato chips, planting his elbow, a cigarette burning in his mouth. "Come on, pussy," he said. Robin just laughed at him. You are invisible, she thought.

Getting out of the Fairlane at one house, Robin saw Roger Dodger, the cop, standing in the driveway next to his cruiser and laughing with some kids. He glanced at Robin and looked away.

In Fairview Park, David Paint planted a series of explosives that he set off one by one using a remote control. A huge crowd watched mud, leaves, and charcoal from a grill leap up in choreographed blows. A crow squawked awake in a nearby tree.

At dawn on the second day, some kid's father offered to buy Robin's Thunderbird.

Somewhere, sometime, a girl with her hair in a bun and a long, Indian-print skirt came up to Robin and showed her a photograph of a very long-haired and bug-eyed Simon Furton standing next to a heavyset, balding, and bearded man who wore a grin that said, I've forgotten what I'm smiling about.

"He met him," the girl said. "Look."

"Who?" Robin asked.

"Baba Ram Dass."

The Duaneiacs appeared at almost every party. One of them had gotten a Les Paul for graduation, and he carried it everywhere in its case, surrounded by the protective phalanx of the other Duaneiacs. Periodically, this boy would pretend to play the Les Paul in perfect imitation of Duane Allman, slouched, ecstatic, as if the poor man had been airlifted from the afterlife and dropped between the strap and the instrument.

In someone's backyard, Robin hung upside down from a child's swing set and Marqueese gathered her hair in his hands and kissed her hard on the mouth. She kissed him back.

In a fetid bathroom somewhere else, Robin stood panting under a bare lightbulb while she examined a cut on Lynn's ear. Lynn sobbed. Robin breathed all over the side of her face. This is foreplay, she thought. Then she walked home.

It was late morning when Robin reached Highland Street. Already the sun was glossy, the air oily. She headed for Freddie's. She'd missed his party, the one his whole family was coming to, the one for which his grandfather made ribs and for which Antoinette got a new dress. Even though she and Freddie hadn't been talking, Robin knew he would have wanted her to come. She hadn't told him about her father yet; he hadn't yet confessed who the boy was. Robin's plan was to get both of those things said. There was nothing she loved better than ticking items off a list, fixing, ordering. Freddie loved it, too.

Robin walked around the side of the Eakinses' house. The bushes Mrs. Eakins had planted years ago had grown, so Robin couldn't see into the backyard. She did hear Freddie's voice, low and slow and friendly. Had Susan Nagler stayed after the party was over? It wasn't that early in the morning. Robin stopped and looked around the bushes.

Freddie was sitting up on the picnic table next to a large boy Robin didn't recognize. The yard was already clean; a dozen overflowing garbage cans dotted the lawn. A broom lay on the patio. The house was dark and quiet. The other boy's back was broader than Freddie's, and he had a fat neck and a wide ass. He was cracking his knuckles and nodding as Freddie talked to him. Robin thought she'd seen the boy before, but he had been thinner, louder. She couldn't place him as someone who would listen to Freddie or even sit quietly on a weekend morning after high school graduation.

Robin walked up to the picnic table. "Happy day," she said to Freddie. She could feel the strain in her smile.

Freddie started, then frowned. "You scared me," he said.

"Hi," Robin said to the other boy. He had a meaty face and a worried, puckered brow.

"Where were you?" Freddie asked. "You didn't need a special invitation, but I sent one anyway."

"Sorry," Robin said. She looked back and forth from Freddie to the boy, and as she did, she remembered him. He was the boy at Tree's party so long ago, the guy who disgraced himself off the football team because of Quaaludes and then teamed up with Stansell, only to fall out of favor when he straightened up, sometime before Robin became a serious part of the entourage. Rocwicz. Carl Rocwicz, who used to wear a letter sweater with an old pill bottle of drugs in the pocket. Was Freddie tutoring him? Robin had heard that Carl wanted to finish school.

"I remember you," Carl said. His face didn't change, though. He looked as if he were deep into despair.

"Oh, for god's sake," Freddie said. Now he was smiling. "Is there anyone you don't know?" he asked Robin.

"Lots of people," Robin said, staring at Carl. The boy had huge hands with thick fingers.

"I guess you graduated, too," Carl said glumly. "Everybody did. And then there's college." He looked at Freddie.

"Hey, man," Freddie said quietly. "I told you, come visit."

"I'm not going either," Robin said. Freddie had looked away. Robin felt a surge of envy, jealousy, anger: to have desire quenched, no matter how roughly, to have one person all your own, to have a secret that somebody else knows, too. Both these boys before her were big; they were men; they were strong enough to cause and to take just a little pain.

"So you're the guy," Robin said, smiling as best she could. Shimmers of heat rose from the road.

"You know," Freddie said, "it can be a trial and a tribulation to be your friend."

∽

For graduation, Heath gave Robin three hundred dollars in cash, stuck inside a signed first edition of *Howl* he'd had since his year in Berkeley;

he left the money and book on the kitchen table on his way out of town. Parts unknown again. Robin called Freddie, and then she heard the distance, and the solidity, in his voice and read the first few pages of "Howl" and cried. She had to pin it all down, get her father back from Stansell, get the one thing for her own life: Lynn.

Robin was still crying when she called Lynn and asked her to come over. They were all recovering from the parties, so Robin promised quiet, no booze or pot, no boys, but when Lynn arrived in her mother's Buick, she got out carrying a bag of Doritos and a six-pack.

"This is so cool," Lynn said, sitting cross-legged on Robin's bed. "We're going to have a real girls' night." She pulled a small bag of pot out of her purse. "Roll one, will you?" she asked. "You're so good at it."

"Okay, but I don't want any," Robin said.

Robin rolled two joints and placed two opened beers on the windowsill next to the bed. She sat down facing Lynn and ate some Doritos. She wanted to be very awake.

Lynn said, "Charlene Agnos came up to me the other night and she's like, stay away from my boyfriend. And I said, 'I don't even know who he is, for god's sake!'"

The odor of oil and mud came wafting in from the shed.

"I have to work at my father's law office starting next week," Lynn said. "Eight fucking A.M. I have to be there. He says he'll drive me, but he just wants me in the car to yell at me."

"I don't understand what his problem is with you," Robin said. Whenever she saw Mr. Nielsen, he always asked her where she lived and what her father did for a living. The next time she saw him, he'd ask her again. Robin suspected he asked not because he'd forgotten or because he didn't know what else to say but because he hoped one day she'd give a different answer.

"My dad," Lynn said. "See, he took this class for criminal defense lawyers that's supposed to show you what drugs your clients are on and what the drugs do and what wasted people look like."

"So he sees you looking that way only he's too afraid to say anything. Because you're his daughter."

"That's it! Exactly." Lynn pointed her finger at Robin. "You always know. My dad's okay, though."

It wasn't working. For all her thinking, planning, her clever ways to get Lynn to confess about Mr. Tomasini and to feel contrite and to make it up to Robin, her best friend, Robin couldn't proceed. At least not subtly. Lynn wore a blue halter top with a cluster of wooden cherries pinned at the cleavage. Her cheeks were downy, and she had a tiny scab on her ear.

"What did you get in Humanities?" Robin blurted.

"I know what you got," Lynn said. "I never have to ask."

"I asked you. You said it was hard."

"It was," Lynn said, looking down. "Mr. Tomasini liked you."

"Did he tell you that?" Robin asked.

"No! But he called on you all the time and said you were right. You always were." Lynn lit one of the joints.

"What did you get?" Robin asked again.

"Nobody would believe me," Lynn said.

"I would. What?"

"An A."

"You're not stupid, Lynnie. I've always known that." Robin rubbed Lynn's knee. She felt a kind of moral sloshing inside; her conscience splashed from sympathetic to cruel and back again. She wanted to believe there were special rules for such beautiful girls, and she wanted to believe the girls deserved them.

"What do you talk about?" Robin asked. "Art? Jazz, maybe?"

"With who?" Lynn asked. Her tongue was orange from the Doritos, her face a little smeared from the beer and pot. Strands of her hair drifted up in the breeze from the window.

"What's Mr. Tomasini's first name?" Robin asked brightly. "I think it's Robert."

Lynn winced. "I told him people would know. I said that to him."

"Well, you were right," Robin said.

"He could get fired," Lynn said. "I could get thrown out."

"You graduated, honey," Robin said, taking Lynn's hand. "There's no place to throw you out of."

"But we were together at school. During school. Sometimes at school."

"How long?" Robin asked.

"Since junior year," Lynn said.

Since Robin and Lynn had been friends.

"They could take away my diploma, I guess," Lynn said.

"They're not going to do that." Robin rubbed the backs of both of Lynn's hands, her fingers moving over the long, thin bones, her thumbs sliding up and over Lynn's wrists.

"Who did you tell?" Lynn asked. She gave Robin a challenging look. Lynn knew the power of their friendship, but not all of it.

"Nobody!" Robin acted shocked. "And I won't tell anybody."

"I couldn't have a better best friend," Lynn said, smiling her big smile, using all her teeth, her voice up in the greeting card register, the one that said kittens and flowers and ribbons and a fondness that would last forever. Oh, but it didn't matter: there was the curve of her breast.

"Lynnie, listen," Robin whispered. She cursed her house, her yard: she smelled twenty years of dripping 30-weight oil.

"I don't know why I never told you," Lynn said. "I can tell you everything."

"Yes," Robin said. "Listen, Lynn." She worked her fingers over the girl's wrist bones again, and this time she moved her hands up Lynn's forearms. One string of the halter top tied around Lynn's neck, the other across her back.

"He's even smarter than in class, Rob," Lynn said, ignoring Robin's fingers. "We go to Chicago sometimes and look at buildings. Just like we did in class that one time, only we have dinner and we talk, and then he shows me stuff in the city. We smoke weed together, too."

"You need to listen to me," Robin said.

Lynn finished her beer. "That one weekend I told everybody I was going to visit my cousins in Indianapolis? Robert and I were downtown, all weekend. He got a hotel. My parents didn't even know!"

Now she was Lynn from the hallways, Lynn from parties and the girls' room, bubbly and confiding and warm. Lynn's bare shoulders were as brown and smooth, as firm and round, as river rocks. Robin leaned forward, pressing her lips to Lynn's left shoulder.

When Robin leaned back, Lynn was smiling. She doesn't get it, Robin thought. How could she not get it? "It's not good, honey," Robin said. "You can't keep letting guys do this to you." She thought she could bring some insight to Lynn, read her like she read her father, save her like you saved a girl in a fairy tale.

"Do what?" Lynn asked

"Well, just, you know, think of you like a body. Just use you. You know."

Lynn sat up against the wall and sighed. "Everybody's always telling me that! My mom? And my dad! When I was like twelve, they had a family conference and said I had to be careful, that I was becoming a 'young woman' and all that bullshit, and I had to watch out for guys. People act like I'm going to get hit by a car or something. Watch out! Here comes a guy and he's out of control!" She laughed.

"Well," Robin said.

"It's not like that, though! Why doesn't anybody believe that I know what I'm doing?"

"Maybe because you're fucking your Humanities teacher, Lynn," Robin said. "And what's wrong with *him*? He's a guy who's going out with high school girls. Even my dad never did that."

"Okay, I've got to say something. You know what's weird? Okay, I'm just not going to pretend guys don't like me."

"Jesus, I hope not!" Robin said. She rubbed Lynn's knees, all in the name of friendship.

"But you know what they think?" Lynn asked. "They think because they're into you that that's the whole point of being together, of getting it on and shit. I mean, like their attraction is in the middle of everything you do. It runs everything."

"I'm not quite following you."

Lynn opened another beer and took a sip. "Guys think that girls they think are pretty don't have any sex feelings of their own. They never care whether you're having a good time or not. It's like you're made for them to do it to and nothing else."

"I think they're probably like that with all girls," Robin said. She held Lynn's knees.

Lynn shook her head violently. "No. No. I know they're not like that with everybody. Nobody ever asks me how I feel! They just go right on ahead."

"That's terrible," Robin said. "And that's what I was talking about."

"Except Mr. Tomasini. Robert."

Now Robin shook her head. Somehow they'd gone in a circle. Did she lead Lynn here? There'd never been a time in school when she couldn't reason or talk her way into or out of an idea. Robin stroked the sides of Lynn's thighs. Maybe there was no idea here, just the experience and meaning of action.

Robin rose to her knees and embraced Lynn. "How does that feel?" she whispered in her ear. Lynn was stiff in her arms.

Be Do Go. Robin put a hand on Lynn's breast and drew her thumb across the nipple. Lynn sucked in air. Robin put her other hand on the back of Lynn's neck and lifted her hair, then ran her fingers down her spine. Lynn's breath grew deeper.

"How does that feel?" Robin asked. Lynn's eyes looked beyond her face. She wasn't too drunk, or too dreamy; she was merely practiced. Robin could feel Lynn step back inside herself.

Robin's palm to Lynn's warm back, her fingers under the tie, the tips of her fingers just reaching down into the back of Lynn's jeans— she had to get the girl's attention. Robin's other hand worked the nipple, then the whole breast. Lynn held her breath.

"You," whispered Robin, her breath on Lynn's cheek, then her lips. Her fingers worked the tie under Lynn's hair. She pulled off Lynn's top, sliding its fabric between their pressed bodies.

And then Lynn moved her face so that their lips met. Her eyes were closed. The muscle of Lynn's tongue worked into Robin's mouth until Robin could taste beer, smoke, Doritos, all backed by the singular taste of this girl. In one moment, just one and then it was gone, Robin felt a delicious suspension of vigilance. Thinking stopped and feeling took its place.

"How does that feel?" Robin whispered.

She lay Lynn down on the bed and, kissing her, she unbuttoned Lynn's jeans and Lynn quickly pulled them off. She was naked underneath. Then Lynn, eyes closed, spread her body out below Robin. It was an opening and an invitation, but it was also a habit. Lynn bent her legs and Robin fell between them.

Robin grabbed Lynn's breasts with her mouth, one and then the other, and she pulled, gently. Lynn moaned, her hands on Robin's head. Robin ran her tongue along Lynn's ribs, breathed in the cut-grass scent of Lynn's armpits, put her lips on the tiny mole; she circled Lynn's waist and lifted, feeling the strength in her arms and shoulders as she brought Lynn's hips to her mouth.

And then her mind stippled and shifted because in one second she had grabbed Lynn's ass and had dropped her face into Lynn's crotch. The hair there was like a ruffled collar around a tender neck. At which Robin nibbled, at first tentatively, then with large movements of her lips and jaw. She thought, but she couldn't say, How does that feel.

Robin brought her hands back to Lynn's breasts, which filled her palms.

"Aye," Lynn said, sucking in breath. "Aye," she said.

And finally, there was movement in Lynn's hips: she pressed them against Robin's mouth; there was a rush of salty liquid. Robin, still in her jeans and tee shirt, felt the workings of her own body. She felt the flow of her blood, the twitch of her muscles, the shaking of her brain, the flutter of her heart, but those sensations quickly disappeared. She saw above her the girl she loved, rising fast and settling, but suddenly she was blind to that, too. By the end, there was only one thing she held between her hands and that was desire.

∼

The phone calls started the night after Lynn's visit. Nasty ringing and then hang-ups. No one was home at Lynn's or Stansell's or even Billy Tree's.

After a few hours, Goldie took the phone off the hook. "Kids," she said, going back to her pinochle game.

The men around the table were quiet because she was talking about dating her lawyer.

"Cline," Goldie said. "Tall and funny. And he's Norwegian, too. He thinks the Bogdanas women are going nowhere fast. He says they're holding out for some guilt money from George and the old man, some 'alienation of affection,' they call it—don't you love that?—but still they want to stay married. I could care less."

Robin lay on the couch all day reading Kafka. Another recommendation from Mrs. Kopopolous. She'd never worked so hard at something only to have it come apart in her hands. She hadn't thought of a word to say to Lynn afterward. They had lay frozen, side-by-side, until Lynn put on her clothes and left. At one point, Robin thought Lynn might be crying, but apparently her friend couldn't even rouse that bit of feeling. Robin couldn't shake her own lack of emotion, lack of thought, the nothingness that was really everything, every moment of want she'd ever had for Lynn, separate and floating. Now that her desire had been fulfilled, she couldn't accept the fact that that same desire might be mobile. Applicable. Able to attach to others. Maybe her love for Lynn wasn't what made her a lover of girls. Maybe her love for girls was the essence of her desire: she worked to fulfill the feeling rather than to covet the subject.

Over and over, Robin read the same page of Kafka. She didn't get out of the castle until her father came home at dark with a bag of hamburgers.

"I can't eat these," he said, dropping them onto Robin's lap. "Hi, kiddo."

"Where did you go?" Robin asked.

"Out," Heath said. He was coked out, looking ready to stomp on anyone who got in his way. "Now I'm going upstairs."

Robin dialed Stansell's private number. He answered and she hung up.

The phone calls started again immediately, but when Goldie and Robin asked Heath the next day if they could change the number, he wouldn't let them.

"I need it for business," he said.

Grandma snorted. "I'm running a business, too, but this is ridiculous." She waved the receiver at Heath.

For two days, the Simonsens turned off the phone's ringer, and at idle moments, they picked up the receiver and answered. Sometimes it was business; most of the time they heard a click and then nothing.

After two days, the calls stopped. Robin believed it was Lynn, who had no words for what they'd done. But every time she called the Nielsens', Lynn's parents or little sisters said she wasn't there.

There was no time to worry. Robin's plan was a book half-read, a paper half-written—she had to finish. On a day she knew her father was out and Goldie in Chicago with the lawyer, Robin drove the T-Bird to the Lilac police station. She still didn't have a license. The two-man detective team knew who Robin was, which didn't surprise her. She told the detectives about her exploited father (this produced smirks), about how her father was being compromised by a boy she knew from high school, a rich kid. His name was Steve Stansell, Robin said, thinking the mere mention of Steve's name would send the cops into action, but they didn't even write it on their pads. They veered back to Heath. How much was he dealing? they asked. How much money was he making? Did he sell to minors? Where did he get his stuff? They seemed disappointed when Robin couldn't answer. Didn't she know what was going on in her own house?

"Stansell's the problem," Robin said. "Steven, the kid. You know his dad. They're loaded, and this kid, he doesn't care. He's the money here. My dad wouldn't be dealing if he didn't have this kid's money."

"Your father has been a person of interest to us for a year or so," Detective Bruni said. He chewed gum and wore a black suit, just like detectives on TV.

"A *year*?" Robin asked, and then she shut up. Almost a decade of dealing, yet somehow her father had stayed out of range.

"Your father's rise in income has not gone unnoticed by us or by your neighbors," Detective Nicholas said. He was trying to grow a mustache. He looked like a Lilac High football star from a few years back.

"Fuck the neighbors," Robin heard herself say.

"Watch it now," Bruni said.

Robin excused herself and went to the women's room. It looked like it had never been used. The beige paint was free of scratches and graffiti. Only Robin's face in the mirror looked prematurely worn, pinched and thin, brown from the sun, her mouth slightly open over her small, straight teeth. She was a slight, angled shape, unchanged by years of worry and sadness. And here was something else new: she no longer looked like her mother, but like herself.

Robin returned to the detectives' office and explained, as calmly as she could, what she would do for her father and how she wanted them to help her. She made it clear that if they followed her plan, the cops would get Stansell, the guy behind it all. She told them where, how.

"Tomorrow," Detective Bruni said, standing up to shake her hand.

Robin went home and took stock, preparing as if for a move or a trip. She liked to clear off surfaces in order to think. First she cleaned her room, what there was of it, dusting her dresser and child's desk. She found a frame for the photograph of Rex, Pinky, and Miguel, and set it next to the studio portrait of her mother. She also framed a photograph of Goldie from one of her vaudeville acts. In the picture, Goldie wore a tight-fitting angel costume; she blew kisses at a fat man in a plaid suit and a bowler. Finally, on the glass of her mother's photo, Robin taped an old Polaroid of her father taken by one of his dates. In the picture, a gorgeous man in a ripped tee shirt and jeans, with a wide, white smile and wavy blond hair flowing over his shoulders, sat in the sun on the bumper of an old truck, just like any hardworking dad.

That night, Robin made dinner for Goldie and the men.

"What's the occasion, kitten?" Grandma asked.

"Who cares?" Larry said. "She's making sirloins."

"You know what I miss?" Tommy asked. "A good schnitzel. I love schnitzel like you wouldn't believe."

"Cline took me to Berghoff's the other day," Goldie said. She slapped cards down on her solitaire hand. "Have they got schnitzel. But the grease! A few more meals there and I'll get one of those fat German cans."

"My ex-wife used to make veal medallions you'd as like to kill for," Larry Pike said. "Course she served them as my goodbye meal."

"We're having steak!" Robin yelled, slamming a screwdriver down on the counter. She'd been stabbing at the years of grease and char that had sealed shut the broiler door. "And salad," Robin added. "And I'm boiling potatoes."

"All right, pumpkin," Goldie said. "We can't wait."

∼

There was no good reason a drug bust couldn't occur in the daytime. When Robin got up the next morning and saw the sun, honeyed and already sizzling away the dew, she paused for a moment, imagining her father being led away under the hot light of a summer afternoon, the neighbors watering their lawns and later reeling in their hoses along with their convictions about Heath. Robin took the silence of her immediate world, meaning of Stansell and Lynn, as further proof that she was on her own.

Goldie left after breakfast, while Heath was still upstairs asleep. Grandma carried a leather briefcase she had bought for her "paperwork," which was comprised of a page of scrawled notes from Cline's phone calls, directions to his office on LaSalle Street, some letterhead Goldie had stolen from him, and a copy of *Screen World* in case the waiting room had only *National Geographic* or *The New Yorker*. Robin stood in the driveway and waved as Goldie pulled the Cadillac onto Highland and roared away. Then she went to her room and got out a small folded packet, Stansell's straw, and the framed photograph of Kim Novak, all of which she took to the kitchen and put on a chair. Then she looked at her watch.

Robin went up to her father's room with a cup of coffee.

"I'm not hungry," he said groggily.

"Do you see any food here?" Robin asked. "Get up, Dad. I want to ask you something."

Heath sat up against the headboard. He now had a box spring, a frame, even a matching nightstand with a working lamp. Robin knew her father was naked under the sheet. Coke had changed his body: he was thin, but not like the skeleton he had been on junk; now muscles strained against the skin of his stomach and arms, long, tight muscles like those of an underfed laborer. His weightlifting drew the muscles finer instead of building them thicker.

"Hey, listen, Rob," Heath said, lighting a Panatela, "I've got a lead on a Stickley dining room set out in Huntley. You know, Arts and Crafts. It's nice shit. You interested? You could start with that."

"Maybe," Robin said. "Is this somebody selling out?"

"Not exactly. The son. He owes me some favors, some money, whatever." Her father pulled his hair back into a ponytail. "That's better," he said, yawning. He hadn't seen a dentist yet; the gaps and black teeth were still there.

"Come downstairs," Robin said, leaving the room.

"Why?" her father called.

She descended the stairs and sat at the table, waiting. She knew her father would come.

He arrived in a pair of jeans and nothing else. Swallows swooped past the kitchen window.

"Look, there's a nest under the eaves," Robin said.

"How about that?" her father said, craning his neck. The living room stereo played "Fortunate Son." "This is my favorite Creedence song," Heath said. "Turn it up." He sat at the kitchen table.

Robin ignored him. The coke and the paraphernalia sat on the chair next to her.

"Where's Goldie?" Heath asked. "Wait, I should know."

"The lawyer," Robin said. She'd never felt so nervous in front of her father. All the years he said he'd given her complete freedom closed up behind her; now she felt trapped, stuck in her own plan, a plan which now seemed ludicrous, as exploitative as Stansell's. Her father looked sleepy, happy; he looked like himself when you took out all the foreign substances.

"So I could go out with you first," her father was saying. "To Huntley to look at the Stickley. That way you'd know what to do next time. Would you like that? We have to get you a truck."

"Dad," Robin said, "I've got to tell you something." She pulled the Kim Novak photo and the packet and the straw from the chair and placed them on the table between her and her father.

Her father took a drag on his cigar and nodded. He blinked rapidly. "Okay, kiddo. Like it's not really a surprise, is it?"

"Maybe it is," Robin said.

"Just be careful, honey. Really. There's some guys that aren't as good as me hooked up in all this."

"I know," Robin said. She poured the coke onto Kim Novak's face and used the straw to separate it into two fat lines. This was Stansell's, a little she'd stolen from his car after graduation. She'd get it this time before her father put his mark on it.

"You know, Rob," Heath said. "I feel kind of funny about this. Are you sure?"

"I'll go first," Robin said.

"Watch your hair, honey," her father said.

The line was so big that it took two runs to get it. The effects were immediate. There was that Supergirl feeling, but jacked up, a whine in her frontal lobe. Right now Robin could take down the swallows' nest, count the babies, and stick it back up in between the arcing flight of the parent birds. Right now she could sand off the last rust from the T-Bird, remove the old, ripped seats, ratchet in new ones, and show the car. She handed the straw to her father and watched him take up the rest. There was another thing Robin could do: she could snort coke with her father from now until the end of time and still save him. But it was too late for that.

"Are you okay?" Heath asked.

Robin felt the moisture on her face before she realized she was crying. She had planned to tell him about Lynn, about Freddie, to spill all her secrets and pave the way for him to go. She thought of Lynn's hips rising to her mouth; Goldie stroking her arm, holding her neck, playing with her clothes, so many years ago. She thought of her mother taking her into her lap, decades ago, in another life. Clean out the house, she thought. Despite the coke, her father still looked like himself, intelligent, listening, reaching for her hand. He might have information she needed. "Dad?" Robin asked. "What do you do when you have to love someone, but you just can't bear it?"

The cops must have parked down the street. When they came in, without knocking, Heath stood and swept the table clean. He looked around, but there was nowhere for him to go, just a stunning morning outside the window, swallows knitting chains in the air, and his daughter's smile fading as the first officer in the room lowered his gun and grabbed her father by the wrist.

chapter thirteen

~

Even before the trial, Marilyn Stansell showed up at the house. Robin returned home from her job selling auto parts at Sears, a job Mr. Eakins, out of pity, had wrangled for her, and she found the black Mercedes in the driveway. Larry, Curly, and Moe raced around the yard, their collars chiming like bells.

"Don't call the cops," Mrs. Stansell said, raising her hands.

Robin didn't smile. She knew from the Lilac paper and from an article in the west suburban edition of the *Tribune* that Stansell wouldn't get more than community service. Nothing but a minor possession count, despite the fact that they ransacked his reeking room. The result of a pile of shut-up money that left Steve Stansell a baby in the crib, right up to the end.

"What do you want?" Robin asked. Marilyn followed her into the house.

"Don't you lock the door?" she asked.

Robin took an Old Style out of the refrigerator. She untucked her blouse and sat at the kitchen table. Marilyn waited by the island.

"This is not as bad as I thought," Marilyn said, nodding.

The phone rang a few times, but Robin ignored it.

"Okay, this is it," Mrs. Stansell said. She took a deep breath. "Your dad's in jail."

"Yeah, that's right," Robin said, gearing up to blame this woman's son. But Marilyn stopped her by raising her hands again. Surrender.

"And I know your mom's been dead a long time." Marilyn paused, possibly to wait for some reaction from Robin. "Your grandmother," Marilyn continued. "Well, your grandmother. I met her at the arraignment and I have to say I have my doubts about whether she could keep the house going. And she seems to have her own problems lately."

"She's handling them," Robin said. By falling in love with her lawyer and making a Scandinavian saga out of her defamation suit— but Robin didn't mention that. Steve's mother was dressed in black and pink golf attire, black sunglasses on top of her head. Dark, wiry hair sprang from her bare legs.

Those hands raised again. Did she think Robin was going to come at her? "All I'm saying," said Marilyn, "is that maybe with everything that's going on and with your dad maybe not going to be home for a while, you might want a safe place to stay. Someplace more stable."

Robin sipped her beer and didn't say anything. Out in the front yard, one of the dogs took a dump under the willow tree.

"Robin, I'm asking if you'd like to come and stay at the house. Our house."

Robin burst out laughing, her torso bowing over the tabletop. "You. Cannot. Be. Serious," she said.

"Live with us for a while," Marilyn said. "Just until you know where you're going."

Was this guilt? Pity? Or largesse? Or the closest Marilyn could get to acknowledging her son's role in Heath's final demise?

"Steven's left," Marilyn said quickly. Hands up. "Both Mr. Stansell and I thought it would be best. He's living in an apartment with his friends Billy and Mark. He wouldn't be there, Robin. And he doesn't know I'm here." She looked away. "Neither does my husband," she said.

This woman was in Robin's house now. Not Goldie's house, not even Heath's, but the house Robin had rescued from the manipulations of this woman's only son. There was something else, though. Something sandy in the air that shifted, shaping a thought.

"I think we get along," Marilyn said. "Don't you?" She laughed. "I mean, who else in Lilac loves old movies like you and me? You know what was on the other night? *Johnny Guitar.* You would have loved it."

Robin had seen it years ago, late one night while her grandmother was in her bedroom with a Bogdanas: Joan Crawford with a whip and another tough woman—the same woman who looked like a boy in *Touch of Evil.*

"Rent free," Marilyn was saying. "I can't pretend we need the money. And all the room we have! Especially now that Susan's staying at school for the summer." Marilyn was talking as if Robin had already said yes.

"I have a job," Robin said quietly, though she meant to say something else. The words for what she should have said took shape as Marilyn replied.

"I thought you did," she said. "I've never seen you in those kind of clothes." Robin thought Marilyn was going to put up her hands again, but instead her arms dropped. "You look nice," she said.

The sand filled a form, a hard sphere of desire with Robin at its center and the hands of Steve Stansell's mother doing the shaping. This woman wanted her.

Robin immediately turned polite, said no, got up from the kitchen table and herded Marilyn outside, smiled and thanked her, ignored her confusion and embarrassment, watched her whistle for the three dogs, but then she waited in the driveway to make sure Marilyn really did back out her filthy car and speed away.

∼

Robin stayed in Lilac until the end of her father's trial, late in the fall, and then there were no more reasons to stay. Heath got five years for possession. Goldie's city lawyer had recommended a three-hundred-pound Lithuanian who had grown up near the Stockyards and who was fresh out of Northwestern Law School; he turned out to be tougher and smarter than Robin expected. Stavius came through with an extraordinary performance for Grandma's benefit. Goldie appeared every day of Heath's trial wearing a new outfit, and the closer they got to sentencing, the more cleavage she displayed. By the time Stavius made his closing arguments, the jury could barely keep their eyes on him. In the end, the lawyer blew the dealing charge off the table like so much white powder.

Despite Robin's worst fears, her father survived in prison. They cut off his hair, and the sight of his naked head caused Robin to burst into tears on the first visiting day. Heath said not to worry, he had a lot of time to read; he was going through a lot of law books, and he was thinking about law school once he got out. He thought he'd make a good attorney.

Robin cried nonstop during her first few visits to Joliet. She loved her father more than she thought possible, and now that her life with him consisted primarily of memories, he had become a figure not unlike her dead mother: a beloved face, a blameless figure, another missing limb of a family she finally had a firm grip on.

It never occurred to Heath to blame Robin for his arrest. He assumed Stansell had snitched, because, in Heath's words, "I was doing too good. Jealousy, you know." The worst part, though, was that Robin's father actively credited Stansell for his survival.

"Kiddo, I was going to die," he said. "I was in bad shape. Heroin is not like anything else, and Steve paid to get it out of me. Steve even sent me to South America. Do you believe it? I brought the first shipment back for ten grand and then I got some to sell. That's what got me going."

"Dad," Robin said, scowling.

Heath shook his head. "Power of money, Rob," he said.

Every trip, Robin left her father a grocery bag full of Panatelas, a gift from Larry Pike. After a while, Robin's visits tapered off, and Heath sent letters. "The weed in here is pretty good," he wrote. "And I'm on the football team. Do you believe it?"

The city lawyer asked Goldie to move in with him while they continued their endless litigation against the Bogdanas women, who still lived with their cheating husbands as if nothing was wrong. To Robin's surprise, her grandmother refused the lawyer's offer.

"I know *here*," she told Robin. The men at the kitchen table smiled. In September, Tommy Boy moved into the downstairs spare room with the strict understanding that he was just a friendly, semi-permanent guest.

"He can't—you know," Grandma whispered to Robin, while Tommy was making dinner one evening. She gestured toward her crotch.

"I'm making cabbage!" Tommy called from the stove. "Here I go, turning into my granny, my *Bobe,* in my old age."

Tommy took on all the cooking and cleaning; Robin came home from Sears one day to find him ironing one of her blouses.

She had other plans. She would move to the city and eventually go to school. Somewhere, maybe in the *Tribune,* Robin had read about a neighborhood in Chicago filled with people who lived as she wanted to, a place overflowing with women to love.

Freddie sent Robin letters from Yale, full, at first, of how sorry he was about her dad, how his father said she was so good at Sears. Sad letters, full of missing Carl, who tried to write but couldn't say how he felt. Carl's letters tapered off, as did Freddie's letters to Robin. Then there was a new flurry: Freddie loved his classes, and he'd joined the black student group on campus; he was second trumpet in the big Yale orchestra. He had met a French horn player, Samuel, and they had taken the train to New York City to hear the Philharmonic. Schubert, Freddie's letters said. Mendelssohn. There was Samuel, and then a new professor, a black man, the first black man Freddie had ever seen in front of a classroom. When could Robin get away?

~

In November, before she moved to Chicago, as the last of the leaves formed a crackling, brown carpet under the tires of the Thunderbird, Robin drove to Lynn's house. She parked down the street. The cottonwood on the Nielsens' parkway was bare, its branches thrown up and out, away from the neat, beige house.

It was a cold, clear day, so if they had wanted to, all the Nielsens could have looked out their picture window and seen the lawbreaker, the daughter of the dealer, the dyke. Robin wondered what they knew. Lynn had never called her after their night together, never come over, never written. It hadn't been her hanging up. A few days after Heath's arrest, Robin rolled up the garage door to see the front of her car bashed in. Stansell. But whether he had smashed the T-Bird over the arrest or over Lynn, Robin wasn't sure. She figured that to Stansell they were betrayals of the same magnitude. Either way, Lynn's silence indicated that she had told, and then had stepped aside or kept quiet, or had lain with her eyes closed and her legs inching open until Stansell found the appropriate response. Robin had heard that Mr. Nielsen pulled some strings and got Lynn into Circle Campus at the last minute. Leaves blew in eddies underneath a new Gremlin in the Nielsens' driveway.

Robin sat in the Thunderbird for half an hour, struck by the dead quiet of Parkside Street, the total absence of movement or life. One car drove by. At least on Highland, the neighbors had Heath Simonsen to watch and worry over. Here, there was nothing, all the houses buttoned up. Finally, the Nielsens' front door opened and Lynn came out and opened the door of the Gremlin. She rummaged in the glove compartment. Robin wondered if she hid dope there, or booze, or even condoms.

Lynn slammed the car door and, without a glance, walked back to the house. Her hair glowed in the slanting orange sunshine. She wore jeans and a tight white sweater that Robin recognized from a long-ago party. Her legs were slim, her breasts high, her eyes, Robin knew, still blue and round and guileless.

As Robin watched Lynn cut across the yard, a familiar shape grew inside of her. It was hard and joyous, terrifying, almost hideous in its beauty, and Robin possessed it fiercely. It was hers to give away.

acknowledgments

Special thanks go to my friends in Fort Collins, all of them talented writers and staunch allies: Leslee Becker, Ellen Brinks, Lisa Langstraat, Steven Schwartz, and Sarah Sloane, my one-woman family. I would like to thank the Department of English at Colorado State University for providing me time, a place to work, and the most congenial pack of academics I will ever meet. All of my fellow faculty members in the Warren Wilson MFA Program for Writers have given me advice and inspiration.

For their generous support I'd also like to thank the National Endowment for the Arts, the MacDowell Colony, and the Corporation of Yaddo, as well as the Tacoma Arts Commission and Artist Trust.

Thanks to Rosie, Dusty, Sparky, and the late Molly and Hannah for their unconditional love.

Finally, I'd like to express my enduring gratitude to Jin Auh and everyone at Wylie for their patience, loyalty, and hard work on my behalf.

Text design by Mary H. Sexton

Typesetting by Delmastype, Ann Arbor, Michigan

Text and ornament font is Minion, a 1990 Adobe Originals typeface by Robert Slimbach. Inspired by classical, old style typefaces of the late Renaissance, Minion combines the aesthetic and functional qualities that make text type highly readable, with the versatility of digital technology.
—Courtesy www.adobe.com